ECHOES IN THE VOID

Ben Hafer

Library of Congress Cataloging-in-Publication Data

Names: Hafer, Ben, author
Title: Echoes in the Void:a novel / Ben Hafer
Identifiers: ISBN 979-8-3482-4447-7 (print)
ISBN 979-8-3413-6520-9 (paperback)
ISBN 979-8-3413-6643-5 (hardcover)
ISBN 979-8-3482-4482-8 (jacketed)
ISBN 979-8-3484-0734-6 (ebook)
Subjects: GSAFD: Science fiction

Published in the United States

CHAPTER ONE

The vessel Perevian quaked as it plunged through the turbulent waves of stellar winds and radiation emanating from the Trapezium Cluster. Outside, space was alive with the raw, violent energy of newborn stars. Brilliant arcs of glowing gas, illuminated by the intense radiation from the young stars at the cluster's heart, twisted through the vastness of the Orion Nebula like tendrils of some immense, unseen force. The Trapezium Cluster, a group of fiercely hot, massive stars in the early stages of their lives, was driving powerful winds that sculpted the surrounding gas and dust. These winds moved at thousands of kilometers per second, carving the Orion Nebula into swirling knots of gas aglow with the ultraviolet radiation from the stars still forming within.

Captain Jonathan Reed stood at the center of the bridge, his eyes locked on the hypnotic beauty displayed on the ship's viewscreen. His tall, broad frame seemed immovable, a calm contrast to the tumult outside. He watched as luminous clouds shifted, their colors a kaleidoscope of glowing greens and deep reds.

"Structural integrity is holding," Lieutenant Commander Maya Chen called from her console. Her fingers moved swiftly across the controls. "Shields are at eighty percent. Radiation levels are spiking as we pass through denser regions of the nebula."

Her dark eyes, sharp and calculating, glanced between data streams. Reed could see the concentration on her face as she constantly recalibrated the ship's systems. The Orion Nebula was a stellar nursery, teeming with the birth of stars. The region was filled with dense clouds of gas and dust, creating pockets of extreme radiation that posed significant threats to their ship.

Lieutenant Carolyn Addison, seated at the helm, cast a quick glance at the viewscreen, her lips pressed into a thin line. "This isn't exactly a smooth ride, Captain," she muttered, her hands tight on the flight controls. Her green eyes, normally bright with amusement, were now narrowed with concentration. The storm outside wasn't just beautiful—it was dangerous.

The ship trembled as a shockwave from the cluster's stellar winds struck, rippling the hull like a pebble tossed into a pond. The stars, which usually remained as steady pinpricks against the backdrop, were distorted, stretching into faint, blurred lines under the pressure of the immense particle bombardment.

"Take us thirty degrees to port, Lieutenant," Reed commanded, his voice calm despite the groaning protest of the ship. "Get us clear of the densest gas clouds, but keep us close enough for optimal sensor readings."

"Aye, Captain," Addison replied, immediately adjusting the ship's trajectory, guiding Perevian as if it were an extension of her own body.

On the viewscreen, vast tendrils of glowing gas twisted in

mesmerizing patterns, their colors shifting from emerald green to fiery red, the hallmarks of star formation. Massive chunks of nebular debris drifted aimlessly, their jagged surfaces faintly glowing under the radiation from the cluster. One colossal fragment, its surface dark and cratered, loomed ahead, sparking with residual energy as it slowly tumbled through space. The ship veered just in time, the debris passing close enough to send flickers of light dancing across Perevian's shields.

In the corner of the bridge, Dr. Liam Russo hunched over his console, his brown curls hanging loosely over his forehead as he studied the readings. His eyes darted between the displays, scanning the radiation levels and energy patterns that painted a deeply unsettling picture.

"These radiation spikes are much more intense than we had expected," Russo said, his voice barely audible over the hum of the ship's systems. "The nebula should be dispersing this energy more evenly, but I'm detecting concentrated hotspots—almost as if energy is being funneled into specific areas by the stellar winds."

Reed turned from the viewscreen to the scientist, his brow furrowed in thought. "What are you saying, Doctor?"

Russo adjusted his glasses and tapped a command on his console. The viewscreen shifted, now displaying a detailed visual of the surrounding radiation fields. Waves of energy moved across space like the ripples of a massive, invisible storm, pooling in certain areas rather than spreading evenly.

"There's definitely a pattern," Russo said, his voice filled with disbelief. "It's like the Trapezium Cluster is still fueling these pockets, producing radiation bursts more often than we'd anticipate from young stars. But the winds—they're erratic, almost as if these stars are far more unstable than they should be at this stage."

Chen's head snapped up from her console, her expression skeptical. "Localized radiation spikes? That doesn't make sense. A young nebula like this should be turbulent, sure, but not creating new sources of intense radiation. The stars should be dispersing this energy, not focusing it."

Before anyone could respond, the ship jolted violently. Addison's hands flew across the controls, stabilizing their course, but the bridge lights flickered, casting the room in ghostly shadows. A deep, resonant hum vibrated through the hull, as though the very fabric of space was compressing around them.

"Captain," Chen called out, her calm exterior cracking for the first time. "The radiation field is intensifying. Shields are down to sixty percent. If this keeps up, we'll be cooked."

Addison fought to maintain control, beads of sweat forming on her forehead. "The stellar winds are making it nearly impossible to hold course. We're getting hammered from all sides."

Reed's eyes narrowed as he turned back to the viewscreen. The swirling remnants of the Orion Nebula glowed brighter, the radiation from the stars lighting up the dense gas. And yet, something about the scene felt... off. The energy wasn't dispersing evenly, and there was an unsettling rhythm to the chaos outside.

"Very well," Reed said quietly. "Addison, engage full thrusters. Get us clear."

"Aye, Captain." Her hands moved quickly, and the engines roared in protest, pushing against the turbulent stellar winds with all they had.

The ship trembled violently, the forces outside pressing down on them. Reed felt it, like a weight dragging them backward through space. Addison's jaw tightened as she fought to maintain control, her eyes flicking between her displays and the swirling storm on the viewscreen.

"We're stuck in a current, we can't escape," Addison growled through clenched teeth. "If we don't break through soon, we'll be torn apart."

Chen's voice cut through the tension. "The winds are fluctuating, Captain. The shields are holding, but the plasma bursts are trapping us. If we don't shift power to the forward thrusters now, we won't have enough momentum to break through."

Russo glanced up, urgency clear in his voice. "She's right. We need to concentrate all thrust forward to push through."

Reed's mind raced. "Chen, can we manipulate the Alcubierre drive without a full warp? Just enough to distort space around us, give us the push we need to break free?"

Chen's eyes widened momentarily before narrowing in concentration. "It's possible, but we'd need a precise, controlled burst. A localized warp bubble could reduce the drag on the ship, but if it lasts too long, we risk destabilizing the space-time fabric around us."

Reed's jaw clenched. "Can you control it?"

Chen nodded, her voice growing steadier. "I can create a one-second pulse. That should be enough to give us the slingshot effect we need, but the timing has to be exact."

Addison's hands moved swiftly, calculating the trajectory. "Give me that pulse, and I'll ride it out of here."

Reed looked between his crew, his trust in them unwavering. "Do it."

Chen's fingers flew across the controls, rerouting power to the Alcubierre drive. The faint hum of the drive grew louder beneath the bridge floor as energy was redirected to its systems.

"Pulsing drive in three… two… one—now!" Chen activated the burst.

Perevian lurched violently, and for a brief second, the space around them bent, compressing the plasma field like a bubble of water bursting in slow motion. The stars outside twisted unnaturally, and Addison gripped the controls as the ship slungshot forward.

The engines roared, but this time they weren't fighting against the pull—they were gliding through it, using the bubble's momentum to cut free of the plasma field. The ship surged forward, faster and faster, until with a final crack, they broke through.

Perevian shot through the remnants of the nebula, the charged particle field finally releasing its grip. The ship lurched forward, accelerating as it left the chaos behind, and the viewscreen cleared, revealing the vast, open expanse of space once more.

"Shields stabilizing at sixty percent," Chen called, relief evident in her voice. "We're clear, but the engines took damage. We'll need time to run full repairs."

Addison let out a long breath, slumping back in her seat.

"Remind me to never sign up for another nebula survey."

Reed glanced to the viewscreen, where the remnants blazed with an eerie beauty. The swirling mass of debris and radiation, glowing in slow, mesmerizing waves, cast long, fractured shadows across the bridge. Deep within the pulsing light, the heart of the energy still throbbed like a dying ember, its radiant core flickering with strange, otherworldly hues—brilliant whites and shimmering violets blending into angry reds, all swirling together in a cosmic dance.

There was something unnatural about it. The way the light twisted and warped, as if it were being bent by some unseen force. Flares of energy shot out sporadically, only to be drawn back inward. It wasn't just the beauty of the scene that held Reed's attention—it was the feeling of raw, untapped power.

At the center, where the stars should have been swirling in smooth orbits, there was chaos. Reed couldn't look away. His mind struggled to comprehend it—a flicker of motion, or perhaps a pulse, something just at the edge of vision. The light seemed to fold in on itself, creating shapes that almost took form before dispersing again.

For a brief moment, Reed thought he saw something—long, twisting forms swirling in rhythm with the pulses. Dark, serpentine shapes coiled and uncoiled in the heart of the nebula, moving as if they were alive, just beyond the limits of comprehension, shifting and bending with the light itself.

A low, steady hum reverberated through the hull, almost as if Perevian itself could feel the pull. Reed's pulse quickened, his heart beating in sync with the slow rhythm of the core, as though it were calling to him. He knew the dangers—but despite the risk, something in him was drawn to the heart of the storm.

The nebula was more than a phenomenon of physics. It was a mystery, and mysteries like this were what pushed humanity forward. His crew were still catching their breath, but Reed couldn't shake the feeling. This wasn't just the aftermath of a celestial event. This was something far more significant—perhaps even a message from the universe itself, encoded in the light and energy, waiting for someone to decipher it.

Ever the explorer, Reed felt it deep within him—an urge, a compulsion to turn back. The core pulsed again, its glow brightening as if it had sensed his attention. The thing within seemed to shift, almost beckoning, waiting to be understood.

Straightening in his seat, Reed made his decision. "Addison, plot a course away from the Trapezium Cluster. We've done enough for today."

Addison turned her head toward him, a flash of relief crossing her features, though she quickly hid it behind her usual smirk. "No arguments here, Captain."

Reed's voice remained resolute. "No matter how much I want to solve this puzzle, we're just not equipped for what we've been put through. We'll have NASA send in Empyrea to complete the survey." He glanced around the bridge, taking in the expressions of his crew. Chen's face remained neutral, her unreadable eyes fixed on her console, while Russo's brow furrowed in quiet thought, his earlier curiosity tempered by the gravity of what they had just encountered.

Addison tapped her controls, the ship turning slowly away from the pulsing light of the Orion Nebula. "Course plotted,

Captain. We'll be clear in a few hours."

Reed gave a slow nod, his gaze lingering on the viewscreen. The glowing heart of the nebula was growing smaller now, the mesmerizing waves of energy and light slowly fading into the distance. But the pull of it, the allure of what they had nearly uncovered, still lingered in his mind.

Chen broke the silence. "Do you want to send a report to NASA?"

Reed nodded, his mind already moving ahead to the next steps, a habit born out of years of meticulous command and survival training. "We'll file our report," he said. "But first, I want full diagnostics on the ship. Make sure we're back to one hundred percent."

He stood up from his chair, the weight of the recent encounter with the nebula still fresh in his mind. The vibrant energy field they had passed through had been unlike anything they'd ever encountered, and safety of his crew and the integrity of Perevian came first, always. If there was any damage, even the smallest anomaly, they needed to find it— and fast.

"Run a full systems check—reactors, navigation, life support, all of it," he continued, pacing to the central console where diagnostic data was displayed. He could already hear the hum of the ship's processors kicking into overdrive as they began scanning every component of the vessel, inside and out.

Chen watched him, knowing this was more than just protocol for Reed. He wasn't only thinking about the report for NASA or the crew's physical safety. There was something deeper in his expression, a hint of concern that hadn't been there before. She could observe it in the way he now moved, his behavior marked with an urgency she wasn't used to seeing.

"You think the field affected more than just the ship's systems, don't you?" she asked quietly, eyeing him carefully.

Reed didn't look up immediately. Instead, he let out a breath, hands resting on the edge of the console. "I don't know," he finally replied, his voice lower now, more contemplative. "But that was no ordinary phenomenon out there, Chen. And I'm not about to assume everything's fine just because the lights are still on." He straightened, his gaze meeting hers. "We're not taking any chances."

Chen nodded in understanding. "I'll get on it," she said, tapping into her own console to initiate further diagnostics across all major systems. "But Captain, if there's anything we missed..."

"I know," he interrupted, his voice sharper than intended. He softened his tone after a brief pause. "I know. That's why we need to be thorough. Every system, every connection— double-check it all."

As the ship's automated systems began scanning and diagnosing, Reed crossed his arms and stared at the readouts, waiting for confirmation that everything was in working order. He couldn't shake the feeling that something wasn't right. It was more than just the usual post-incident precaution. The nebula, with its strange and inexplicable energy waves, had unsettled him in ways he wasn't ready to admit out loud.

Reed's eyes never left the diminishing glow on the viewscreen. "We'll get answers to our scientific questions, but not today." He straightened in his chair.

Addison shook her head, a small, wry smile tugging at her lips. "And here I was thinking you were ready to turnaround and go back."

Reed allowed himself a faint smile in return. "Not when my ship and crew are in danger, Lieutenant."

As Perevian slipped further from the remnants of the Trapezium Cluster, Reed let the tension in his shoulders ease, though the weight of what they'd encountered stayed with him. Whatever waited out there, beyond the edge of known space, had shown itself just enough to keep them exploring.

But for now, they would move forward, away from the mystery of the nebula, and toward the next.

CHAPTER TWO

A week later, things were back to normal. Captain Reed stood on the bridge, his hands resting lightly on the back of his chair. The ship's wide viewscreen revealed a sea of stars, an endless expanse that stretched far beyond the reach of known space. Space was vast, and though humanity had reached for it for centuries, it still held countless mysteries, each waiting to be unraveled. Reed's expression was calm, his gaze steady as he looked out at the horizon.

Perevian, one of many ships in the S.T.A.R.S. fleet, was tasked with a monumental mission of exploration and discovery: venturing into the uncharted reaches of the Milky Way galaxy, gathering data, and seeking new opportunities. Perevian was around 70 meters in length, with its arrowhead-like body tapering at the bow. At its widest point, near the midsection, it measured about 15 meters, where the angular stabilizers extended from the sides. Its hull was sleek and matte black, built to minimize its radar and thermal signature, with angled panels that helped deflect radiation and debris. It was just large enough to comfortably house its four crewmembers, with each compartment carefully optimized for space and utility.

The interior of the ship was minimalist and practical, every bit of space thoughtfully optimized for efficiency. Perevian's bridge, located near the bow, was a compact yet highly advanced command center. A large viewscreen dominated the front of the room, and the crew's workstations were arranged in a tight semicircle—each equipped with consoles for navigation, communication, engineering, and science. Every station featured holographic displays, providing three-dimensional projections of star charts, system diagnostics, and environmental data. The captain's chair, positioned centrally, reflected the ship's collaborative philosophy, appearing no grander than the other stations. This tight, efficient space kept the crew focused, with all critical information accessible at a glance.

Behind the bridge, a central corridor ran the length of the ship, linking all essential compartments. Lining the corridor were individual crew quarters. Each crewmember had a bunk, a couch, and a desk equipped with a terminal—allowing them to monitor personal projects or work from their own spaces. Storage was built seamlessly into the walls and floor, keeping personal items and equipment securely stowed. Their quarters were designed for long-term missions, providing essential privacy while maximizing space efficiency.

After passing an observation lounge, galley, and gym, was the ship's science lab. Designed with sleek rows of consoles lining the walls, each station was equipped with scanners, analysis equipment, and glowing interfaces constantly streaming data. Containment units housed sensitive or volatile materials in reinforced, temperature-controlled chambers. In the center of the lab stood an examination table with a polished alloy surface, resistant to chemical reactions and heat, embedded with modular slots for diagnostic tools. Robotic arms and manual systems handled the delicate work of organizing and analyzing samples retrieved by drones. Monitors mounted above the workspace displayed real-time imaging, from drone footage to microscopic scans, ensuring the crew could follow experiments or planetary surveys in progress with pinpoint accuracy. The lighting and air filtration systems were carefully controlled, maintaining a sterile, adaptable environment for sensitive research.

At the aft of the ship was the engineering section, where the primary power systems and engines were housed. The steady hum of the Alcubierre drive resonated through the bulkheads, though the system was used sparingly. Maintenance hatches provided easy access to critical systems, allowing the crew to make routine checks and repairs with minimal disruption. The compact, efficient layout of the engineering section allowed for swift monitoring of the ship's vital operations, with AI-assisted diagnostics running continuously to ensure everything functioned smoothly.

Perevian's cargo hold, though small, was equipped for scientific exploration. It housed drones for planetary reconnaissance, deployable satellites, and a variety of tools designed for gathering and analyzing samples from planetary surfaces or asteroids. This section was optimized to store essential mission equipment and scientific specimens, with smart storage systems keeping everything secure and accessible for immediate deployment. The space was designed for efficiency, minimizing excess weight while maximizing the ship's ability to conduct long-term research.

As Reed scanned the bridge, he took in the sight of his crew—individuals bound by mission and purpose, more like family than colleagues. They were the best in their fields, chosen not only for their technical expertise but also for their ability to work seamlessly under pressure. Each of them brought something vital to the table, and as Reed observed them at their stations, he felt a deep sense of trust in their abilities.

Lieutenant Addison sat at the helm, her posture relaxed yet focused, radiating a confidence that came with experience. Her auburn hair was pulled back into a neat ponytail, and her intense green eyes were fixed on the navigation controls, scanning every detail with practiced precision. A faint smirk tugged at the corner of her lips, a sign of her ease in navigating even the most treacherous of space routes. Despite the serious atmosphere, there was an undeniable energy about her—a sense of control and purpose. Her uniform, crisp and unwrinkled, mirrored her discipline and the meticulous attention she brought to her work.

Addison was born to fly—raised in a Navy family, she'd spent her life around cockpits and thrived in high-pressure environments where every second counted, and a single decision could tip the balance between survival and disaster. Her background in high-risk flight missions was evident in the way she handled the ship, navigating the stars with an instinct that went beyond training. Reed had seen her remain calm through the most chaotic situations, and it was this steadiness that made her invaluable. She wasn't just guiding them through space—she was reading the movements of the ship as though it were an extension of herself, making small adjustments to their trajectory, always one step ahead of the next challenge.

To Reed's right, Lieutenant Commander Chen sat at her engineering station, her expression alert. Her straight, shoulder-length black hair was pulled back neatly, revealing a face of sharp, symmetrical features. Her almond-shaped eyes, dark and intelligent, moved quickly over the console, absorbing the data. Her skin had a warm, bronzed tone, and though her demeanor was often serious, there was a quiet strength behind it. Dressed in her uniform, she carried herself with a sense of purpose, her posture straight, reflecting years of discipline. There was an aura of perfection about her—a no-nonsense approach to both her work and her role on the ship. Despite the pressure of their mission, Chen always maintained a composed, thoughtful presence.

With her background in advanced engineering and computer science, Chen had made herself indispensable on this mission. She could break down complex systems in her mind as easily as she could rebuild them with her hands. At the moment, she was monitoring the ship's Alcubierre drive and power output, running diagnostic checks to ensure everything was functioning within optimal parameters. Chen had a reputation for solving problems that others couldn't, often catching potential failures before they even appeared. Reed knew that if anything went wrong with the ship, Chen wouldn't just fix it—she would improve it. Her analytical mind never rested, and her resourcefulness had already saved them more than once. But beyond her technical prowess, there was a calm determination in Chen that gave the crew confidence. When she was at the controls, they knew everything would hold together.

On the opposite side of the bridge, Dr. Russo sat at his console, his tall, lean frame hunched slightly as he studied the data streaming across the screen. His brown, curly hair was tousled, a sign of long hours spent without much concern for appearances. His angular features—especially his high cheekbones and aquiline nose—gave him an intense expression. His dark eyes, framed by thin-rimmed glasses, darted back and forth as he processed the incoming information. Along with his relentless pursuit of knowledge, there was also a boyish energy in his movements, a restlessness that revealed his passion for unraveling the mysteries of the universe. He wore his uniform with the sleeves slightly rolled up as if he was always ready to dive deeper into his work.

The ship's resident astrophysicist, Russo was a master of theoretical physics and space-time mechanics, his mind constantly working on problems most people couldn't even begin to comprehend. Where others saw the cold void of space, Russo saw patterns, equations, and possibilities. He had a deep understanding of the forces that governed the universe, and Reed often felt that Russo's sharp intellect could outthink even the most advanced algorithms the ship had to offer. Today, he was analyzing gravitational fluctuations recently observed in a nearby system, his fingers rapidly inputting data and running simulations. If there were mysteries to be unraveled about the cosmos, Russo was the one who would decode them. Yet, despite his academic brilliance, he had an almost boyish curiosity about the universe—a curiosity that drove him to question everything, constantly searching for answers.

Reed's eyes lingered on the empty captain's chair, a reflection of his own steadfast presence aboard Perevian. Tall and broad-shouldered, Captain Reed carried himself with the quiet authority of a seasoned leader. His short, dark hair was beginning to show hints of gray at the temples, a testament to years of experience. His sharp, blue eyes held a steely determination, always scanning his surroundings with the precision of a military man. Reed's square jaw and strong, rugged features gave him an air of resilience, while the faint lines around his eyes hinted at the weight of command and the countless decisions he had made.

His military background had prepared him for command—years of discipline, strategy, and leadership had forged him into the steady hand that could guide the crew through the unknown. He wasn't just responsible for the ship; he was responsible for the lives of every person aboard. Reed's mind was constantly weighing risks and outcomes, always thinking several steps ahead. Years of military service had taught him to trust his instincts, but also to rely on his team. He knew that the best leaders weren't those who gave orders, but those who empowered their crew to perform at their best. And with this crew, he knew they could face whatever lay ahead.

Together, they were a finely tuned machine. Each member of the crew brought their own expertise to the mission, and in doing so, they formed a unit that was stronger than the sum of its parts. Reed felt a surge of pride as he watched them work, knowing that with this team, they could navigate even the most treacherous of cosmic waters. They weren't just exploring the stars—they were unlocking the secrets of the universe itself.

Addison glanced up from the helm, tapping her fingers lightly on the console. "You know, it's a little eerie when things are this quiet. Almost makes you wish for a minor emergency. Just to keep things interesting."

Chen didn't look up from her station, but a faint smile played on her lips. "Be careful what you wish for. The last time you made a comment like that, we spent two days repairing the sensors after that ion storm near Altair."

Russo chimed in, a teasing edge to his voice. "Yeah, remind me to never let you pick vacation spots. You've got a knack for trouble."

Addison shot him a mock glare. "Hey, it's not my fault the universe likes a bit of excitement."

Russo leaned back in his seat, folding his arms. "I think it's you. Trouble has a way of following you, Lieutenant."

Reed raised an eyebrow, watching the exchange unfold. "If that's the case, maybe we should start keeping a tally."

"Oh, come on," Addison said with a grin. "A little excitement never hurt anyone."

Chen glanced over at her. "You're saying that now, but the moment something goes wrong, you'll be the first one complaining."

Before Addison could respond, the steady hum of the ship was interrupted by a soft alert tone. The crew fell silent, immediately snapping back to attention.

"Spoke too soon," Russo muttered under his breath, earning a smirk from Addison.

Chen's hands moved swiftly across her console. "Captain, we've got an incoming message from NASA."

Russo gave Addison a pointed look. "Maybe you got your wish after all."

Addison sighed dramatically. "I'm never going to live this down, am I?"

"Very well. Patch it through," replied Reed.

A burst of static crackled through the speakers, followed by the voice of Director Eliza March from NASA's deep-space exploration division. "Perevian, this is Director March. I'll keep it brief—we need you to assist Aetherion."

Reed leaned forward slightly. "What's the problem?"

"Aetherion was sent to the Vela Supernova Remnant," March began "It's a volatile region. The explosion left behind not only gas and dust, but also a sprawling asteroid belt made up of debris from nearby star systems. Initially, deep space scans suggested the presence of rare resources—minerals and other elements."

"So, Aetherion was there to confirm the resource potential?" asked Reed.

"That's correct," March continued. "But they found something unexpected. Some of the larger asteroids are hollow, with vast cave systems extending deep inside. These caverns could hold valuable materials, possibly even new geological phenomena. But more critically, we need to understand how these hollow structures formed."

Russo's voice broke through. "How hollow are we talking? What's the structural integrity of these asteroids?"

"That's the issue," March replied. "The caverns are

extremely unstable. Aetherion's initial surveys indicate gravitational shifts from nearby planetary bodies are affecting the cave systems. Rockslides and collapses are happening frequently. Their equipment isn't advanced enough to safely conduct a full survey."

A brief pause, then Addison chimed in. "Aetherion wasn't designed for that."

"Exactly," March confirmed. "That's why we're sending Perevian. Your ship's advanced geological analysis drones make you the best suited for this mission. Your task is twofold: first, conduct a thorough survey of the cave systems and determine if they're safe for further exploration. Second, assist Aetherion in retrieving critical data before the asteroids destabilize further."

A pause followed, and March continued. "Aetherion already lost contact with several drones they sent into the deeper caverns. We're not sure if it was rockslides or gravitational interference, but they're not risking any more until the situation stabilizes."

Addison paused for a moment, then shook her head. "Well, that's just perfect," she muttered, frustration creeping into her tone.

March's voice returned. "I have full confidence in your team, Captain. Remember, safety is your priority, but we need that data. Good luck."

With a soft click, the transmission ended.

Reed turned to Addison. "Lieutenant, plot a course to rendezvous with Aetherion."

Addison's hands were already moving over her console,

inputting coordinates and adjusting their trajectory. "Already on it, Captain," she replied. She glanced at the projected flight path, her brow furrowing slightly. "I'll run continuous scans along the way. If there's even a hint of trouble, we'll be ready to adjust course. But the region ahead is volatile—any miscalculation could slow us down."

"Chen, start preparing what you need for the mission," Reed added.

Chen nodded. "I'll recalibrate the seismic scanners and run a full systems check on the deep-core drill. The subsurface imaging array will need to be tuned for the unique composition of the asteroids, especially given the gravitational shifts in the area. Once we're on-site, we can deploy the ground-penetrating radar and map out the cave networks in real time. I'll also configure the geological density analyzers to account for any anomalies in the asteroid's composition, and we'll be able to assess the stability of the structures before we move in too deep."

She paused, tapping commands into her console as a detailed list of their geological tools flashed across the screen. "I'll also get the plasma cutters and remote excavation drones ready in case we need to remove any debris or widen access points. If those caverns are as unstable as Aetherion indicated, we'll need all our equipment in top condition. The margin for error down there will be slim."

Finally, Reed looked at Russo. "Prepare any data models or gravitational forecasts you have based on what NASA shared. We need to know exactly what we're dealing with when it comes to those shifts."

Russo tapped a few commands on his console, pulling up a series of complex charts and readings. His fingers moved deftly across the interface, bringing up planetary alignment data and cross-referencing it with the latest gravitational patterns from the region. He nodded thoughtfully before speaking.

"I'll factor in nearby planetary alignments, gravitational influences, and any anomalies we've documented from our previous missions," Russo said. "If these shifts are as volatile as they seem, we'll need multiple contingency plans ready to go."

Reed nodded. "Aetherion found something important, but it's dangerous down there. We're going to help them finish the job, and we're going to do it safely. Understood?"

"Aye, Captain," the crew responded.

Reed allowed himself a moment to process the gravity of the mission. They had faced challenging environments before, but the unpredictability of the asteroid caverns and the potential for catastrophic collapse weighed heavily on him. Still, Perevian was the best-equipped ship for the job, and he trusted his crew.

"All systems go, Captain," Chen announced.

"Alright," Reed said. "Let's engage the drive."

Addison glanced up, her fingers poised over the final sequence. "Engaging the Alcubierre drive," she said.

The bridge seemed to hold its collective breath as the familiar hum of the ship's systems intensified. The lights dimmed slightly, casting the crew in a soft, otherworldly glow. Then came the deep, resonant pulse that reverberated through the hull—subtle yet unmistakable. It was the sound of space itself being twisted and manipulated, a profound shift in the very fabric of reality.

Reed's gaze remained fixed on the viewscreen as the stars—normally fixed in place—began to shimmer. The vast, static canvas of the cosmos seemed to tremble, as though preparing to shift in a way that defied conventional understanding. The stars, once perfect pinpricks of light, appeared to quiver under the strain of the warp field forming around the ship.

"Warp field forming," Chen confirmed as data streamed across her console in rapid bursts. "Power levels are stable. We're good to go."

Outside, the stars no longer stood still. They vibrated, as if tugged by some invisible force. Then, suddenly, they began to stretch, pulling into long, glowing streaks across the blackness of space like brushstrokes dragged across a dark canvas. It was as though reality itself had been softened, smeared by the intense distortion of the Alcubierre drive. The universe bent around them, the ship no longer a part of it, but instead moving through it, slicing through space-time with an elegance that masked the immense forces at work.

The ship itself felt suspended—motionless despite the universe twisting around them. There was no sensation of acceleration, no turbulence to indicate the incredible speeds they were reaching. It was a paradox, a stillness in the heart of a storm of energy and light. The Alcubierre drive reverberated through the ship, the only indication that they were pushing the limits of physics. By contracting the space ahead and expanding it behind, Perevian moved forward, carried along by a wave of distorted space.

"We're locked into the bubble," Addison reported, her hands dancing across the controls. "Velocity is holding steady."

Russo, seated at his station, was absorbed in the gravitational data streaming across his screen. His eyes were wide, filled with wonder as he muttered under his breath, "Perfect compression… We're moving through folded space." The science he had studied for years was now unfolding before him, tangible and real, a fusion of theoretical physics and cutting-edge technology. It was one thing to theorize about it—another to experience it firsthand.

Reed watched the viewscreen, the intangible beauty of the distorted stars playing out before him. "How long until we reach the remnant?" he asked, his voice relaxed despite the surreal visuals unfolding around them.

Addison glanced at her instruments. "Ninety-six point four two hours, Captain."

Reed nodded, leaning back in his chair. They were on their way to the Vela Supernova Remnant, not just as explorers, but as masters of the space-time continuum, pushing the very limits of what was possible.

As the hours stretched on, the crew fell into a rhythm. Addison remained attentive at the helm, occasionally making minute adjustments to their trajectory as they navigated through small gravitational fluctuations. Every so often, she would stretch her arms, roll her shoulders, and mutter something to herself about the smoothness of their path.

Chen left her station on the bridge, descending to the cargo hold where the ship's advanced geological analysis and excavation tools were housed. There, she conducted another round of thorough checks on the equipment they would rely on once inside the asteroid caverns. These tools weren't just scanners; they were the cutting edge of excavation technology—spectral analyzers capable of assessing mineral compositions from kilometers away, and tunneling drones designed to safely navigate unstable rock formations.

"Perevian," Chen said as she activated the diagnostic terminal. "Run a full systems check on all excavation tools. Focus on power output and sensor integrity."

"Diagnostic initiated," the AI responded smoothly. A moment later, holographic displays lit up across the hold, showing detailed readouts of each machine. "All systems are operational. Spectral analyzers calibrated to 99.8% accuracy. Tunneling drones report stable feedback loops and error-free mobility."

Chen moved from one piece of equipment to the next, cross-referencing the AI's data with her own visual inspections. "Recalibrate the spectral analyzers to account for magnetic interference. The asteroid's composition might affect signal clarity."

"Recalibration in progress," the AI acknowledged. "Adjustment complete. Accuracy improved by 0.2%."

Chen nodded to herself, her hands brushing along the smooth casing of the tunneling drones. "Simulate drone stability in a collapsing environment. I need to know how they'll respond to unexpected shifts."

"Simulating…" the AI said. After a pause, it added, "Results indicate 87% success in maintaining operational stability under sudden rock collapses. Additional reinforcements to stabilizer protocols are recommended."

"Make the changes," Chen ordered. The soft hum of the equipment around her was a soothing counterpoint to the tension on the bridge, and she felt a growing confidence in their preparation as the AI reported back.

"Changes applied. Stabilizer protocols updated."

Russo, meanwhile, was seated in his quarters, his mind working relentlessly as he ran complex simulations based on the limited data Aetherion had transmitted. His holographic display was alive with shifting graphs and mathematical models. Pausing to adjust a variable, he leaned back and frowned at the projections.

"Perevian," Russo called out. "Input updated gravitational data from the Vela Supernova Remnant and run new models based on high-density dark matter pockets."

"Updating models," the AI responded. "Incorporating recent data. Revised simulations now available."

Russo studied the updated projections as they streamed across his display. "The anomalies are worse than expected," he muttered. "Identify scenarios with the highest risk of gravitational collapse and calculate escape vectors for each."

The AI processed the request quickly. "Fourteen scenarios identified with collapse probability exceeding 60%. Escape vectors calculated for each, with an average survival rate of 72%."

"Not good enough," Russo murmured, swiping through

the data. "Optimize survival rates by rebalancing propulsion energy output and shielding configuration. Add a margin for energy fluctuations caused by magnetic interference."

"Optimization in progress," the AI replied. After a pause, it updated, "Survival rates increased to 84%. Adjustments may compromise long-term shielding durability."

Russo sighed, pinching the bridge of his nose. "Not ideal, but better than nothing. Save the updated scenarios and prepare them for integration into the ship's tactical system."

"Scenarios saved and integrated," the AI confirmed.

After several hours, Russo stepped away from his work to clear his head. He wandered down the narrow corridor of Perevian, heading toward the observation lounge. The faint glow of distant stars through the viewport offered a momentary reprieve from the relentless calculations and looming uncertainties.

The lounge offered the crew an escape from the confines of the ship. Here, the vast expanse of space spread out before them, a reminder of the enormity of the universe they navigated. Russo found Chen already there, a tablet in hand as she reviewed geological data.

"You don't leave work behind either, huh?" Russo said, stepping beside her.

Chen gave him a small smile. "I figured I'd catch up on some analysis while the equipment calibrates. What about you? Thought you'd be knee-deep in your equations."

"I was," Russo sighed, rubbing his eyes. "Just needed a break. The figures start to blur after a while."

"Think we're ready for what's out there?" Chen asked

quietly, her voice barely above a whisper.

Russo hesitated, watching the distortion of light play tricks on his eyes. "I've run the numbers a dozen times, and still… it's hard to predict what we'll find."

Chen glanced at him. "You're usually more certain than that. What's bothering you?"

Russo sighed, leaning against the railing that lined the lounge. "It's not the numbers—it's what they can't tell us. The gravitational anomalies, the way the fabric of space is bending in the Vela Remnant… It's beyond anything I've modeled before. We're entering a region of space where the laws of physics might not apply. And that's what gets to me."

Chen looked back out at the endless swirl of light outside the ship. "So, it's not just the unpredictability. It's the unknown variables—things we don't even know to look for yet."

"Exactly." Russo's voice was quiet, reflective. "You can't plan for what you don't understand. And while I can create contingencies for every scenario I think we might face, there's always the possibility that something completely unforeseen will throw me."

Chen nodded, her face thoughtful. "It's strange, isn't it? We've been traveling through the stars for so long, solving problems we never thought we'd face. And yet, every time we step into a new part of the galaxy it feels like we're starting all over again."

Russo chuckled softly. "The more we know, the more we realize we don't. The universe just keeps finding ways to surprise us."

Chen smiled slightly. "At least it keeps things interesting."

"Interesting is one way to put it," Russo replied with a smirk. "But in the Vela Remnant… interesting could be deadly. The gravitational anomalies alone could rip the ship apart if we're not careful. And that's not even considering whatever else we might run into out there."

Chen was silent for a moment, her gaze distant. "Do you ever wonder if we've pushed too far? If there are places we just aren't meant to go?"

Russo's eyes flickered with the weight of her words. "Sometimes. But we wouldn't be out here if we weren't willing to face it head-on."

Chen looked back at him. "I guess you're right. And no matter what happens out there, we'll handle it. We always do."

Russo smiled, the tension easing. "We always do."

Reed sat in his quarters, the dim lighting casting a soft glow on the holographic display before him. He leaned back in his chair, eyes fixed on the mission brief as the data continued to scroll. Aetherion's transmissions detailed their initial findings, beginning with routine data—analysis of gravitational anomalies, asteroid density, and mineral scans. But as they delved deeper into the asteroid belt, the tone of the reports began to shift. The crew's excitement at discovering vast, hollowed-out caverns gave way to cautious concern as the gravity shifts increased in intensity.

Reed's brow furrowed as he reviewed Aetherion's mineral scans. The composition of the asteroids was unlike anything recorded in known space. Rare earth elements, complex silicates, and traces of metals they hadn't yet identified. But the real discovery, one that had piqued the interest of every scientist back on Earth, was the detection of unknown elements within the core of the larger asteroids. These elements showed potential densities far beyond conventional materials. If harnessed, they could revolutionize energy production, but they also posed an unpredictable risk.

Reed's jaw tightened as he scanned through the sections of the report describing the unstable conditions within the caverns. The hollow asteroids were riddled with fractures, likely caused by gravitational anomalies from nearby planetary bodies. Rockslides and cave-ins had already caused Aetherion's crew to reroute multiple times, making exploration difficult and dangerous. But despite the instability, they had pushed on, intrigued by the promise of discovery.

Reed paused the display, focusing on a series of transmissions from Aetherion's Captain, Commander William Townsend. One report caught Reed's attention—a detailed scan of an unusually large cavern, deep within one of the asteroids. Townsend's crew had detected strange quantum anomalies—subatomic particles behaving unpredictably—emanating from its walls, something that didn't match any natural phenomenon. Reed zoomed in on the data, trying to make sense of it. The energy readings were faint but consistent, almost like a pulse, but there was no clear source. Townsend's crew had only just begun investigating when the transmissions ended.

Reed sighed, leaning back in his chair. Aetherion's team had made incredible progress, but now it was Perevian's turn to take the mission further. The data suggested immense potential—new materials, unexplained energy phenomena, and a deeper understanding of the Vela Supernova's impact on the region. But the risks were equally high. Unpredictable gravitational shifts, the possibility of further collapses, and the eerie energy signatures in the caverns all loomed over the mission like a shadow.

Reed stood and slowly made his way back to the bridge, the dull hum of the ship's systems greeting him. The viewscreen now displayed the edge of the Vela Supernova Remnant in full view. A swirling mass of debris, gas, and cosmic dust. They were close now—close enough that Reed could feel the shift in the atmosphere aboard the ship.

Addison was sitting at the helm, as she would always be as much as possible when the drive was engaged. "Captain," she said. "I wanted to run a few ideas by you about how we approach the remnant."

Reed leaned back in his chair, gesturing for her to continue. "Go ahead."

Addison pulled up a detailed map of the remnant on the main viewscreen. "I suggest we take a more conservative approach as we enter. I propose we bring Perevian to a near stop just outside the outer edge. If the gravitational shifts are as volatile as Russo's predicting, we need to be cautious. We'll have better control if we minimize speed before we navigate the heart of the remnant."

Reed studied the display as she spoke, his fingers tapping lightly on the armrest. "Agreed," he said, nodding thoughtfully. "We can't afford any mistakes. Playing it slow is the best move. What about our drive? Any concerns there?"

Addison shook her head, glancing over at the readouts.

"Not with the current trajectory. We'll drop out of warp at the outer edge, then switch to conventional propulsion. It'll give us better maneuverability in an environment like this, even if it means slower progress. Warp's too unpredictable near these kinds of gravitational shifts."

Reed nodded again. "Good thinking," he said. "Let's stay on top of this. The moment you see anything out of the ordinary, bring it to my attention. No surprises."

Addison gave a quick nod and adjusted the display, marking their projected route through the debris field. "Aye, Captain."

"Time to drop out of warp?"

Addison looked at her console. "Just under fourteen hours," she replied. They were getting close. Days had passed in preparation, and now it was time to get to work.

CHAPTER THREE

As Perevian neared its destination, the crew prepared for the delicate maneuver of exiting the warp bubble. Addison's hands were steady on the controls, her eyes fixed on the readouts displayed in front of her.

"Approaching final coordinates," she announced. "Prepare to disengage the Alcubierre drive."

The crew braced themselves for the transition, knowing the moment would be both subtle and profound. Around them, the swirling tunnel of stretched starlight began to shift, the stars slowly reverting from streaks to their natural pinpricks of light. There was no sudden jolt or lurch—just the faintest shudder as space-time released its grip on the ship, returning them to the familiar flow of the cosmos.

"All systems nominal," Chen confirmed, scanning her instruments. "Warp bubble collapse was clean. No anomalies."

The viewscreen flickered for a moment before the stars snapped back into place—brilliant, steady, and unnervingly still. The chaos of their journey gave way to the vast emptiness of the universe, the stars now distant and cold, just as they had been before they'd engaged the drive.

"We've returned to normal space," Addison said with

relief. "Dropping to sublight speed. We should be right on the outer boundary of the Vela Supernova Remnant."

Chen's fingers flew across her console as she checked their coordinates. "Confirmed," she said. "We're exactly where we should be. No drift."

Reed stood from his chair, moving to the center of the bridge, his eyes fixed on the viewscreen. "Great work, Addison."

Perevian drifted closer to the swirling chaos before them.

The viewscreen displayed a kaleidoscope of colors as gas clouds rippled and shifted, casting shades of crimson, amber, and violet across the debris field. Glowing strands of superheated gas wove through the scene, pulsating and swirling like cosmic rivers through the void, illuminating the chaotic landscape while patches of dust and rock lurked in the distance. As the ship ventured deeper, the stars dimmed, and the region took on the feel of a shattered battlefield, silent but charged with an ominous energy as if the violence of the past still echoed.

Beyond the vibrant clouds, debris thickened; chunks of asteroids and celestial remnants collided, sending plumes of dust spiraling outward. Occasional bursts of light flashed as rocks clashed or gas met solid matter, crackling with energy. Reed observed distant lightning-like arcs rippling through the gas clouds, remnants of electromagnetic forces. The entire region seemed to throb with the memory of the star's violent death.

What lay ahead wasn't just a field of debris—it was a cosmic graveyard, the remnants of a star that had once shone brilliantly, now reduced to fragmented asteroids and swirling clouds of gas. Massive chunks of shattered planetary bodies floated in the void. Some pieces were small, barely larger than the ship itself, while others were towering monoliths of rock and metal, tumbling lazily in the weightlessness of space.

Russo's voice broke the stillness. "Captain, sensors are picking up gravitational anomalies across the region. As we enter the outer edges of the remnant, things will start getting tricky."

Reed nodded. "Keep us steady, Addison. Chen, monitor the structural integrity of the ship. We don't know what kind of gravitational distortions we're dealing with yet."

"We're approaching the outer edge of the asteroid belt," Addison reported, her hands steady on the controls as she guided the ship carefully through the dense field of debris. "It's going to get tight."

Reed stepped closer to the viewscreen, studying the field ahead. "Engage thrusters," he ordered. "Addison, take it slow and steady." His eyes remained fixed on the swirling debris. The ship moved with precision, avoiding chunks of debris and pockets of cosmic dust. He could feel the tension in the air as they neared their target.

"Chen, open a channel to Aetherion," continued Reed. "Let them know we've arrived."

Chen's fingers moved across the console, and a soft chime indicated the connection had been established.

"Aetherion, this is Perevian," Reed said. "We've arrived at the Vela Supernova Remnant. What's your status?"

The bridge fell silent as they waited for Aetherion's

response.

Then, a burst of static filled the air before a familiar voice broke through.

"Perevian, this is Aetherion," came the voice of Commander Townsend. His voice seemed edged with fatigue. "It's good to hear from you. We've been holding position near the inner edge of the belt, but it's getting rough out here. The gravitational anomalies are getting worse."

Reed exchanged a glance with Chen before responding. "Will, this is Jonathan. We're enroute to your position. What's your condition?"

There was a pause on the other end before Townsend's voice came back, lower and more serious. "Our initial scans confirmed resource-rich asteroids, but the instability in the region makes it impossible to continue. We've been mapping the caverns inside some of the larger asteroids, but it's becoming too dangerous to proceed without help. Rockslides are frequent, and we've lost a number of drones already. We need your help to get the rest of the data and get out of here in one piece."

Reed nodded. "Understood. Once we rendezvous, we'll assist with the scans and complete the survey. How long can you hold your position?"

"Not long," Townsend admitted. "We've sustained some damage from smaller debris, but our shields are holding for now. We'll wait for your approach, but we need to move fast if we want to stay safe."

Reed's mind raced. The entire area was a minefield of gravitational distortions, cosmic dust, and asteroid fragments—

one wrong move could mean disaster.

"Hang tight, Aetherion. We'll be there soon."

"Copy that, Perevian," Townsend replied. "Transmitting our coordinates now. We'll be ready. Aetherion out."

The connection cut off with a soft click, leaving the bridge in silence.

Addison turned her head, her expression serious. "Captain, we've now entered the outer belt and we'll arrive at Aetherion's coordinates within the next four hours. We'll have to navigate through some of the densest parts of the belt."

Reed nodded. "Take it slow, Lieutenant. Keep an eye out for any sudden shifts in the debris."

The ship slowed to a cautious crawl as it entered the asteroid belt, the thrusters firing in short bursts to keep them steady. The asteroids drifted lazily around them, but Reed knew better than to let his guard down. Long minutes passed as they maneuvered through the shifting debris. One sudden fluctuation, and they could be crushed in an instant.

Chen's voice cut through the quiet. "Captain, we're entering a high-risk zone. Sensors are picking up erratic movement from some of the larger fragments."

Reed's gaze remained fixed on the viewscreen as the swirling chaos of the Vela Supernova Remnant seemed to press in around them. The vast field appeared deceptively still at a distance, but as they moved closer, it was clear that the remnants of the ancient explosion were anything but stable. Jagged pieces of rock and metal drifted aimlessly, colliding and splitting apart, sending smaller fragments spinning off in unpredictable directions. Some of the asteroids were colossal, their surfaces riddled with craters and fractures, while others were smaller but no less dangerous, darting through space like shrapnel.

"Chen," Reed said. "How bad are we talking?"

Chen scanned the real-time data streaming across her console. "We're seeing gravitational fluctuations from the remnants of the supernova. It's causing chunks of debris to shift unexpectedly, almost like they're being pushed and pulled by invisible hands. The larger asteroids are more stable, but the smaller fragments are constantly on the move. If we get too close…"

She didn't need to finish the sentence. Reed understood the risk all too well. The slightest collision with one of those smaller fragments could compromise the ship's hull, and in this environment, there would be no margin for error.

Russo chimed in from his station as he analyzed the gravitational data. "It's more than just debris movement. These gravitational distortions are fluctuating unpredictably. One moment they're weak, the next, they're pulling in every direction. It's like this whole region is a battlefield of competing forces."

Reed leaned forward, his hands gripping the edge of his console. "Are we in danger?"

"Not yet," Russo replied. "But if those fluctuations get stronger as we go deeper, we'll have to watch our trajectory closely."

"Chen, keep monitoring," Reed ordered. "If those gravitational shifts start affecting us, I want to know immediately."

"Aye, Captain," Chen responded, her hands a blur on her console. "I'll set the sensors to maximum sensitivity. Any significant fluctuation, and we'll get an early warning."

Reed nodded, his eyes returning to the viewscreen. The swirling clouds of gas and dust seemed to glow with an eerie light, casting strange shadows across the bridge. Time seemed to stretch as the debris field thickened. He could feel the tension building, the anticipation of what lay ahead.

At the helm, Addison's fingers pressed the controls, adjusting Perevian's trajectory. The ship responded to every small input, its engines humming as they navigated through the shifting gravitational forces. Invisible pockets of pressure tugged at the hull, causing the ship to tremble slightly underfoot. The inertial dampeners compensated, but Reed could still feel the subtle pulls.

Outside, the debris field began to thicken. Fragments of rock and metal drifted lazily. Addison adjusted the course again, threading the ship through the growing maze. A steady ping of impacts on the shields echoed through the bridge.

"We're approaching the first significant debris field," Chen reported. "It's dense, but navigable."

"Steady as she goes," Reed replied, gripping the armrest of his chair.

Perevian weaved through the dense belt, the ship's path narrowing as the asteroids grew in size. Some were colossal, drifting just beyond reach, while others floated deceptively still. Addison remained focused, her fingers working the controls. Each turn, each adjustment, was made with the utmost care, the ship skirting danger at every corner.

The bridge was quiet, save for the sound of the ship's systems and the occasional shudder as gravitational forces pulled at the hull. The shadows cast by the debris flickered across the viewscreen, creating an almost hypnotic rhythm.

A massive asteroid loomed ahead, slowly rotating as it drifted in their path. Its surface was pocked with craters, scars from long-forgotten impacts. Addison nudged the controls, guiding the ship around its edge, careful to avoid its gravitational pull. Perevian groaned slightly as it passed, the proximity triggering another small tremor through the deck.

Another asteroid drifted past, its size dwarfing the ship as they moved through the increasingly tight spaces between debris. Perevian shuddered again, the inertial dampeners struggling to keep up with the constant pressure changes. Reed remained silent, his attention split between the viewscreen and his crew's movements. Every action had to be perfect, every decision precise.

Without warning, a cluster of smaller rocks scattered across their path, forcing Addison to adjust course rapidly. Perevian tilted slightly, the stars on the viewscreen shifting as the ship narrowly avoided the incoming debris. Reed felt the tension rise, but Addison stayed composed, navigating through the chaos.

Time passed as the ship advanced deeper into the asteroid field. Reed watched with a clenched jaw. There was no turning back now. Each move had to be more exacting than the last, the stakes rising with every passing second.

Addison made another adjustment, the ship narrowly avoiding a large chunk of rock that had veered suddenly into their path. Reed exhaled slowly. They were getting closer, but the worst was still ahead.

"Captain," Addison said, "I've got a clear path to the inner belt. We'll be in range to Aetherion in about an hour."

"Very well," Reed replied.

Addison adjusted Perevian's course as it approached Aetherion, careful to maintain a calculated distance. The massive asteroids drifted slowly, their gravitational pulls creating subtle shifts in the ship's trajectory. Reed stood watching the holographic display while Addison navigated through the field, using constant thruster bursts to counteract gravitational perturbations. Every movement required a careful balance of speed, distance, and timing.

"We're approaching Aetherion," Addison reported. "Distance is now within ten kilometers."

Perevian slid into position alongside, the enormous asteroids of the belt looming like dark giants in the distance. Aetherion hovered in the darkness, its sleek hull reflecting faint starlight. Though it shared the same streamlined silhouette as Perevian, its design bore the marks of a different era—its edges slightly more angular, its panels less flush with the body. The engines, though clearly more robust, were mounted wider, giving the ship a bulkier appearance.

As the two ships neared, they held a separation of just over a kilometer—close enough for communication and data sharing, but far enough to avoid mutual gravitational interference. The asteroid field was dense but navigable, and the real challenge was staying ahead of the constantly shifting debris patterns.

"We're in position, Captain," Addison reported as the ship locked onto its final trajectory. "Aetherion is holding steady, and there's no major debris between us."

Reed nodded. "Chen, give me a full sweep. I want a complete analysis before we do anything."

Chen tapped a series of commands into the system. "Aye, Captain. I'll have preliminary data in a few moments."

The ship's sensors hummed to life, scanning the surrounding asteroid field and sending waves of data to the bridge. Reed studied the viewscreen. The belt around them was dense with asteroids clustered together in unpredictable orbits. Several of the larger ones—marked in red on the map—were hollow, with deep cave systems running through them.

"Captain, we're receiving a signal from Aetherion," said Chen.

"Put them through," Reed replied.

The main screen blinked to life, revealing Commander Townsend with a short salt-and-pepper beard framing his weary face. Dark circles under his eyes betrayed the exhaustion from weeks of navigating the treacherous asteroid belt. Though his uniform was neat, his tense jaw and tousled hair hinted at days without rest. Behind him, the dim, flickering lights of Aetherion's bridge cast long shadows, hinting at the strain his crew must be feeling as they pressed on through the volatile region. "Jonathan," Townsend said with a tired smile, "good to see you."

"Will," Reed replied, nodding in return. "Looks like you've been busy."

"You could say that," Townsend said, glancing at a console to his side. "We've mapped most of the major features of the belt, but these cave systems… they're something else. We've barely scratched the surface."

"We're here to help with that," Reed said. "I've read your preliminary findings, but I'd like to get your input before we move forward. What have you learned since then?"

Townsend's expression darkened. "The caverns are vast. Some of the asteroids have cave systems running hundreds of kilometers deep. But they're unstable. The belt's orbit takes it through a region with heavy gravitational interference from a nearby gas giant. It's been wreaking havoc on the caverns. We've recorded tremors and minor collapses every time the asteroid field passes too close."

Reed turned to Russo. "Thoughts?"

Russo was fixed on the data streaming across the screen from Aetherion. "That gas giant's gravitational pull would be more than enough to cause trouble. Its sheer size is going to create massive tidal forces, and those effects get amplified as the asteroids move closer. The tremors Commander Townsend reported aren't just random—they're a direct result of the gravitational shifts." He paused, analyzing further. "Given the uneven mass distribution in the belt—some of these asteroids probably have dense metal cores—it's no wonder we're seeing stronger effects. Those concentrated metal deposits would make them much more sensitive to gravitational tides."

He leaned in closer to the display, running simulations in real-time. "As the belt passes closer to the gas giant's orbit, the asteroids with higher densities would experience more pronounced shifts."

Reed nodded, following Russo's train of thought. "So, it's not just their size, but the makeup of the asteroids themselves."

"Exactly," Russo replied. "That could make some of those cave systems even more unstable."

Reed nodded. "How much warning can we expect before they destabilize?"

Russo tapped on his console. "Minimal. We're talking minutes—if we're lucky. I'll run continuous simulations based on the readings we get from Aetherion and our own sensors."

Reed looked back at Townsend. "We'll assist with the deeper survey, but I want to be cautious. We can't afford to lose more equipment—or worse."

"Agreed," Townsend replied. "We've been holding off on a specific section of the cave network. It's too deep, and our equipment couldn't handle it. I'm sending over the coordinates now. It's one of the largest caverns we've detected."

Reed's console blinked as the data transfer completed. He glanced down, then back at Townsend. "We'll take it from here. Thank you for the brief."

Townsend gave a nod. "We'll share the rest of the data we've collected. It should give you a better idea of which sections of the asteroid belt are the most unstable."

"Appreciated," Reed said. "Let's stay in close communication. We'll proceed with the survey, and I'll update you with any findings."

"Good luck, Jonathan. We'll be monitoring from here."

The screen went dark. Reed turned to his crew. "Alright, we've got our target. Addison, set a course to

Aetherion's asteroid."

Addison's fingers moved smoothly over the console. "Course set, Captain. We'll be within range in two hours."

Perevian began its careful approach, the ship's thrusters firing in controlled bursts. On the viewscreen, the asteroid belt stretched out, vast and menacing. Addison made minute adjustments, guiding the ship through the dense field of smaller debris that orbited larger asteroids like moons around a planet. Each adjustment was subtle, the thrusters firing briefly to keep the course steady. The process was painstaking, each correction ensuring Perevian avoided a potentially catastrophic collision.

Outside, clouds of dust and small fragments of rock swirled past, some clinking faintly against the ship's hull. The closer they got, the more ominous the asteroid appeared. Massive fractures cut jagged paths along its face, some wide enough to swallow their ship whole, while others stretched into narrow, deep fissures that seemed to reach the asteroid's core. The rock face, rough and unforgiving, was a stark reminder of the violent forces that had shaped it.

As the ship continued to edge closer to Aetherion's asteroid, its silhouette grew larger on the viewscreen, a hulking mass that dwarfed everything around it. The rough, uneven terrain stretched endlessly, a mottled gray surface streaked with veins of darker, metallic hues. These veins hinted at valuable minerals—potential riches buried within—but they were overshadowed by the asteroid's raw, dangerous presence.

Chen examined the incoming data, her eyes narrowing as she processed the information. "Captain, this asteroid is massive—roughly 525 kilometers in diameter. The surface is riddled with craters and deep fissures, likely from countless impacts. But what's more concerning is the internal structure. These caverns make the asteroid incredibly unstable."

She tapped a few keys, pulling up a more detailed image. "From what I can see so far it looks like the asteroid is composed of a mix of dense rock and lighter materials, with irregular layers throughout. This thing isn't solid—it's a web of fragile corridors and voids."

Reed nodded as he absorbed the information. "So, it's not just a rock—it's a labyrinth."

"Yes, Captain," said Chen. "These corridors weren't just caused by impacts—there are signs of ancient volcanic activity. It looks like, early in its formation, molten material may have flowed beneath the surface, creating tunnels and caverns that have since cooled and hollowed out. Over time, as the asteroid aged, the surface collapsed in places, making these fragile tunnels even more unstable."

The asteroid's surface, now fully visible on the viewscreen, seemed to stretch endlessly in every direction, its uneven texture a blend of jagged ridges and sunken craters. Some craters were shallow, their rims partially eroded by time, while others were deep enough to disappear into shadow. Streaks of metallic veins traced erratic patterns across the rock face, standing out against the dull gray of the surrounding material. Despite the allure of potential resources, the asteroid's appearance was anything but inviting.

Addison adjusted the ship's trajectory slightly, her hands steady on the controls. "We're threading the needle here," she said. "Every piece of debris out there feels like it's got our name on it."

Chen continued to refine the scans. "This asteroid isn't just unstable—it's precarious. The hollow corridors inside create pressure points. A minor disturbance, maybe even our presence, could be enough to set off a chain reaction."

Reed frowned, his eyes fixed on the rotating model of the asteroid displayed on the main console. "Let's hope it doesn't come to that. Proceed cautiously."

The asteroid loomed ever larger, its gravitational pull subtly affecting Perevian's trajectory. The occasional impacts against the hull grew more frequent, though still minor—dust and fragments from the surrounding debris cloud brushing against the ship's exterior.

Outside, the asteroid's fractured surface seemed to shift subtly in the changing light, shadows deepening as they approached.

CHAPTER FOUR

We've arrived at the target coordinates, Captain," Addison called out from her station. "Bring us into a stable orbit just outside the gravity well," Reed ordered.

"Aye, Captain," replied Addison. "Preparing to enter synchronized orbit."

Perevian's thrusters engaged in a series of controlled bursts, each one calculated to counteract the asteroid's weak gravitational pull. The ship's trajectory adjusted slowly, matching velocity with the asteroid while keeping a safe distance to avoid any unforeseen fluctuations in its gravity. Addison used the ship's inertial guidance system to ensure the approach was smooth and steady.

Perevian gradually slowed, slipping into a stable orbit just beyond the asteroid's influence. Outside, the massive rock rotated lazily, its irregular shape generating small but unpredictable gravitational variances that kept the ship's sensors working constantly to adjust their position.

"We've stabilized our orbit," Addison reported, her hands still poised over the controls, ready for any sudden changes. "Minimal gravitational interference, but we're holding steady."

"Very well," Reed said, his eyes scanning the displays.

"Maintain this orbit and keep all sensors on full alert."

Reed turned back to the viewscreen, looking out at the asteroid. It was an awe-inspiring sight, this massive chunk of rock suspended in space, hiding an entire world within. But it was also dangerous, and the thought of venturing into those unstable caverns made his stomach twist.

The ship's external floodlights swept over the asteroid's surface, revealing it in startling detail. The rock was far more imposing up close than any sensor readout or distant observation could have captured. The asteroid's surface wasn't just pitted and scarred—it was a brutal landscape shaped by millennia of collisions and cosmic forces.

As the lights continued to sweep over the asteroid, they revealed the cave. A massive, gaping hole, black as the void itself. The entrance was jagged and uneven, as though a colossal giant had clawed its way through the rock, leaving behind a gaping wound that led deep into the asteroid's dark, mysterious interior. The ship's lights didn't even come close to piercing the darkness inside, but what little could be seen revealed walls that seemed to twist and coil deep into the asteroid's core.

"Holding position just outside the entrance," Addison said quietly.

Reed rose from his chair and stepped forward, standing at the very edge of the bridge's platform. His eyes were locked on the screen, studying the massive formation that loomed before them. The asteroid's sheer size was overwhelming, and the mouth of the cave seemed to beckon them in—an invitation to explore, or perhaps a warning to stay away. "Alright, Chen, send in the drones. Let's see what we're dealing with inside."

With a quick tap on her console, Chen sent the drones whirring into action. The faint sound of the small, multi-legged machines reverberated through Perevian's hull as they launched, swiftly vanishing into the cavernous mouth of the asteroid. Their tiny lights blinked against the shadows, briefly illuminating the rock formations before they disappeared completely into the abyss.

On the bridge, the main screen flickered to life with the drone video feeds, as well as a three-dimensional holovision projection in the center of the room. The feed from the four drones showed a stark and detailed view as they plunged deeper into the asteroid—narrow, winding tunnels, walls rough and irregular, scarred by ancient impacts and fissures. The drones' floodlights cast long, ghostly shadows, bringing fleeting glimpses of glistening mineral veins that ran like arteries through the rock. The entire cave system seemed to pulse with an otherworldly energy, as though it were alive.

"Feeds look good," Chen reported, her fingers adjusting the drones' paths. They glided silently through the tunnels, their cameras feeding back crisp, high-definition images to the crew.

Drone Alpha's path opened into a wide, cathedral-like chamber, its sheer scale breathtaking. The ceiling arched high above them, lost in shadow, while the walls were a strange blend of angular, natural rock and smooth, almost glassy surfaces. Massive cracks and crevices ran through the chamber, evidence of volcanic or tectonic forces that had once torn through the asteroid. Precious ores shimmered like threads of silver and gold, embedded deep within the walls, their glow reflecting off the dark surfaces.

The drone's lights swept across the chamber, revealing towering rock formations that jutted upward like spires, their surfaces slick with condensation. The ground was uneven, pocked with deep craters and strange crystalline structures that rose up in clusters, their facets gleaming as they caught the light. These formations were like nothing Reed had ever seen before—unearthly, almost organic in their appearance.

Chen leaned closer to the screen. "We'll need a full geological scan of Alpha's crystals," she said.

As Drone Bravo ventured deeper, its light illuminated a colossal fissure that ran the length of the floor of another cavern. The rift descended into an abyss of inky blackness, seemingly endless. It was as if the asteroid had been cracked from the inside out, a scar from an ancient, violent event.

Russo, who had been poring over gravitational data at his station, spoke up. "Bravo's fissure... it's aligned almost perfectly with the gravitational anomalies I've been tracking. There's a definite correlation here. We're seeing shifts in the asteroid's core—this entire region is unstable."

Chen's voice remained steady as she monitored the drones' progress. "The deeper they go, the more stress fractures I'm picking up. These rock formations are holding for now, but any sudden shift could trigger a collapse."

Drone Charlie navigated a narrow offshoot from the main chamber, its light flickering over what looked like glittering veins of crystal embedded in the rock. The crystals seemed to pulse faintly, as if they held some internal energy. As the drone drew closer, the light it emitted refracted off the crystals in dazzling patterns, casting beams of light across the walls.

"Captain," Chen said. "This chamber's structural integrity is fragile at best. If we disturb anything, we could cause a chain reaction of collapses. These crystals... they may be unstable too. I'm running full scans now."

Russo, his eyes glued to his station, chimed in. "I'll overlay the drone feed with gravitational data. If anything starts shifting—even slightly—we'll know ahead of time. But the deeper they go, the more unpredictable these fluctuations become."

The visuals on the holovision display captivated the crew as the drones navigated through the asteroid's labyrinthine tunnels. The three-dimensional projection expanded around them, mapping the cave system in striking detail. Tight passageways gave way to towering rock formations that glistened with frost, casting reflective glints in the surrounding space. The drones pushed deeper, their lights revealing the intricate, multi-leveled structure of the asteroid's caverns, each passage twisting and turning like the veins of a vast, ancient colony.

At one point, the holovision adjusted its perspective, showing Drone Delta passing over a ledge that revealed a vast underground reservoir far below. The crew leaned forward in their seats, captivated by the sight. The projection highlighted the glistening surface of liquid trapped within the asteroid's depths, its smooth, mirror-like surface untouched for millennia. The liquid seemed impossibly still, shimmering in the faint light cast by the crystals embedded in the surrounding rock.

Russo quickly pulled up readings, his expression shifting

from surprise to curiosity. "That's not water," he reported, his fingers flying over the console. "It's pure liquid ammonia, heavily saturated with salts and other chemicals." He scanned the data in front of him, a growing excitement in his voice. "This… this is incredible. The composition alone could reveal so much about the asteroid's past."

Addison, still at the helm, glanced up from her controls. "How can a liquid exist inside an asteroid?"

Russo looked up from the screen, his eyes gleaming with discovery. "Large asteroids, like this one, have their own gravity. It's weaker than what you'd feel on a moon or planet, but it's still enough to influence the materials inside. That gravity helps create the pressure needed to maintain liquid in the core, similar to how planets and moons have internal layers of molten material beneath their surfaces. The asteroid's mass may not be enormous, but it's enough to create its own internal environment, keeping things like liquid ammonia stable."

"Ammonia has a much lower freezing point than water," Chen added. "The internal heat from radioactive decay could be just enough to keep it from freezing solid, while the surrounding rock and ice layers act as insulation. Even in these extreme conditions, liquid ammonia can remain stable as long as the temperature stays low and the pressure remains consistent."

Reed, standing at the center of the bridge, watched the holovision display in silent awe. "That's extraordinary," he said quietly, his voice tinged with wonder. "We could be looking at something that's been undisturbed for millions of years."

Chen's fingers moved swiftly across her console,

analyzing the mineral composition from the drone's sensors. "The readings suggest the surrounding rock is rich in metals and rare minerals," she said, excitement building in her tone. "Whatever process formed this asteroid must have been incredibly complex."

Russo nodded, already preparing more detailed analysis. "We need a full report on the chemical composition of that liquid. Liquid ammonia like this could give us insight into similar environments on moons, like Jupiter's Titan."

The crew buzzed with renewed energy as the drone hovered over the ammonia lake, its sensors sweeping the surface in careful patterns. As they worked, layers of data began to appear on the holovision display—chemical compositions, temperature, pressure readings—all adding to the growing picture of the asteroid's internal structure and the unique environmental conditions that preserved this liquid ammonia reservoir.

The projection made it feel as if the crew stood on the edge of the cave themselves, looking down at the reflective, mirror-like surface. The stillness of the liquid gave the scene an otherworldly quality, magnifying the sense of wonder—and danger—lurking within the asteroid's depths.

The drones pressed on, venturing deeper into the asteroid's heart, revealing chambers of unearthly beauty and hidden threats. As they moved further into the depths, the cave system began to show its age. Cracks lined the walls, and the floor was uneven and crumbling, clear evidence of past rockslides. Small tremors occasionally shook loose debris, though nothing major... yet.

"Structural integrity is low in several places," Chen said, her voice cautious. "There's a lot of strain on the surrounding rock. If the gravitational forces shift again, we could see major collapses."

"Gravitational shifts expected soon?" Reed asked.

Russo tapped into the data streaming from the drones. "Yes. The gas giant is nearing its closest approach to this region of the asteroid belt, and the gravitational pull from the planet is increasing. Based on current projections, we have an hour or two before significant movement begins. But given the instability of the surrounding rock, it could accelerate without much warning."

Reed tightened his grip on the console. "Let's keep this quick, then. I want to know exactly what we're dealing with before the next gravitational shift hits."

The drones pushed deeper into the cavernous depths of the asteroid. As they scanned the rock walls, their sensors detected elevated concentrations of iridium and palladium—rare metals typically formed only in cataclysmic conditions. These elements were not just present; they were embedded in quantities that defied all known models of asteroid formation.

"These metals," Russo began, his voice barely concealing his astonishment, "are elements that require both extreme pressure and heat, typical of the aftermath of a supernova. What we're seeing here is beyond rare. This asteroid's core contains metals that suggest it was at the heart of a dying star before it was scattered across space by the explosion."

The drones continued deeper, revealing chambers so high they vanished into shadow. The metallic walls shimmered under the drone lights, the product of intense pressure and extreme thermal conditions from the explosion that shaped this asteroid.

"This is like peering into the guts of a star," Russo muttered, fascinated by the display. "These reflective surfaces are metallic alloys formed under pressures we can barely replicate in labs. If we can get a sample, we might be able to study their atomic structures to understand conditions inside a supernova."

The farther the drones ventured, the more the asteroid's tortured geological past became evident. Dust and small rocks cascaded from the ceilings of the caverns with increasing frequency, their fragile state made clear by the drones' laser scanners. This asteroid, while stable enough for now, was on the verge of structural failure. And yet, amidst the danger, the beauty of the formations stood out.

Enormous quartz and garnet crystals protruded from the cave walls. These crystals had been compressed into their current forms by unimaginable forces, some of them exhibiting clear signs of annealing—where high pressure has allowed them to recrystallize into their current forms. The minerals shimmered in shades of red and purple, casting a faint glow through the dust-filled air. The walls also displayed layers of basalt and feldspar, formed during the turbulent cooling process after the asteroid was violently expelled from the supernova's core.

"This asteroid is a geological treasure," Russo said, awe evident in his voice. "The mineral composition alone is unprecedented. I'm seeing traces of osmium, ruthenium, and rhodium—platinum group elements in concentrations that defy conventional models."

The drones' spectrometers began to pick up unusual energy signatures from deep within the asteroid. Russo zoomed in on the readings. One of the data sets indicated the presence of a highly unstable metallic isotope that had never been cataloged before. Its electron configuration was volatile.

"Look at this," Russo said. "This isotopic structure… it's beyond anything I've ever seen. This element shouldn't exist outside the core of a star. The fact that it's here means we're looking at remnants of the nucleosynthesis process that formed the universe's heavy elements."

Russo paused, studying the volatility of the isotopic structure. "It's possible this isotope formed under such extreme compression and heat that it can't survive outside those conditions for long. Any disturbance could trigger its decay, and we don't know what kind of energy release that might cause."

As the drones ventured ever deeper into the asteroid, the geological complexity intensified. The rock layers became denser, with heavier elements like thorium and uranium appearing in the scans. Some cave walls were rich in iron-nickel alloys, similar to those found in metallic meteorites.

"Captain," Chen said, "we're detecting increased radiation levels deeper in. It's likely from the uranium deposits scattered through the core. We'll need to monitor closely for any critical levels of decay, but these readings are still within operational limits for now."

Drone Charlie transmitted a new set of images, revealing

a massive central chamber, its walls lined with enormous crystalline structures gleaming in the dim light. They appeared to be composed of an unfamiliar compound, likely a byproduct of the asteroid's unique chemical composition and the extreme conditions caused by the Vela Supernova Remnant. Their sheer size—some stretching up to a kilometer in length—suggested a slow growth process, possibly influenced by the aftermath of the supernova over millions of years.

Russo's brow furrowed as he analyzed the readings. "These crystals… they're emitting a faint electromagnetic field. That shouldn't be possible unless they've been exposed to strong magnetic forces over time. Given that this asteroid was likely formed from debris in the remnant, it's possible it passed through intense magnetic fields or was shaped by the supernova's explosion."

The discovery of these magnetized crystals added another layer of intrigue to the mission. As the drone continued to scan the chamber, the crew began to realize that this asteroid was not just a geological oddity—it was a cosmic relic, shaped by forces and events far beyond anything humanity had previously studied.

As the drone neared the farthest point of the main chamber, the walls of the cave trembled, their surfaces crisscrossed with widening cracks that groaned under the immense pressure. A low rumble reverberated through the underground network, vibrating the rock as dust and pebbles cascaded from above, forming swirling clouds illuminated by the drone's lights. The once stable walls now threatened to cave, and the tension on the bridge matched the instability below.

"That's not good," Addison muttered. "Rockslide?"

Chen's gaze darted between her displays. "Small for now," she replied. "But it's escalating. Gravitational forces are building. If we don't pull the drones out, they could be buried under tons of debris."

Reed didn't need a second thought. "Start sending them back, Chen. Addison, prep the ship for an immediate withdrawal in case orbit becomes unstable."

The drones instantly began to retreat, their thrusters igniting in a brilliant blue as they sped through the winding labyrinth of tunnels. Leading the way, Drone Alpha surged forward, its sensors scanning every rockface for signs of collapse. The walls seemed to close in, jagged edges jutting out as fractured stone glistened in the dim light. Small rocks clattered onto the path ahead as the drone nimbly darted through the tightest gaps, its hull barely clearing the outcroppings. It swerved hard to avoid a fresh rockfall, its sensors quickly recalibrating as it weaved around another narrow bend.

"Drone Alpha's nearing the entrance," Chen reported, eyes locked on the data flooding her screen. "But Bravo's in trouble—there's been a major rockfall in Tunnel Three, blocking its route."

On the screen, Drone Bravo twisted sharply to avoid a falling boulder that crashed down from above, exploding into a shower of fragments.

Chen tapped at the console. "I'm rerouting Drone Bravo through a secondary passage," she said. "It's unstable, but it's the only way out."

The drone banked hard through a tight side tunnel as more rocks tumbled behind it. Its cameras revealed a narrow passage barely enough room for it to maneuver. Each twist seemed to bring it closer to danger.

Drone Charlie, meanwhile, was struggling further behind. It had been sent deeper into the most treacherous part of the cave system, and now it faced an obstacle course of shifting rock. Its camera feed flickered as it dodged another set of boulders that had broken loose from the ceiling, the ground beneath it trembling violently. The drone's thrusters fired in short bursts, navigating through a web of deep fissures that snaked across the floor, some of them wide enough to swallow it whole.

"Charlie's stuck," Chen muttered under her breath, her eyes widening as the screen showed a massive wall of debris ahead. "I'm boosting its thrusters."

With a sudden surge of power, Drone Charlie sped forward, banking left as a section of the ceiling collapsed just behind it. The drone narrowly dodged the falling rocks, its path ahead shrouded in thick dust. The cracks in the walls were growing wider, and the floor beneath it crumbled into deep crevices. The drone pitched upward, firing its thrusters hard to avoid the growing abyss below.

Russo studied the data on his screen. "The asteroid's core is collapsing. If we don't move now, we're looking at a catastrophic implosion."

"Chen, status of the drones?" Reed asked, his eyes glued to the images on the screen.

"Alpha is almost clear," she replied, "but Delta's a lost

cause—it's completely buried under the collapse in Sector Eight. Bravo's making progress, but Charlie's facing more blockages."

"Leave Delta," Reed said through gritted teeth. "Focus on getting the others out."

Drone Alpha sped through the final tunnel, its sensors adjusting to the dust cloud that had formed as the cave collapsed behind it. The mouth of the cave loomed ahead, the dark void of open space just beyond. With a final burst of speed, Alpha shot out into the vacuum, its hull dusted with fragments of the asteroid's surface as it ascended toward Perevian.

"Alpha is clear," Chen confirmed, but her attention immediately shifted to the other drones still in danger.

Drone Bravo was next, navigating the narrow passage Chen had rerouted it through. The drone's camera showed the walls trembling, rocks breaking away from the ceiling in chunks that smashed into the tunnel floor, creating obstacles at every turn. A massive boulder suddenly dropped from above, but Bravo reacted quickly, twisting to the side and rocketing through a gap that was closing fast. As the cave continued to collapse behind it, the drone picked up speed, shooting out of the tunnel just as the walls caved in.

"Bravo's out," Chen reported, her voice tinged with relief.

But Drone Charlie was still deep inside the labyrinth, struggling to find a clear path as debris continued to rain down. The screen flickered violently, and the drone's cameras captured the chaos ahead—massive rock formations splintering, large cracks tearing through the ground, and jagged stones tumbling into the cave. The drone swerved sharply to avoid being crushed, its path twisting and turning with increasing speed.

"Charlie's in trouble," Addison warned, her hands gripping the helm. "The whole tunnel's about to collapse."

Russo's console beeped with an alert as the gravitational forces spiked again. "We're running out of time," he said. "The asteroid's core is shifting rapidly."

Reed's eyes locked on the screen as he watched Charlie struggle through the falling debris. "Chen, you have ten seconds. Then we're leaving it."

The drone's thrusters flared at full power as the tunnel behind it crumbled into dust. Charlie twisted through a collapsing corridor, narrowly avoiding a massive boulder that smashed into the ground where it had been just moments before.

"We're losing stability in the chamber!" Russo shouted as the seismic tremors intensified, vibrating through the ship.

Chen's grip tightened on the controls. "Hold together, just hold together..." she muttered under her breath as she maneuvered the drone through the claustrophobic, winding path. The walls around it trembled, fragments of rock bouncing off Charlie as the collapsing cave roared behind.

Suddenly, a violent tremor ripped through the asteroid, sending a cascade of boulders crashing down ahead, blocking the route. Charlie's sensors screamed with warnings on the viewscreen, but Chen didn't flinch. She jammed the thrusters forward, pushing the drone into a desperate nosedive. The rocks above crashed mere inches from the drone's tail, slamming down in a deafening explosion of debris that engulfed the passage in a cloud of dust.

"Dang it!" Chen growled. She jerked the controls hard to the left, weaving Charlie through a tight crevice as the walls on either side began to collapse inward. The drone shot through the narrow gap, scraping against edges of rock.

"We're close," Chen murmured as she adjusted the drone's course. The final stretch loomed ahead, but another section of the tunnel caved in, sending more rubble tumbling directly into Charlie's path.

With a final desperate lunge, she directed Charlie into a steep vertical climb. The drone shot upward just as a massive slab of rock crashed down, clipping one of its rear thrusters. Sparks flew. Alarms blared. Chen's heart raced as she fought to regain control, her hands moving to stabilize the damaged drone.

"Come on, Charlie…" she muttered.

With a final burst of speed it shot through the cave's mouth, emerging into the black void of space. A massive cloud of dust billowed out from the entrance, following its trail, but the drone was safe, its thrusters still firing as it headed toward Perevian.

"Charlie's out," Chen said, exhaling as the last drone cleared the collapsing asteroid.

As the drones made their way back to Perevian, the crew watched in tense silence, eyes locked on the holovision display showing the unfolding disaster. The asteroid, with its towering crystalline structures and complex passageways, began to buckle under the immense strain. Fissures spread rapidly across its surface, splitting the rock with violent cracks. It trembled, sending deep vibrations through its structure, which reverberated through the ship's hull. Before the crew's eyes, the cave system began to collapse in on itself, sending plumes of debris into the void.

Reed gripped the armrest of his chair. "Addison, pull us back to a safe distance," he ordered.

Addison nodded sharply. "Aye Captain," her hands moving rapidly over the controls. The hum of the ship's thrusters filled the air as Perevian began to back away from the asteroid. The ship's sensors warned of incoming debris as larger chunks of rock were torn free from the surface, thrown into space by the sheer force of the collapse.

The crew held their breath as the ship reversed. The asteroid visibly strained under the pressure, with rock faces collapsing and scattering into space like shrapnel, the force of the implosion propelling debris outward. Addison made careful adjustments, keeping Perevian steady and clear of the spreading danger. The thrusters fired in quick bursts, pushing the ship further away from the unstable asteroid.

For a moment, it seemed as though it might break apart entirely. Large fissures snaked across its surface. Every shift of rock sent new tremors through the area, and the crew could feel the faint vibrations as debris glanced off the ship's shields. Perevian rocked slightly, but Addison held the ship firm, maneuvering through the chaos.

"We're clear of the immediate danger zone," Addison reported.

Reed exhaled slowly, allowing the tension to leave his body. "Good work," he said. "Everyone, let's take a moment to assess the data. We need to understand what we got before I make any decisions."

As Perevian pulled further away, Reed couldn't shake the feeling that they had only just begun to scratch the surface of the dangers lurking within the belt. The gravitational shifts were growing more unpredictable.

But they had their orders. The mission wasn't over, and Reed knew they couldn't turn back now.

CHAPTER FIVE

The interior of the hollow asteroid had revealed far more than anyone had anticipated. The data collected by the drones was now being analyzed by the crew, each new piece of information further expanding the scope of their discovery. Vast, unstable caverns, intricate veins of rare minerals, and dangerously widening rock fissures formed the fragile internal structure. The latest readings confirmed what the visuals had already suggested—this asteroid was a geological time bomb, its integrity on the verge of collapse. The gravitational anomalies in the region were accelerating, and the clock was ticking.

The crew worked in silence as they processed the information. Layers of data flashed across the holovision display: temperature fluctuations, stress points in the rock, and seismic activity spikes. The weight of the situation began to settle over the bridge like a gathering storm.

Russo let out a low whistle as he studied the stress maps projected on his console. "Captain, I've seen unstable systems before, but this? It's like trying to hold back an avalanche with a broom. Every reading I pull up makes it look worse."

Chen, leaning over her console, added, "It's not just the asteroid. The entire belt is interacting in ways we haven't seen before. The gravitational forces from the gas giant are creating waves that are propagating through the whole field. If the initial collapse spreads, it could trigger a cascade across hundreds of kilometers of space."

Reed frowned, his eyes scanning the endless streams of data. "If that happens, we're looking at a region-wide disaster. Everything in the vicinity would be pulverized—and that includes us."

Suddenly, alarms blared throughout the bridge.

"Status report!" Reed barked.

Russo, his hands flying across the console, quickly processed the data. "The gravitational waves from the gas giant have triggered a cascading collapse. Multiple asteroids are destabilizing simultaneously. If we don't pull out now, we're going to be caught in a massive debris storm."

The main viewscreen lit up with red warning markers, tracking the trajectory of the debris. Reed's jaw tightened as the realization hit—this wasn't just one asteroid; the entire belt was reacting to the gravitational forces. A chain reaction was underway, and Perevian was dangerously close to being caught in the fallout.

"Alright, Lieutenant, reverse course back to Aetherion," Reed ordered, his voice steady despite the chaos unfolding around them.

Addison's fingers flew over the navigation controls. "Aye, Captain. It's going to be rough—this much debris will make it hard to maneuver, but I'll get us there."

The ship shuddered as another massive chunk of asteroid exploded, sending shards of rock careening toward Perevian.

The shields absorbed most of the impact, but the rumble through the hull told Reed just how close they were to disaster.

"Captain, the instability is spreading fast," Russo warned. "The asteroids closest to us are starting to break apart. We need to do something or both ships could be caught in the fallout."

Reed glanced at the holographic display showing the chaos expanding around them. "Chen," he said, his voice tight, "boost shields to maximum and reroute auxiliary power to thrusters."

"Aye, Captain."

Reed glanced at the sensor display on Addison's console. The readings showed Aetherion's position as a faint blip, steadily moving toward the outer edges of the field, carefully navigating through the growing turbulence.

"Chen, open a channel to Aetherion," Reed ordered.

A moment later, Townsend's face appeared on the screen, his expression troubled. "We're picking up the same thing, Jonathon. This whole section of the belt's going under. We're pulling out—what's your status?"

"We're moving as well," Reed said. "We'll meet at the outer edge. Just keep an eye on those shifts—the gravitational forces are throwing the larger asteroids into complete disarray."

Townsend gave a curt nod. "Understood. We'll meet you at the rendezvous. Aetherion out."

The screen blinked off, and Reed turned back to his crew. "Alright, let's move fast. Addison, take us through, slow and steady. Chen, manage shields and monitor the ship's systems and flag any irregularities. Russo, keep scanning for gravitational shifts and incoming debris."

Perevian began pushing through the increasingly volatile

debris field, its thrusters firing in precise, controlled bursts. Addison gripped the helm, her eyes locked on the navigation display. Around them, massive chunks of shattered asteroids careened past. Smaller rocks, sharp as razors, hurtled through the void, clashing together with devastating force. The space outside the ship was alive with destruction.

"Captain," Russo's voice cut through the tension, "the gravitational shifts are reaching critical levels. The entire belt is destabilizing. If we don't clear this field soon, we'll be trapped."

Reed kept his face composed, though the magnitude of the situation weighed heavily on him. "Addison, increase speed—but keep it under control. There's no room for error."

Addison responded with a nod. Her fingers moved over the controls, pushing Perevian through the treacherous field. The ship picked up speed, its thrusters firing harder as it weaved between massive chunks of rock. The proximity alarms were screaming, but Addison silenced them, her instincts taking over. Each turn was precise, every maneuver calculated down to the millisecond.

The bridge was a cacophony of warning sirens, fluctuating shield reports, and the low rumble of stressed metal. Russo muttered to himself as he monitored gravitational flux readings. "It's like the entire belt's in freefall, Captain. I've never seen shifts this erratic—gravity wells collapsing and reforming within seconds. We're flying blind here."

Chen glanced over. "Then we need more eyes. Captain, recommend deploying the recon drones. They won't survive long, but we can use their feeds to map a more precise route."

Reed nodded sharply. "Do it."

Chen tapped a series of commands into her console. Moments later, three sleek drones launched from Perevian's side bays, disappearing into the swirling chaos. Their feeds appeared on the main viewscreen, showing fractured paths of debris and unstable gravitational pockets ahead.

"Plotting updated vectors now," Chen announced. "Addison, watch for these markers—drones are picking up new safe zones, but they're fleeting."

Outside, a massive asteroid—several kilometers wide—shattered with an explosion as it impacted a neighboring rock. Colossal fragments tumbled toward the ship. Addison's pulse quickened. She fired the starboard thrusters, sending Perevian into a sharp roll. The ship narrowly avoided the first chunk, the rock grazing past the hull. A second piece spiraled toward them, and Addison yanked the controls hard to port, ducking the ship just in time.

"Three o'clock!" Chen yelled, adjusting the ship's shields as another massive fragment hurtled toward them.

Addison veered left, narrowly dodging a chunk the size of a building as it smashed into where they had been moments earlier, disintegrating into a cloud of smaller debris. The ship shuddered as the shockwave rippled through the void, but Addison quickly regained control.

Reed gripped the armrests of his chair, his knuckles white. "Keep talking to me!"

Addison didn't look up, her eyes locked on the navigation screen. "There's a corridor opening up. If I time it right, we can ride the gravitational push and slingshot out of this cluster. If I time it wrong…" Her voice trailed off, leaving the obvious unsaid.

"You won't time it wrong," Reed replied.

Behind them, the asteroid belt was collapsing in on itself. Massive slabs of rock collided in bursts of energy. The explosions echoed like thunder through space, and the once-majestic belt was now a swirling tempest of destruction. Dust clouds billowed outward, blotting out the stars.

"Structural integrity holding," Chen reported, though tension was clear in her voice. "We're almost clear. Another hundred thousand kilometers, and we'll be through the worst of it."

"Captain, if the belt's collapse accelerates, the safe zones could disappear entirely," added Russo. "We're playing a dangerous game here."

Reed turned to him, his expression unreadable. "Noted, Russo. But unless you have a faster way out, we stick to the plan."

Russo hesitated, then nodded. "Aye, Captain."

Addison fired the aft thrusters, pushing Perevian forward with another burst of speed. The ship lurched as it dodged an incoming fragment, the hull groaning under the strain. The alarms blared, but Addison had blocked everything out—her entire world was the ship, the controls, and the debris field she was navigating through.

Suddenly, a massive asteroid on their right detonated with a blinding explosion. The viewscreen flashed with light as chunks of rock hurtled toward the ship.

"Brace for impact!" Reed shouted. The ship rolled

violently to avoid the incoming shards, the maneuver forcing the crew back into their seats. Perevian twisted through the debris with only meters to spare, a smaller piece clipping the shield and sending a shudder through the hull.

But Addison kept them steady, her grip firm on the controls as she pushed the ship forward.

"We're getting boxed in," Chen warned. "The debris is piling up ahead of us. Gravity's pulling everything into a choke point."

Reed's body tensed as he saw the narrowing gap on the viewscreen. The collapsing asteroid belt had funneled the largest fragments into the center of the field, creating a blockade of tumbling rocks spiraling out of control, crashing into each other with brutal force. The collisions sent smaller fragments flying in every direction as the debris field churned with relentless energy.

Amidst the chaos, Aetherion appeared just ahead in the distance, its hull faintly visible. But the route ahead was anything but clear. Enormous shards of rock tumbled as gravitational forces pulled them into erratic orbits. Some moved with alarming speed, while others drifted slowly but menacingly, rotating just enough to threaten collision. The gaps were fleeting, closing as quickly as they opened.

"There's no clear path," Russo said grimly. "If we get caught in the middle of that, we'll be crushed."

"Addison, full stop," Reed ordered.

Addison eased back the thrusters, the ship's momentum carrying them dangerously close to the swirling mass.

"We're getting sucked in," Chen said, her voice low with

dread. "It's too strong to fight."

The ship rocked again as another collision sent a shockwave through the hull. The path they had taken to enter the field was now completely blocked, and the only way forward was equally treacherous. From the corner of the screen, Aetherion remained distant but visible, apparently stuck in the same gravitational currents.

"We're trapped," Addison said through gritted teeth, her hands desperately gripping the controls.

Suddenly the comms crackled to life and Townsend's voice came through. "Perevian, this is Aetherion. We've sustained critical damage. Shields are nearly gone, and our thrusters are on the edge of collapse. We can't hold out any longer."

"Chen, status of Aetherion?" ordered Reed.

She reviewed the data streaming in. "They're in bad shape. Their shields are weakening. Propulsion systems are close to failing. If they take a big hit… they won't make it."

Russo looked over at Reed. "Captain, I can't see them surviving another wave."

Reed exchanged a pained look with Russo before speaking. "What's the plan, Will?"

Townsend's voice carried a note of resignation. "We're going to make a final push into the debris field. We're redirecting all remaining power to the thrusters. We'll clear the largest fragments, but we won't survive the maneuver. Jonathon, we'll buy you time to escape."

Reed's stomach turned. The bridge fell into stunned silence. Chen's hands hovered over her console, her expression one of disbelief. "Captain, they can't—" she started, but stopped at the look on Reed's face.

"Will, you can't be serious!" said Reed.

"There isn't another option, Jonathon." Townsend replied. "We've gone over every possible scenario. If we don't do this, we both die. This is the only way to give you a chance."

Reed gripped the edge of the console, the cold metal grounding him as his mind raced for alternatives. "You're suggesting flying straight into that mess. There's no coming back from that."

"We know," Townsend said, his voice softening with a finality that twisted Reed's gut. "But this is the reality we're facing. My crew is prepared. We've made peace with it."

Reed's voice took on a sharp edge. "No, there has to be another way. We could deploy our drones to clear a path, or use the mining lasers to break apart the largest fragments! We've got to try something—we're not leaving you behind to—"

Townsend cut him off. "We're not asking, Jonathon. There's just no time. This is the reality we're facing. You need to accept it. Perevian can still make it, but we have to make this move. It's your only chance."

Reed's heart pounded in his chest. He shook his head, trying to find the right words. His voice, when it came, was rough with emotion. "You're asking me to sit here and watch your ship—watch you—"

"Look, Jonathon," Townsend interrupted again, his voice filled with unspoken emotion. "If you try to save us, you'll doom both ships. You know that. We've been through too much together. Let us do this… think of your crew."

Reed closed his eyes, the weight pressing down on him. He forced himself to accept the reality before him. Finally, he opened his eyes and took a deep breath. "Will, you're right. But don't think for a second this makes it any easier."

"I know," Townsend said. "It's been an honor, Captain. Now get your crew out of here. Don't let our sacrifice go to waste."

Reed swallowed hard, his words catching in his throat before he finally found his voice. "Understood, Aetherion," he said quietly. "We'll see you in the next life."

The comms fell silent, and Reed stood motionless, watching as Aetherion prepared for its final maneuver. The ship's thrusters roared with power, and it surged forward, heading straight for the largest fragments of debris. The crew on Perevian watched in silent awe as their sister ship made its final charge.

"Addison," Reed said, his voice barely above a whisper. "Hold steady. Be ready to move as soon as they clear the path."

Addison nodded, her hands on the controls. "Aye, Captain."

On the screen, Aetherion wove through the debris field, its thrusters burning at full capacity as it headed for the largest threats. The ship's shields flickered, sparks flying as pieces of rock collided with the hull. But Aetherion pressed on, driving into the heart of the collapsing asteroid field.

"They're taking out the largest fragments," Chen said quietly, her eyes never leaving the screen. "They can't survive long."

Russo stood frozen at his station, watching the desperate

maneuver. "This is insane," he muttered under his breath. "It's like trying to outrun an avalanche while carrying the mountain on your back."

Chen glanced at him but said nothing. There was no need; the sentiment was shared by everyone on the bridge.

Aetherion collided with the first massive chunk of asteroid, sending it spinning away from the debris field. The impact shook the ship, and its shields finally collapsed under the strain. The hull cracked, but it didn't stop. The crew pushed their ship toward the next threat, determined to clear the way for Perevian.

"They're really doing it," Russo muttered, his voice filled with disbelief.

Another impact, and this time Aetherion's engines sputtered, the ship's hull buckling as it collided with the second massive fragment. But the debris was moving, and the path was clearing.

Aetherion was disintegrating before their eyes. The once-majestic ship, a symbol of endurance and strength, was now being torn apart by the merciless forces surrounding it. Its sleek hull, which had weathered the void of space and the countless trials of deep-space exploration, was now crumpling like paper under the impacts. Jagged rents opened up across the ship's body, spilling metal plating and internal components into the swirling maelstrom. Each new collision sent shockwaves rippling through its frame, splintering off pieces of the proud vessel.

The vast, dark void was filled with the remains of the ship, pieces spinning and colliding like shattered glass. Reed could see the ship's skeleton—the inner framework torn, beams bent at impossible angles, hanging precariously before they too succumbed to the relentless assault. Aetherion was now a ghostly shadow of itself, its integrity fully compromised, drifting aimlessly toward the heart of the vortex.

Reed's heart clenched as he watched the devastation unfold, helpless to stop it. Electrical sparks crackled from exposed conduits, momentarily illuminating the wreckage as the ship began to break apart in slow, agonizing stages. The midsection collapsed inward under the weight of its structural failure.

Asteroids smashed into what remained, sending plumes of debris spiraling into the blackness of space. Each impact was met with a shower of metal and fire as gases vented from the few remaining intact sections, creating fleeting bursts of light in the darkness. The ship, now little more than a collection of twisted wreckage, was being consumed by the chaos.

Reed's jaw tightened, his hands clenched into fists as he stood frozen, watching the slow-motion destruction. A mix of disbelief and sorrow washed over him as he saw Aetherion's final moments play out. The great ship that had served so faithfully was being erased, its existence reduced to a scattering of debris lost in the swirling tempest.

The crew of Perevian sat in solemn silence, the reality of the sacrifice sinking in. Aetherion was no more.

"They've done it," Chen whispered, her voice thick with emotion. "The way is clear."

"Addison," Reed said with a deep, unspoken grief. "Take us through."

With a low rumble, Perevian's engines roared to life, and the ship surged forward, propelled by the fortitude of its crew and the path Aetherion had sacrificed itself to clear. The debris field now swirled in eddies around them, but the largest and most dangerous pieces had been obliterated by Aetherion's final act of defiance. Through the viewscreen, asteroids, now smaller and less formidable, spiraled in slow, disorganized patterns. The ship moved steadily through the treacherous terrain, guided by Addison's capable hands.

Reed sat tall, his expression a mask of steely resolve, but the weight of what had just transpired sat heavily on his shoulders. He could feel the unspoken sorrow that gripped the crew, a collective grief that hung in the air, thick and suffocating. Aetherion was gone. Will Townsend, a friend, a fellow captain, was gone. Reed's chest tightened at the thought, but he swallowed his pain, knowing he couldn't afford to dwell on it—not yet. There was still a job to do. They were alive because of the ultimate sacrifice Aetherion had made, and now it was up to them to ensure that sacrifice wasn't in vain.

The hum of Perevian's thrusters filled the bridge as they accelerated. Reed's eyes remained locked on the viewscreen, watching as the last of the debris drifted past, the shattered remains of asteroids and celestial bodies slowly fading behind them. His grip on the chair tightened, his mind racing with the enormity of what lay ahead. They had been given a second chance, but the path forward was no less dangerous.

"They didn't die for nothing," Reed said quietly, his voice barely audible. His words were meant as much for himself as they were for the crew. They all felt the weight of what had just happened—felt it in their bones. But they pressed on, professionals to the core, because that's what Aetherion would have wanted.

The debris field continued to thin out, the swirling chaos giving way to the cold emptiness of space. It was quiet now, the violent collisions that had once reverberated through the ship reduced to distant echoes. But the silence wasn't peaceful.

As Perevian cleared the final remnants of the debris field, Reed stared at the empty space where Aetherion had once been. The wreckage of the ship, and the lives they lost with it, lingered in the silence behind them. It wasn't just the ship they left behind—it was pieces of themselves, fragments that would never be whole again.

Reed's jaw tightened as he looked ahead into the endless expanse. Without another word, Perevian continued forward, carrying not just their mission, but the memory of Aetherion— a reminder that survival wasn't just about living, but about honoring those who couldn't.

CHAPTER SIX

The aftermath of Aetherion's sacrifice still hung heavily in the air. The debris field behind them continued to churn, with smaller fragments spinning harmlessly off into space. Perevian pressed on, its engines pushing them further from the danger zone, toward the outer edge of the Vela Supernova Remnant.

The silence on the bridge was suffocating, each member of the crew lost in their own thoughts. Aetherion was gone. They had watched it fall apart, taking the brunt of the destruction so that Perevian could survive.

Chen's console beeped softly, breaking the silence. She glanced at the data coming in from the scanners. "Captain, we're clear of the field."

"Gravitational shifts are stabilizing as we move further out," added Russo.

"That's something, at least," Reed said quietly, though his thoughts lingered on the lives lost aboard Aetherion. "Chen, I need a full status report on the ship."

Chen's hands moved over her console, running a full diagnostic. After a moment, her voice broke the silence. "Shields are holding at sixty-five percent, Captain. Structural integrity is stable, though we've taken damage across the hull—mostly surface-level impacts. No breaches detected."

"Engines?" Reed asked.

Addison chimed in from her station. "Main thrusters are fully operational, but our lateral thrusters took a hit. They're down to seventy-five percent efficiency, so maneuvering will be slower until we make repairs."

Reed nodded, processing the information. "What about power levels?"

Chen responded quickly. "We're running at eighty percent capacity, but the debris field caused minor fluctuations in some of the subsystems. I've already rerouted power to essential functions, and we're stabilizing now."

"Life support?"

"Fully operational," Chen confirmed. "No interruptions."

"Very well," Reed replied. He took a deep breath as he addressed the crew.

"I know what we just witnessed, what we endured, weighs heavily on all of us. We lost more than a ship back there—we lost friends, shipmates. And there are no words that can make that easier. But they didn't give their lives so we could fall apart. We owe it to them to keep going, not because it's easy, but because it's the only way to honor their sacrifice. We move forward—step by step. For them."

The crew remained silent as Reed's words hung in the air. He gave a final nod. "Take a moment. Then, we get back to work."

"I knew the astrophysicist on Aetherion, Captain," said Russo after a moment. "It's... hard to process."

Reed nodded. "We all knew this mission would be

dangerous, but that doesn't make it any easier."

Russo looked up at Reed, his eyes clouded with emotion. "We should still analyze the data we've collected. The gas giant is clearly the cause of the disruption, but we need to figure out why—after eons—it all came to a head today of all days."

Reed placed a hand on his shoulder, offering what little comfort he could. "Thanks, Liam."

Turning to Chen he said, "Send out a distress signal. Let NASA know what's happened. We'll need to include a full report."

She nodded. "Aye, Captain."

As Chen sent the signal, the rest of the bridge remained in silence, the asteroid belt receding into the distance. Reed walked the bridge, checking in with each of his crewmembers, ensuring they were holding together. He knew the shock of Aetherion's destruction would hit them all in different ways, but they were professionals—resilient, experienced. They would carry on, even in the face of loss.

As they continued their journey away from the wreckage, Reed found himself staring out into the expanse of space, his mind replaying the last moments of Aetherion over and over. He knew this was the life they had chosen—a life filled with risks, with sacrifice. Reminding him of his own mortality.

"Godspeed, Commander," Reed whispered to himself, his voice barely audible.

He turned back to the bridge, the weight of command settling once more on his shoulders. There was still work to be done. The mission was never over.

* * *

The journey back to a safer region of space had been quiet—too quiet. After the chaos of the asteroid belt's collapse and the loss of Aetherion, the stillness felt almost oppressive. The hum of Perevian's engines and the occasional beeping of the ships systems were the only sounds filling the void.

Reed stood alone in his quarters, staring out the small viewport at the softly blinking stars. The vast emptiness of space had never felt so suffocating. He hadn't slept in the days since the destruction of Aetherion; every time he closed his eyes, he saw the ship disintegrating in slow motion. The faces of its crew—their final moments—haunted him.

He took a deep breath, trying to center himself. He couldn't afford to let grief cloud his judgment. Perevian had received a response from NASA acknowledging the distress signal, and a support vessel was enroute. But it would take time for them to reach the remnant.

A knock at the door broke his thoughts. "Come in."

Russo entered, his face as tired as Reed felt. "Captain, I've finished analyzing the gravitational data from the asteroid belt. I thought you'd want to see it."

Reed gestured for him to sit, and Russo placed a tablet on the table between them. He hesitated for a moment before speaking, his voice quiet, almost as if he were afraid to disturb the solemn atmosphere. "The nearby gas giant's tidal forces had been increasing exponentially from the beginning. Its mass and proximity, coupled with the rotational velocity of the belt, created a resonance effect. The asteroids were essentially being pulled apart by these complex gravitational forces."

Reed scanned the data on the tablet, his brow furrowing

deeper with each passing second. The readout displayed intense gravitational waveforms, each peak representing another destabilizing pulse from the gas giant. "Was this something we could've predicted earlier?"

Russo shook his head, leaning forward to explain. "Not without more advanced equipment. The gravitational shifts were happening at a subatomic level, and the resonance wasn't detectable until we were deep inside the belt. The forces acted in a cyclical pattern. Each time the gas giant's gravity pulled on the belt, it didn't just create a simple shift—it caused micro-strains in the molecular structure of the asteroids themselves. This stress built up over time, eventually exceeding their tensile strength and causing them to break apart. Our sensors weren't sensitive enough to detect the microscopic fractures."

Reed leaned back in his chair, exhaling slowly as he processed the information. "So, it was always going to end like this."

Russo nodded, his voice heavy with regret. "The belt had been destined to collapse under the strain. The asteroid fragments were caught in a gravitational tug-of-war—some were being pulled toward the gas giant, while others were flung outward by centrifugal force. There was no way to know that today was the day it all came to a head. It was out of our hands."

Reed set the tablet down, leaning back as the full weight of their predicament settled in. "So, there was no avoiding this."

"No," Russo admitted. "Aetherion saved us by clearing a path, but the collapse was inevitable. The resonances would've torn the belt apart regardless. We're lucky we made it out at all."

Silence settled between them for a moment. Reed could tell that Russo was still processing the loss of Aetherion and its crew, just like the rest of them. Everyone had their own way of dealing with grief, but Reed felt a deeper responsibility—as Captain, the burden of those lives weighed heavily on him.

"What happens next, Captain?" Russo asked, breaking the silence. Though they had cleared the asteroid belt days ago, the tension still lingered. Reed glanced at the tablet filled with streams of gravitational readings and geological scans.

"We keep moving forward," Reed replied. "Perevian is fully operational, and the mission continues."

Russo gave a small nod, exhaustion evident in his eyes. He had been working tirelessly since their escape, his energy untouched despite the strain.

"Take a break, Russo," Reed said, his tone softening. "You've done a great job with your analysis. We're out of danger, and we all need time to process what happened."

Russo hesitated. "I'll rest when I know everything's accounted for, Captain. We can't afford to miss anything."

Reed watched him for a moment, admiring his determination. He knew Russo wouldn't stop until every piece of data was fully examined and every angle of their mission secured. That's who he was—an unyielding scientist, methodical and relentless in his pursuit of answers. In this moment, he knew it was also how he was coping with the loss.

"Just don't burn yourself out," Reed added quietly as Russo turned to leave. "We'll need you sharp for whatever comes next."

"Aye, Captain," replied Russo over his shoulder.

As Russo exited Reed leaned forward, resting his elbows on his knees. He rubbed his temples, trying to push away the thoughts that crowded his mind. The faces of Aetherion's crew flashed before his eyes again—their final moments, their courage, their sacrifice. Reed couldn't shake the feeling that, as a Captain, he should have been able to do more, should have found another way.

But he knew there was no other way.

Reed was deep in thought when Chen's voice crackled over the comms. "Captain, I've got NASA on the line. You're needed on the bridge."

He took a steadying breath, pushing aside his thoughts. "Acknowledged. On my way." Reed stood and quickly made his way to the bridge.

When he entered, Addison and Chen were chatting quietly. Addison was focused on the helm, while Chen turned in her seat as Reed approached.

"Put it through," he said.

Chen tapped the controls, and Director March's voice came through immediately, clear and direct. "Perevian, we've received your report. We're sending a support vessel, but it's still some time out. In the meantime, your next objective is Kepler-452b."

Reed sighed, not sure why he should be surprised to receive new orders. "Kepler-452b? What's the mission?"

March's voice carried a hint of urgency. "Kepler-452b is a high-priority target. Preliminary scans suggest it could be one of the most Earth-like planets we've ever discovered. We need you to conduct a full survey—terrain, atmosphere, potential resources. We're counting on Perevian to get it done."

Reed hesitated, glancing at the crew around him. "With respect, Director, we've just taken a hit out here. Aetherion's loss is fresh, and my team needs time to recover. Shouldn't we wait for the support ship?"

March's tone softened slightly, but the urgency remained. "I understand, Captain. But we can't afford delays. The window for optimal conditions on Kepler-452b is closing. The support ship will handle recovery operations when they arrive. Right now, Perevian is the only ship in position to conduct this survey. I wouldn't ask if it wasn't critical."

Reed's jaw tightened. He looked at the viewscreen, then back at the crew. After a long pause, he nodded. "Understood. We'll proceed to Kepler-452b."

"Good," March replied. "We'll keep you updated on the support vessel's progress. NASA out."

The line cut, leaving a noticeable silence in the air. Reed turned to face his crew. The shift in their mission weighed on them, but there was no time to dwell on it. "You heard the order. Addison, plot a course for Kepler-452b."

Addison's fingers moved across the console, her hands a blur of practiced skill. The navigation readouts on the screen shifted rapidly, displaying the trajectory she had meticulously plotted.

"Course set, Captain," Addison said, an unmistakable edge of anticipation. She seemed relieved to have something to do—perhaps NASA knew what they were asking of them after all. She glanced briefly at Reed, seeking confirmation before her hands hovered above the final control sequence. "Ready to engage on your command."

Reed took his seat in the command chair. His gaze swept over the bridge, catching the focused expressions of his crew. The hum of the ship's systems filled the air, a reminder of the power under Perevian's hull. He leaned forward slightly, his voice carrying the gravity of their task. "Engage the drive."

As Addison activated the Alcubierre drive, the ship's core systems began to glow with a soft, pulsing energy. The advanced technology began to bend space-time around them. The low hum intensified, resonating through the ship's framework. A vibration rippled under Reed's feet as the drive engaged fully, distorting the space directly ahead of the vessel.

On the main viewscreen, the stars shifted as Perevian entered its warp bubble. They blurred into long, luminous trails, streaking past like shimmering lines on a dark canvas. The ship's hull thrummed with the energy of the drive, its engines cutting through the barriers of conventional travel, pushing them toward Kepler-452b at faster-than-light speeds.

The bridge was bathed in the soft glow of the ship's systems, the quiet beeping of sensors and displays a sharp contrast to the extraordinary feat of physics happening outside. Time seemed to stretch as the ship moved through warped space, cutting across light-years in mere moments.

"Course steady, Captain," Addison confirmed, her hands gliding over the controls. "We're on track for Kepler-452b. Estimated time to arrival is ten days, seventeen hours."

Reed gave a small nod. Whatever awaited them in that distant system—new discoveries, challenges, or threats—they would face it head-on. The mission wasn't over, and with every second, they drew closer to uncovering the next mystery in humanity's journey through the stars.

"We'll carry it," Reed whispered to himself. "We'll carry it all the way."

As the ship raced toward the unknown, Reed felt the weight of the responsibility—of continuing the mission that others had died for. They weren't done yet.

The Alcubierre drive pulsed with a soft glow, the ship's heart beating steadily. Beneath it all, the ship's twin nuclear fusion reactors worked in tandem, generating the immense energy required for faster-than-light travel. Buried deep within the ship's core, the reactors fused deuterium and helium-3, creating a nearly limitless supply of energy by mimicking the fusion processes found in stars. Chen stood at engineering's central console, her eyes moving over the readings.

"Perevian," Chen said, tapping a control panel. "Run a stability check on both reactors. Focus on the containment fields and fuel flow rates."

"Stability check in progress," the AI replied. "Reactor one containment field holding at 99.7% efficiency. Reactor two holding at 99.6%. Fuel flow rates are stable and within expected parameters."

"Looks good," Chen muttered, adjusting a few settings on her display. The drive, housed in reinforced glass and metal, was an imposing structure, a lattice of energy conduits snaking out like veins feeding power into every corner of the ship. The twin reactors supplied the ship's energy needs, with each one serving as a backup to the other. If one reactor ever failed, the other would seamlessly take over, keeping the ship operational.

Russo was a few feet away, crouched near the stabilizer coils, his handheld scanner tracing along the surface of the magnetic field generator. "Perevian, calibrate the stabilizer coils for drift correction. Cross-check alignment with magnetic field generator outputs."

"Calibrating," the AI replied. A moment later, it continued. "Alignment corrected by 0.02%. No further drift detected."

Russo glanced at the readings on his screen, satisfied. "No surprises here," he said. "A few micro-adjustments, but nothing to worry about."

The reactors' electromagnetic containment fields hummed beneath the floor, keeping the volatile fusion reactions safely in check. Chen leaned back against the console, giving the drive one more look. "Perevian, perform a predictive analysis for potential fluctuations during extended FTL operation."

"Predictive analysis underway," the AI responded. After a brief pause, it added, "Projected fluctuations remain within operational tolerances for the next 72 hours of continuous operation. No intervention required."

Chen nodded, satisfied. "Drive's in good shape, then." The reactors had been operating smoothly for years, their fusion processes ensuring that all systems, from life support to shields, remained fully powered.

Russo stood up, pocketing the scanner. "Perevian, prepare a diagnostics report for the conduits. Include current energy transfer efficiency and any signs of wear."

"Diagnostics report prepared," the AI confirmed. "Energy

transfer efficiency is at 98.4%. No significant wear detected in the primary conduits."

Chen said. The pair made their way toward the next section. The low hum of energy passing through the pipes was a constant, a reminder that this vast machine was alive in its own way. The conduits, thick metal tubes lined with insulated conductors, carried the massive output from the reactors to the drive and other ship systems.

As they approached, Chen glanced at the illuminated display along the wall. "Perevian, run a thermal stress analysis on the conduits."

"Thermal stress analysis complete," the AI replied after a brief pause. "Heat distribution is uniform. No hotspots detected."

Chen exchanged a look with Russo. "Let's run a manual inspection just to be safe."

Meanwhile, up in the observation lounge, Addison relaxed near the large, curved window, eyes drifting over the streaks of stars outside as Perevian moved quietly through space. The room was still, the kind of quiet that invited reflection. Addison had always liked this part of the ship, where the vastness outside felt somehow closer.

Reed entered, his footsteps barely audible. He stood next to Addison, his hands resting casually in his pockets. Neither spoke for a moment as they watched the stars slip by.

"I like the view here," Reed said.

Addison let that hang for a second. "Yeah. Sometimes I forget how much I miss just… looking at the sky." She smiled, "Even if the sky is outer space."

They fell into an easy silence again. Reed glanced at her. "What do you think about when you're here?"

Addison gave a half-shrug. "Depends. Mostly nothing. I just let my mind wander."

"Where's it wandering now?"

She smirked, finally turning to face him. "You really want to know?"

Reed raised an eyebrow. "Not if it's going to give me more to worry about."

Addison chuckled lightly. "I was just thinking about how long we've been out here. I mean, we've seen things no one else ever will, and half the time it feels like it's just another day on the job."

Reed smiled. "That's because it is."

Addison shook her head. "Not to most people."

Reed leaned back slightly, crossing his arms. "Getting philosophical?"

"Maybe," she said, turning back to the stars. "But when you're out here this long, things stop surprising you. I just didn't expect that."

Reed didn't answer right away. He leaned forward, resting his arms on the railing. "It's easy to get used to it. But I don't think we're supposed to."

Addison shot him a look. "Getting philosophical, Captain?"

He shrugged, chuckling. "Just saying."

Addison watched him for a moment before leaning back. "I guess you've got a point. Doesn't mean I'm going to start waxing poetic, though."

"Didn't expect you to," Reed replied, the faintest hint of amusement in his tone.

They lapsed into silence again. The ship continued its steady course, the stars outside streaking past in quiet indifference.

After a moment, Addison spoke again. "You ever think about how long this can go on?"

Reed glanced at her, curious. "What do you mean?"

"I mean, this." She waved a hand toward the stars. "The missions, the routine. It feels endless. Even though we've only been out here a few years, sometimes it feels like a thousand."

Reed thought about it, then nodded. "Yeah. But I think that's the point. There's always something more to discover."

Addison tapped her fingers lightly on the armrest of her lounger. "You're not wrong. Just feels like we could be out here forever, and it wouldn't change anything."

Reed's gaze drifted back to the stars. "Maybe that's okay."

Addison chuckled softly, shaking her head. "Spoken like someone who doesn't mind the quiet."

Reed smiled. "It has its moments."

She gave him a sideways glance. "You really don't get tired of it? The same stars, the same procedures?"

Reed shrugged. "It's not about getting tired. It's about knowing what to expect."

Addison leaned forward, resting her chin on her hand as she stared at the streaks of light outside. "I guess that's true. Maybe I'm just missing any kind of spontaneity."

Reed glanced at her, studying her for a moment. "You've always been a free spirit."

She smiled at that. "Yeah. It keeps things interesting."

The silence stretched again, the hum of the ship and the steady motion through space filling the gap. They didn't need to speak anymore; the quiet was enough, filled with the years they'd spent working side by side, the trust that had built over time.

That night, the crew gathered in the galley. Addison leaned back in her chair, half-heartedly picking at her meal. "How long has it been since any of us had something with real flavor?"

Chen, seated across from her, didn't even look up from her tray. "Too long to count," she said simply, taking another bite without much interest.

Russo chuckled, shaking his head. "You're still complaining about the food?"

She shrugged, unfazed. "Complaining is part of the job. Keeps me sharp."

Reed sat at the head of the table, eating quietly but listening. He glanced at Russo. "What do you miss back on Earth?"

Russo tilted his head thoughtfully. "Easy, a real chair. Not these hard things bolted to the deck."

Addison leaned in, amused. "You're thinking too small. Me? I'm going straight for a proper steak. None of this ration pack nonsense."

Chen gave her a look. "You'd be sick within ten minutes."

Addison shrugged. "Worth it."

Russo smirked. "You'll be complaining about your stomach, and I'll be the one relaxing on my recliner."

"Sounds about right," Chen said.

Reed was quiet for a moment before speaking up. "I miss being outside. Fresh air. A breeze."

Addison pointed her fork at Chen. "What about you? What do you miss most?"

Chen set her fork down, thinking for a moment. "I don't know. Maybe just a walk in a park."

Addison leaned back, smiling to herself. "Not a bad idea. Walking under trees again… with the captain's breeze in my hair. I could get behind that."

Chen, with her usual practicality, stood and gathered her tray. "Well, it's not a walk in the park, but I'm going to check the secondary power relays."

Reed watched them slowly filter out, still chatting, the easy rhythm of the crew settling back into place. He lingered a little longer. For now, the mission didn't matter. They were just four friends sharing a brief moment in the endless stretch of space.

CHAPTER SEVEN

Three years earlier, the NASA compound on Earth was a vast labyrinth of activity sprawled across miles of flatlands where concrete gave way to launch towers that stood like sentinels against the blue sky. The distant rumble of engines and the sharp crack of metal echoed through the complex as technicians, engineers, and scientists worked tirelessly. Perevian was among multiple ships scheduled to depart as part of the Solar Taskforce for Advanced Reconnaissance and Survival program, or S.T.A.R.S. Each crew had undergone rigorous training, and the sense of anticipation was palpable. This was the future of space exploration, the next great leap for humanity.

S.T.A.R.S. had been launched in response to the growing uncertainty surrounding Earth's future. Years of environmental decline, resource shortages, and rising friction among the world's superpowers had made it clear that humanity needed to look beyond the planet for survival.

The program wasn't just an exploration initiative—it was a survival plan. The fleet's mission was to venture into the far reaches of the galaxy, identifying potential planets for colonization, uncovering new resources, and developing technologies that would ensure humanity's longevity. NASA knew from the start that this mission would be daunting. The decision to focus on the Milky Way first wasn't arbitrary—it was out of necessity. The galaxy itself was enormous, spanning over 100,000 light-years across and housing more than 100 billion stars. Even with advanced technology, traveling from one end to the other at the speed of light would still take over 100,000 years. The sheer scale of it was enough to humble even the most experienced astronaut.

But beyond the Milky Way lay an even greater expanse. They were only scratching the surface of the universe, a place so vast it held an estimated 2 trillion galaxies. They needed to explore, and they needed to succeed. The future of all humanity was tied to the stars—and this was only the beginning of that journey.

The taskforce wasn't composed of a single ship or a single crew; it was an entire fleet, each ship with a unique mission and specialized team. And while the crews trained for separate disciplines, there was a shared sense of purpose—a collective understanding that what they were doing held far reaching implications.

Jonathan Reed's crew was one of the latest to join the effort. Their mission, like the others, was focused on exploration and reconnaissance, charting new star systems and seeking out resources that could one day sustain human life. It was the culmination of years of scientific breakthroughs, and the technology they were about to deploy had been refined to ensure the highest chance of survival in the most hostile environments.

Reed stood with his crew near one of the towering launch

pads, its metal frame shimmering in the afternoon sun. The roar of distant engines vibrated through the ground beneath his boots. Around them, other teams clustered in small groups, some engaging in final technical briefings, others laughing nervously as they swapped stories. The jokes were thinly veiled attempts to mask the anxiety simmering just beneath the surface.

His team, too, were lost in their own thoughts, focused on what was to come. Reed glanced over at Dr. Russo, whose usually calm demeanor was tinged with excitement today. Russo's eyes were fixed on the distant horizon where the massive launch towers stretched towards the heavens. The sun reflected off the metal surfaces, casting long shadows that seemed to stretch into infinity.

Russo finally broke the silence. "Hard to believe we're finally here, huh?" He folded his arms, looking back at Reed with a grin that belied his serious tone. "All those years of simulations, the tests, the setbacks… and now we're standing on the edge of something historic."

Reed gave a brief nod, though his mind was elsewhere, preoccupied with the endless layers of responsibility that rested on his shoulders. "Yeah. The edge," he echoed, his voice low. His eyes focused on Lieutenant Commander Chen, who, as usual, was absorbed with her tablet. She swiped at the pad, reviewing critical data and system diagnostics before their lives became irrevocably tied to the ship. She was the heartbeat of engineering—every piece of technology would answer to her, and Reed trusted her more than he trusted the systems themselves.

"Chen, you good?" Reed's voice was soft but carried the authority of command.

Chen glanced up briefly. "We're synced across the board. All systems are responding perfectly. Every test we've faced has gone without a hitch. I'm not seeing any issues. We're as ready as we'll ever be." She spoke with confidence, and there was a glimmer of anticipation in her eyes.

Lieutenant Addison stood a few steps away, leaning against the side of a transport vehicle as the wind played with her hair. Reed could see her take a deep breath and signs of tension in her shoulders, but there was also a sense of quiet resolve. Her calm demeanor had always been her strength.

"Lieutenant," Reed said, walking over. "How are you holding up?"

She glanced at him and shrugged lightly. "Tired. We've trained hard for this, Captain. If we're not ready now, we'll never be."

Reed studied her face for a moment, then nodded. "You're right. Everything's lined up. And it's almost time."

Addison smiled. "Let's hope time's on our side."

Russo, overhearing, jumped in with a chuckle. "And if it's not, we'll improvise."

Addison shot him a playful glance. "As long as your improvising doesn't blow us up, I'm all for it."

Reed chuckled softly. It wasn't much, but these small exchanges kept them grounded. In a few weeks, they would be far beyond the reach of Earth, but for now, they were just people—friends, colleagues—sharing a quiet moment.

* * *

The days leading up to the launch were a whirlwind of preparation, the kind that blurred days into nights and left little room for anything but the mission. NASA's compound was a constant hub of activity—an endless churn of people and machine. Training wasn't just intense; it was exhaustive. Every possible scenario, from catastrophic system failures to encounters with unknown cosmic phenomena, was relentlessly drilled into the crew. It wasn't enough to know what to do; they had to embody it, to react without thinking, as though their instincts had been rewired for deep space exploration.

In NASA's vast engineering building, Chen had become a familiar presence, often staying late into the night. The soft hum of machinery and the hiss of pressure valves filled the space as she meticulously reviewed design schematics and performance data, ensuring every system would function flawlessly when the time came.

"This ship—it's going to do things we've only theorized about," Chen said one afternoon, her eyes alight with excitement. She had taken a break from her work to visit Russo in the science building, eager to share her thoughts. "The propulsion systems alone are on a whole different level. We're about to make history."

Russo, seated at a cluttered workstation surrounded by data models and technical readouts, looked up from his notes. His mind was filled with the endless possibilities waiting just beyond the edges of human knowledge. "And that's why this mission matters," he said. "We're not just explorers. The data we collect out there... it could change the course of humanity. Imagine finding alien life forms or discovering new energy sources. Our mission is about leaving a lasting legacy of scientific research."

Chen smiled, sharing his enthusiasm. "And we'll be the ones to see it first."

While Chen and Russo were steeped in the technical and scientific possibilities of the mission, Addison had her focus set on an all-important responsibility—keeping them alive. In the command training center, she spent hours mastering the navigational systems that would guide them through the uncharted reaches of space. Every trajectory, every adjustment to the ship's course, had to be precise. Space was unforgiving, and even a minor miscalculation could spell disaster.

The physical training was just as demanding. Addison led the crew through exercises that tested their stamina and reflexes, pushing them to solve complex problems under extreme pressure. In one drill, the team had to navigate an obstacle course simulating the cramped interior of the ship, all while dealing with simulated system malfunctions. By the time they finished, they were exhausted, their muscles burning, but they had learned to trust one another in ways that went beyond the mission objectives.

There was a moment during one of the more grueling exercises—when the weight of their bodies seemed too much to bear, and their minds were stretched thin—that Addison looked around at the faces of her crewmates. Despite the fatigue, despite the endless training, there was a shared sense of purpose in their eyes. They were pushing through, not just for the mission, but for one another.

It was in those moments that Reed saw the true strength of

his team. Camaraderie had grown naturally, born out of the countless hours spent together, overcoming challenges that would have shattered lesser crews. They had evolved beyond individual roles and specialties—they had become a cohesive unit. The intensity of their preparation had molded them, but the mission had cemented their bond.

In the brief moments of respite, when the sun dipped low over the compound and the relentless pace of preparation slowed for just a moment, the crew would gather outside. They would sit together, backs against the cool metal of the equipment containers, watching the stars slowly blink into existence in the evening sky. It was during these quiet times that the weight of what they were about to do truly settled in.

"I've been thinking," Russo said one evening as they sat in the fading light, "about what it'll be like out there. The silence, the isolation. We've trained for it, but we don't really know what it'll feel like until we're in it."

Addison, leaning back with her arms folded behind her head, glanced over. "I'm not worried about the silence. It's the unknown that'll keep me on edge. We have no idea what's out there."

Chen, sitting cross-legged with a tablet in her lap, looked up. "That's what makes it exciting, though. If we knew what was out there, there'd be no point going."

Reed, standing slightly apart from the group, took a deep breath, the cool night air filling his lungs. He listened to their voices. They were ready—he could feel it in every word, every glance exchanged between them. Whatever they faced out there, they would face it together.

CHAPTER EIGHT

Perevian continued its silent voyage through the vast expanse of space towards Kepler-452b, the distant stars forming a glittering tapestry against the darkness. Although life had settled into a rhythm of routines and duties, strange disturbances had begun to unsettle the crew beneath the surface of normalcy.

It started subtly—a flicker of lights in the corridors, a brief distortion on a monitor, a whispering static over the intercoms. At first, these disturbances were dismissed as minor glitches, the inevitable quirks of technology on a long-duration mission. But as the incidents grew more frequent, concern began to spread.

On the bridge Addison monitored the ship's course. The navigation systems showed them on a steady trajectory toward their known coordinates, but an uneasy feeling gnawed at her.

"Captain, I'm detecting slight deviations in our heading," she reported, turning to face Reed. "It's nothing major, but we seem to be drifting off course intermittently."

Reed raised an eyebrow. "Is it the autopilot malfunctioning?"

"I've checked it twice," Addison replied. "Everything appears to be functioning correctly."

Reed leaned forward in his chair. "Keep a close eye on it. Inform me immediately if it gets worse."

Meanwhile, Chen sat in the heart of engineering, the soft glow of holographic displays casting a bluish tint on her features. The ship's engines provided a constant, soothing backdrop as she examined the intricate schematics floating before her. Lines of code scrolled rapidly alongside three-dimensional renderings of Perevian's systems. Despite her efforts, none of the data explained the strange occurrences plaguing the ship.

Her concentration was broken by the sound of footsteps approaching. Russo entered the room, a tablet clutched in his hand and a concerned expression on his face.

"There's been another power fluctuation in Sector 7," he reported. "That's the third one today, and this time it disrupted the environmental controls for a few seconds."

Chen frowned, her fingers flying over the console as she pulled up the relevant data. "Voltage levels are within normal parameters," she said, puzzled. "There's no spike or drop that would account for these fluctuations. It's as if the energy is being redirected, but there's no record of where it's going."

Just then, the overhead lights flickered, casting fleeting shadows across engineering. A low vibration resonated through the deck plates, growing in intensity before fading. Chen's console flashed erratically, the holographic displays warping into distorted shapes. Briefly, lines of garbled text appeared—symbols and characters that didn't correspond to any known language—before the system stabilized and returned to normal.

She exchanged a concerned glance with Russo. "That

was different."

Russo nodded, his eyes reflecting her concern. "We can't keep attributing this to minor glitches. Something is affecting the ship's systems, and we need to find out what."

"Let's run a full diagnostic on the primary systems," she said. "Focus on the power distribution network and see if there's any irregularity in the energy flow patterns. I want to rule out any hardware failures or software anomalies."

"On it," Russo affirmed, moving to a nearby console. "I'll also cross-reference the timing of the fluctuations with external sensor data, just in case we're missing something."

Chen took a deep breath, trying to quell the growing apprehension. She opened the ship's comm channel. "Chen to Captain Reed."

"Go ahead, Commander," the captain's voice replied.

"Sir, the anomalies are becoming more frequent and affecting multiple systems. I'm initiating a full diagnostic, but we may need to consider all possibilities, including external influences."

"Understood," Reed responded. "Keep me updated on your findings."

"Aye, Captain," Chen acknowledged, signing off.

She glanced over at Russo, who was deeply engrossed in his analysis. "Any luck?" she asked.

He shook his head. "Nothing conclusive yet. But there's a pattern emerging in the electromagnetic fields around the ship. It's subtle, but it could be related."

Chen's eyes narrowed. "Let's hope we can figure this out before it escalates further."

Before he could respond, the ship's intercom crackled to life. A burst of static filled the air, followed by a faint, unintelligible whisper that seemed to echo from the walls themselves.

"That was creepy," Chen muttered, her hands gripping the edge of the table.

The next day the atmosphere was tense as each crewmember sat at the galley table, the soft glow of their tablets illuminating concerned expressions.

"Captain," said Chen. "The issues include power fluctuations, environmental control irregularities, and now auditory phenomena manifesting over the intercom system."

Reed listened intently, his expression unreadable. "And these occurrences are increasing in frequency?"

"Yes, sir," Chen confirmed. "And they seem to be escalating in intensity."

Russo spoke, his tablet displaying a series of complex graphs. "I've analyzed the electromagnetic fields surrounding the ship," he reported. "There are unusual fluctuations that don't correspond to any known natural phenomenon or space weather."

Reed glanced at him. "Could this be an external source affecting our systems?"

"It's possible," Russo acknowledged. "But the patterns are structured. There's a repeating sequence that suggests it might be a signal or some form of communication."

Reed folded his arms, deep in thought. "An unknown electromagnetic field, system anomalies, and now auditory phenomena," he summarized. "This is more than mere coincidence."

Addison spoke up. "Captain, I propose initiating a level-three diagnostic of all ship systems. This would allow us to thoroughly check both hardware and software for any irregularities."

"Additionally," Chen added, "we should attempt to isolate the frequency of the electromagnetic field. If it's a signal, we might be able to decode it or at least determine its origin."

Reed nodded thoughtfully. "Very well. Make it a priority. Russo, focus on the electromagnetic analysis. Work with Chen to see if there's a way to interact with the signal safely."

"Aye, Captain," Russo affirmed.

Reed's eyes swept over his officers. "Keep me informed of any developments, no matter how minor. Dismissed."

As the team dispersed to carry out their tasks, Reed couldn't shake the uneasiness that had settled over him. Perevian was a state-of-the-art vessel, designed to withstand the rigors of deep space exploration. Yet, they were encountering phenomena that defied explanation.

As the ship got closer to Kepler-452b, something new registered on the ship's sensors. At first, it was barely noticeable—a faint blip amidst the usual readings. Russo caught it during one of his routine scans, an energy field so weak it was almost imperceptible. He mentioned it offhandedly to the crew, expecting it to be a transient anomaly, nothing more than a quirk of deep-space physics. But over the next few days, the readings didn't fade. Instead, they intensified.

Russo's curiosity surged. The energy field grew stronger the closer they came to the coordinates, its consistency now undeniable. He ran the data through multiple systems, triple-checking for any sensor malfunctions, but everything came back clean. The energy readings were real, and they were coming from the region of space where they were headed.

"Something's out there," Russo murmured to himself one afternoon, his eyes locked on the console in front of him. The energy field wasn't just a stray signal; it was concentrated, focused. Whatever was generating it was stable, persistent, and now, undeniably in their path.

He shared the readings with Chen, who quickly began scanning the data.

"It's faint, but it's not natural," she said after a moment. "No known celestial body or phenomenon should emit energy at these levels without being more noticeable on our scans. And yet... here it is."

They exchanged a brief glance, neither daring to voice their growing unease.

One evening on the bridge, while reviewing navigation logs, Addison noticed something unusual. A jump in coordinates had just occurred—something that should have been impossible given their position and velocity, yet the readings were unmistakable. It was as if the ship had briefly been... somewhere else.

"Captain," Addison called from her station. "You might want to take a look at this."

Reed joined her at the helm, scanning the data. "Explain

this to me."

"We were here," Addison pointed at the map. "But for exactly 3.72 seconds, we registered as being nearly two light-years away—only to return here as if nothing happened."

Reed's pulse quickened. "How is that possible?"

"That's what I'm trying to figure out. Navigation systems show no error, no course corrections. It's like we never left this spot, except we weren't here."

Russo examined the readings. "It's impossible," he muttered. "Unless—"

"Unless what?" Reed pressed.

"Unless it's tied to that energy field we've been tracking."

Chen shook her head. "But how? The field is faint, and even now, it barely registers on the sensors."

"Exactly," Russo said, his eyes narrowing. "Which makes it all the more suspicious."

"I want all sensors set to maximum sensitivity," said Reed. "Russo, I need you to run a deep scan of that energy field. Chen, check every inch of the ship for anomalies. Addison, give them a hand. If you find anything I want to know immediately."

The crew exchanged anxious glances but nodded in unison. The silence that followed was heavy.

Later in the science lab, Russo, Chen, and Addison were engrossed in their analysis. "Look at this," Russo said, pointing to a waveform oscillating on the main screen. His voice carried a mix of curiosity and concern. "It's repeating at regular intervals—exactly every forty-two seconds."

"Almost like a heartbeat," Addison observed, leaning

closer. The rhythmic pulses on the display seemed almost alive, a steady cadence against the backdrop of fluctuating data.

Chen adjusted the parameters on her console, her fingers moving over the holographic interface. "Perevian, analyze the waveform. Apply decryption algorithms and cross-reference with the universal translation matrix for recognizable patterns."

"Analyzing," the AI replied. The waveform on the display began to shift, the jagged lines smoothing into coherent peaks and valleys. Patterns started to emerge—repetitive sequences that hinted at a deliberate structure.

Russo leaned forward, his excitement growing. "It's a signal," he declared. "And it's structured. Perevian, confirm: does this match any known forms of communication?"

"Signal analysis complete," the AI responded. "No direct match found in the ship's communication database. However, the structure exhibits characteristics consistent with intelligence."

Addison's eyes widened. "Could it be a distress call?" she speculated. "Maybe a beacon from another vessel?"

"Or an attempt at communication," Chen mused. "From an unknown source."

Suddenly, the lights dimmed without warning, casting the lab into semi-darkness. The monitors flickered erratically, their displays momentarily distorting into static before stabilizing. A cold chill swept through the room, causing Addison to shiver.

"Perevian," Addison said. "Report on environmental conditions. Is there a malfunction?"

"Environmental controls are functioning within normal parameters," the AI replied. "However, a localized temperature drop of five degrees has been detected in this section. Cause unknown."

Chen frowned, her eyes scanning the diagnostic readouts. "Perform a deeper analysis of life support systems. Look for anomalies that could explain the fluctuation."

"Analysis in progress," the AI replied. A moment later, it reported. "Life support systems are operating normally. No anomalies detected. Temperature fluctuation is isolated to this section."

Equipment around them began to emit a low hum, almost imperceptible at first but growing steadily louder. The oscilloscopes displayed erratic spikes, and the electromagnetic readings fluctuated wildly.

"This doesn't make any sense," Russo muttered. "Perevian, check for electromagnetic interference or external influences on the ship's systems."

"Electromagnetic fluctuations detected," the AI confirmed. "Localized to this section. No external sources identified."

Addison tapped into the ship's internal sensors. "I'm detecting minor fluctuations in the ship's gravitational field localized to this section," she reported. "Perevian, verify these readings."

"Gravitational field fluctuations confirmed," the AI replied. "Localized distortions detected. Cause unknown."

Chen's expression grew more serious. "We need to alert the captain."

"Captain is requested in the Science Lab," announced the AI over ship's comms.

A few minutes later, Reed stepped into the room. "Report," he commanded.

"Captain," Chen replied. "We've identified a structured signal repeating at regular intervals coming from the direction of the energy field. During our analysis we experienced simultaneous environmental anomalies—temperature drops, lighting fluctuations, and irregular equipment behavior."

Reed's gaze swept over the equipment. "Any idea what's causing it?"

"We suspect the signal may be interacting with our systems," Russo explained. "But we haven't determined whether it's intentional or a byproduct of its nature."

"It's possible that our attempts to decode the signal are amplifying its effects," Addison added.

Reed considered this. "Do you believe there's any immediate danger to us or the ship?"

"Not at present," Chen replied. "But if the disturbances increase in intensity, they could pose a risk."

"Very well," Reed said. "Cease any active analysis of the signal for now. Let's focus on gathering data passively until we understand more."

"Understood," Chen agreed. "We'll compile all the data we've collected so far."

Reed nodded. "Good. Keep me informed of any developments."

As the captain departed, the trio exchanged thoughtful glances.

"This is turning into quite the puzzle," Russo remarked, his fingers drumming lightly on the console.

"One that we need to solve carefully," Chen cautioned. "We don't want to inadvertently escalate the situation."

Russo tapped a few keys, bringing up comparative data. "I'll start cross-referencing our readings with known phenomena and previous encounters. Maybe we'll find something that sheds light on this."

Chen gave a small nod. "I'll focus on analyzing the environmental data. There might be clues in the way the anomalies manifested."

"I'll assist with the sensor logs," Addison offered. "Perhaps we can triangulate the signal's origin or at least understand its propagation."

With a plan in place, they each delved into their respective tasks. The lab hummed softly as they worked, the screens displaying a steady stream of information.

The next morning, the air was thick with anticipation—making every creak of the ship sound louder. The usual sound of the engines had taken on a sharper edge, almost as if the ship itself was bracing for something. Then, without warning, ship's sensors detected a sudden spike in the energy field. The ship jolted slightly, as though a great force had brushed against them. Alarms rang out across the bridge, and the crew scrambled to respond.

"Captain!" Chen called out, pulling Reed's attention to her station. "We've got an incoming transmission."

"NASA?" Reed asked.

"No," Chen's voice faltered. "It's... it's coming from the direction of the energy field."

Reed's heart raced. "On speaker."

A crackling hiss filled the room—static, thick and garbled. At first, it was hard to distinguish anything, just noise. Then, beneath the distortion, came a voice. Broken. Faint. But unmistakable.

"…help… us."

The bridge fell silent as the crew processed what they'd heard.

Russo's eyes were wide with disbelief. "Captain… that voice. It's… it's Commander Townsend."

CHAPTER NINE

The bridge remained in stunned silence as the garbled transmission dissolved into static. Reed's mind raced, trying to process the impossible. Aetherion? It couldn't be. Yet, the voice was unmistakable. Reed had heard it enough times to know without a doubt: the voice on the transmission was Will Townsend.

"Impossible," he muttered, as if trying to convince himself otherwise.

Chen, her fingers working furiously, ran the transmission through multiple filters, amplifying and clarifying it as much as she could. The harsh static began to fade, leaving behind a clearer signal, but it brought no comfort. "There's no doubt, Captain. The vocal print matches Commander Townsend exactly."

Russo was the first to break the silence. "But how?" His voice trembled slightly. He turned back to his console, almost as if hoping the data might offer a rational explanation, but the empty screen only deepened the unease settling over him.

"Maybe it's not really Commander Townsend," Addison said quietly, though her voice sounded doubtful. The absurdity of what they were experiencing clawed at her. She'd always been the first to question, to challenge the unknown, but even this felt beyond comprehension.

The mention of Townsend brought the grim reality of Aetherion back to the surface—the wreckage, the destruction, the helplessness they had all felt watching a fellow ship swallowed into the cold void of space. The final transmission from Aetherion had been haunting enough, but to now hear Townsend's voice again after his death… it was agonizing.

Reed could sense the shift in the room. They had all mourned the loss of Aetherion. The destruction had been total—no chance of survival. They had come to terms with it. Or so they thought.

Yet now, Townsend's voice echoed through the bridge, shattering the fragile acceptance they had built. It pulled at each of them in different ways—fear, disbelief, and a nagging hope that perhaps they had been wrong, that somehow Townsend and his crew had survived against all odds. But that hope felt dangerous, like a false light in a nightmare that could pull them deeper into the dream.

Chen's usually composed face tightened as she continued to work at her station. "I don't understand… we all saw what happened to Aetherion. It was torn apart. There's no way…" Her voice trailed off. She didn't need to finish; they all knew. Whatever they were hearing, it wasn't supposed to be real.

Russo leaned forward as a new thought struck him. "But even if that were somehow Commander Townsend… how is it even possible for a transmission to reach us here? We're light-years away from where Aetherion was last seen."

Chen nodded, the disbelief deepening. "Exactly. There's no known way for a signal to travel that far unless…" Her voice faltered, unwilling to finish the thought. The implications were too disturbing.

Reed's gaze hardened as he considered the unsettling reality. "Unless it didn't come from Aetherion at all. But if it didn't… then what?"

Addison clenched her jaw, her eyes drifting back to the empty view outside the bridge. She had tried to push Aetherion's destruction from her mind, convincing herself that they couldn't dwell on the past if they wanted to survive. But now, the past was calling to them in a voice they couldn't ignore. "We all saw it happen," she muttered, her hands tightening into fists. "This doesn't make any sense."

Russo struggled to reconcile the data in front of him with the grim reality they had witnessed. "If Aetherion somehow survived, there should have been signs—escape pods, distress beacons, life support signals, anything. But we saw nothing. What if it's some kind of interference from past transmissions, like an echo?"

Chen shook her head. "I've reviewed the transmission log. There's no indication of interference or lingering signals. This isn't an echo—it's something else."

Reed, though outwardly calm, felt the same sinking dread rising in his chest. He had led his crew through countless dangers, but nothing had prepared him for this—the horror of confronting what should have been impossible. "We need answers," he said finally. He glanced at Chen, as if hoping the technology might somehow offer clarity. "Run another analysis on the signal."

"But, Captain…" she hesitated.

"Just do it, Chen."

Chen nodded, though the task felt hollow. She knew the result would be the same. The voice was Townsend's, and nothing she could do would change that fact. She ran the analysis again and glanced over at Reed. "It's him, Captain. Whatever this is… it's Townsend."

The realization settled over them, heavy and suffocating. Aetherion was gone, yet somehow, Townsend's voice lingered—a ghost from a ship that had been lost to the void, stirring up memories they thought had been buried with the wreckage. And with it came the crushing fear that their own fate might soon mirror the one they had barely survived witnessing.

Russo, still fixated on the data, slowly looked up, his voice hesitant. "What if… what we're hearing isn't Townsend at all? What if this energy field—whatever it is—has the ability to mimic his voice?"

Chen's eyes widened. "You're saying the field is using Commander Townsend's voice because it somehow absorbed or replicated his transmissions?"

Reed rubbed his temples. "Possible. And the question is, why? Why would this—whatever it is—use Will's voice to communicate with us?"

Russo turned his attention to the data scrolling across his terminal. "If this field is capable of mimicking him, it could also be trying to manipulate us. It might be using the voice of someone we trust to lure us closer to it."

Reed felt a pit form in his stomach. "We can't rule that out," he said, glancing back at Chen. "Have you pinpointed the exact origin of the signal?"

Chen shook her head, frustration creeping into her voice. "It's coming from within the energy field, but there's no clear source. It's almost as if the entire field itself is broadcasting the message."

Reed's mind raced. They had been chasing disturbances for days, but this was the first clear indication that something— or someone—was aware of their presence. And if it really was Commander Townsend, then something had gone terribly wrong.

"We need to proceed cautiously," Reed said finally. "Whatever is out there, it's not a simple anomaly."

Russo leaned forward. "Captain, we should send a probe closer to the energy field and start gathering detailed data."

Reed considered the suggestion. A probe would give them critical insight without putting the crew at immediate risk. But if this entity could manipulate signals and even simulate voices, there was a chance it could infiltrate their systems as well.

"Very well," Reed said after a long pause. "But it must be completely isolated from Perevian's systems. No direct link— air-gapped entirely. It should send data back in short, encrypted bursts to minimize any chance of interference."

Chen nodded, considering the security layers. "I'll build a fully self-contained system with no external access points. It'll run autonomous diagnostics and use an onboard buffer to store data before transmitting it in brief, encrypted bursts. I'll also add a kill switch—if any anomaly tries to breach the probe's systems, it'll shut down immediately."

"Proceed."

Chen nodded. "I'll get started on the modifications. Give me a few hours."

Several hours later, Reed leaned over Chen's shoulder as she made the final adjustments to the probe's systems.

"Completely isolated, as ordered," Chen said, stepping back from the console. "No network connection to Perevian, and data will only be transmitted in brief, encrypted bursts. The probe will operate autonomously."

Reed turned to Addison. "Disengage the Alcubierre drive."

Addison nodded, quickly bringing up the warp drive panel on her console. "Aye, Captain. Beginning drive disengagement sequence."

The ship shuddered as the warp bubble around Perevian collapsed. A subtle, high-pitched tone faded, signaling the end of the faster-than-light travel. Space around them shifted, the stars returning to their normal positions as the ship exited the bubble. The crew felt a brief jolt as the ship stabilized, now adrift at sublight speeds.

"Drive fully disengaged," Addison confirmed. "We're in standard space now."

Chen's eyes scanned the system readouts, ensuring no residual energy from the warp bubble lingered. "Everything looks good, Captain. We're clear to deploy."

As the ship settled into normal space, the view of the energy field on the display shifted. What had been a distorted, chaotic swirl while in warp now appeared more defined—its edges distinct, the colors less blurred. The instruments began registering new data, previously masked by the warp distortions.

Russo raised an eyebrow at the console. "We're seeing something different now… clearer. It's not just a field—it's… complex."

Reed leaned in, his eyes narrowing. "Send in the probe. I want to know exactly what we're dealing with."

The probe detached from Perevian, slipping silently into the void. As it moved toward the energy field, the crew watched the data streams flood in from its sensors. They all hoped for answers—but dreaded what they might find.

The vast emptiness around them felt oddly charged, as if the void itself was on the verge of revealing something hidden. Now and then, a brief glance passed between the crew, each one asking the same silent question: *What if the unknown is anything but safe?*

Hours seemed to stretch unnaturally. The ship's systems hummed in the background, while faces were illuminated by the dim glow of their consoles.

As the probe neared the edge of the energy field, tension aboard Perevian grew almost unbearable. The once-steady stream of data began to fluctuate, subtle shifts in the readings catching everyone's attention. Reed leaned forward in his chair. Every eye was glued to the displays, the distance between the probe and the energy field shrinking with each second.

"Approaching the anomaly," Addison said, her eyes fixed on the navigation data. "The probe's still holding steady."

On the main viewscreen, the energy field came into view—an ethereal, shimmering distortion in the fabric of space, its edges flickering with a strange, otherworldly light. It was beautiful, in a way, but there was something about it that felt… wrong.

Chen leaned over her terminal as she adjusted the probe's sensors. "The energy patterns are becoming more complex," she muttered, half to herself. "They're shifting."

Suddenly, the viewscreen flickered, and the probe's feed cut out. The bridge was plunged into darkness.

"What the hell just happened?" Reed demanded, his voice cutting through the silence.

Chen's fingers flew across her console. "The probe's systems were compromised. It's not responding to any commands."

"Could the field have disabled it?" Russo asked.

"Possibly," Chen replied as she tried to reestablish contact. "But it happened too fast. One second everything was fine, and then—nothing."

Reed stared at the blank viewscreen, his mind racing. "We need to know what happened out there. Run a full diagnostic on the probe's last transmission."

Chen pulled up the data. "There's something…" she said after a long moment.

Reed stepped closer. "What did you find?"

Chen didn't answer immediately. Instead, she magnified the final moments of the transmission, the feed jittering slightly as it neared the end. "Just before the signal cut out… the probe picked up an object inside the energy field."

Reed's brow creased. "An object?" he repeated.

Chen zoomed in further, the object slowly coming into

focus. The silhouette emerged, faint at first, but undeniably there. The blurred shape grew clearer, the silhouette unmistakable. The view expanded, revealing more detail—enough for Reed to recognize the contours, the structure. The image filled the viewscreen, and a cold shiver ran down his spine.

It was a ship.

More specifically, it was Aetherion.

Aetherion appeared intact, floating within the energy field like a ghostly apparition. Its hull gleamed under the faint light of distant stars, yet the ship drifted aimlessly, devoid of power. It was as if it had been abandoned, left to the mercy of the void.

Reed's heart pounded in his chest. "What the hell is going on?"

Russo shook his head, his eyes wide with disbelief. "I have no idea. There's no logical explanation for this. It's as if they somehow survived."

Chen, working furiously at her station, ran a deep scan. "The ship is intact… and real. No warp signatures, no temporal anomalies, nothing that suggests how it got here. It's physically there, but I have no idea how or why."

Reed turned to her. "How does a ship jump light-years without any warp trail? No power signatures? And after it's been blown to pieces?"

Chen tapped furiously at her controls. "I don't see any propulsion history on their end. If Aetherion moved, it wasn't by conventional means."

Russo leaned over. "Captain, we're talking about a ship

that was destroyed. Not just stranded or disabled—destroyed. And now it's here, fully intact."

Reed's mind raced. The energy field. Could it somehow be responsible for this? Had it dragged Aetherion across light-years of space? And what had happened to Townsend and his crew?

Chen's voice cut through the silence. "I'm picking up a faint life support signal. It's weak, but there could be survivors aboard."

"Survivors?" Reed repeated. "How could they have survived?"

"We need to find out," Russo said, his expression grim. "We need to board Aetherion and figure out what happened."

Reed hesitated, calculating the risks. He glanced at the drive controls and then back at the viewscreen, where Aetherion loomed like a spectral figure from the past. Every instinct screamed something was wrong, that nothing about this situation was normal—but they couldn't ignore what was right in front of them. Docking two ships in this energy field was risky—especially given what they knew about its effects on their systems. But if there were survivors aboard Aetherion, they couldn't just leave them to their fate.

"All right," Reed said finally. "We're going to find out what happened on that ship."

As Perevian closed the distance, Reed felt a knot of anxiety tighten in his chest. The derelict ship, once a beacon of exploration, now loomed like a ghost in the void. Its hull, dark and unlit, appeared lifeless, a stark contrast to the vibrant energy it once held. The closer Perevian drifted, the more unsettling the sight became.

Perevian floated just off the starboard side, positioning itself parallel to the dark silhouette of Aetherion. It was a precise maneuver, each thruster firing in calculated bursts, holding the ships in delicate proximity. The only sound in Perevian's bridge was the low hum of the ship's systems and the faint creaks of the hull adjusting to the movement.

Reed leaned forward. "Chen," he called. "Initiate system handshake with Aetherion. I want full diagnostics before we even consider stepping onboard."

Chen swiftly activated the subspace communication systems. "Perevian, initiate a low-energy subspace handshake with Aetherion. Monitor for anomalies in their response protocols."

"Handshake initiated," the AI replied. "Subspace link established. Awaiting response from Aetherion's systems."

The initial connection fluctuated as the damaged Aetherion struggled to respond. Chen fine-tuned the handshake parameters, her fingers moving across her console. "Adapt to Aetherion's degraded communication protocols. Adjust handshake timing to accommodate fragmented data streams."

"Adjustments applied," the AI confirmed. "Data exchange stabilizing. Aetherion's systems are responding intermittently."

Chen stared at the incoming data. "Their core systems are heavily fragmented—likely running on isolated clusters, each barely maintaining minimal functionality. Perevian, analyze the structure of their distributed network and identify the most stable nodes for data exchange."

"Analysis complete," the AI reported. "Stable nodes identified. Redirecting handshake to prioritize stable communication pathways."

The rhythmic sound of Perevian's core AI filled the bridge as it worked to stabilize the link. Data packets from Aetherion's network began to trickle in, riddled with inconsistencies and errors. Chen frowned, scanning the streams. "Perevian, deploy advanced error-correction algorithms. Smooth over the inconsistencies and reconstruct missing data where possible."

"Error-correction protocols deployed," the AI responded. "Reconstructed data is being integrated into the diagnostic stream. Aetherion's systems remain unstable."

Chen continued to adjust parameters as more information flowed in. "Monitor for critical subsystem statuses—life support, power distribution, and hull integrity. Flag any catastrophic failures."

"Monitoring active," the AI said. "Life support functioning at 27%. Power distribution at 18%. Multiple breaches detected in hull integrity."

Reed's expression darkened. "Chen, can you stabilize the link?"

"I'm deploying an adaptive protocol to compensate for their degraded subsystems," Chen said. "Perevian, implement redundancy routing through our subspace array to reinforce the handshake."

"Redundancy routing active," the AI confirmed. "Signal stability improved by 22%."

Chen exhaled slowly, her fingers pausing briefly. "The protocol will smooth over the gaps, but Aetherion's systems are barely operational. We're holding the connection, but they're running on fumes."

Reed watched as data trickled in, slowly stabilizing under Chen's guidance. "What's their status?"

"We've stabilized our connection with Aetherion," Chen reported. "It's operating in emergency mode, likely triggered by catastrophic system failures. Their main processing grid is offline, and it's running on low-powered backup processors. Power levels are critical. Life support is functional but barely sustaining. Perevian, analyze Aetherion's systems for immediate support needs."

The AI processed for a moment before responding. "Critical systems requiring immediate stabilization: power distribution, environmental controls, and AI core integration. Navigation and propulsion systems are offline."

Reed studied the holographic displays that mapped Aetherion's disarrayed power grid. "Can we boost their systems from here?"

Chen's eyes narrowed as she ran a rapid diagnostic. "Perevian, assess feasibility of an auxiliary power transfer to Aetherion's systems. Calculate safe transfer rates to avoid overloading their compromised infrastructure."

"Auxiliary power transfer is feasible," the AI replied. "Recommended transfer rate: 15% of Perevian's auxiliary power capacity. Transfer must be throttled to prevent overload."

Chen nodded, already initiating the process. "I'll throttle the transfer rate and monitor their systems for strain. Prepare an external support module to interface with Aetherion's core

AI. It will assist with stabilizing their processing load."

"Support module configured and ready for deployment," the AI confirmed.

"Do it," Reed said, watching as Perevian's power grid rerouted, preparing to initiate the transfer.

A low, steady vibration coursed through the ship as auxiliary power began flowing to Aetherion. On the displays, Aetherion's power systems flickered and pulsed, showing tentative signs of stabilization as Chen's commands worked through the fractured network.

"Power is stabilizing," Chen reported. "Perevian, monitor the power transfer for fluctuations and alert me if any subsystems show signs of overload."

"Monitoring active," the AI said. "Power transfer stable at current rates. Environmental controls and minimal lighting restored on Aetherion. Life support functionality has improved but remains at critical levels."

Chen's hands moved quickly over the controls. "Offload non-essential tasks from Aetherion's core AI to Perevian's processing nodes. Redistribute the load evenly to minimize stress on their systems."

"Task redistribution complete," the AI replied. "Aetherion's core AI functionality improved by 28%. Stability remains fragile."

Chen exhaled. "We've restored enough stability for boarding, Captain. But this situation is delicate. One misstep and their systems could spiral again."

Reed's gaze shifted between the displays. Aetherion's systems, though no longer critical, were precariously balanced, held together by the support of Perevian's advanced infrastructure. "We proceed carefully. No unnecessary risks. Keep monitoring their systems, and let me know the moment anything changes."

"Understood," the AI replied. "Continuing to monitor Aetherion's status and support module performance."

Chen leaned back slightly, her eyes scanning the stabilized but fragile network. "We've bought some time, but we're still walking a fine line, Captain. Their systems are barely hanging on."

Reed nodded. "Then let's not waste a second. Prepare the airlock for docking."

Chen quickly tapped at her console, syncing Perevian's docking protocols with Aetherion. The docking procedure initiated, and Perevian's automated systems responded.

Addison fired the ship's thrusters in controlled, minute bursts, nudging Perevian closer to Aetherion. The two ships needed to align perfectly, a process that required utmost precision. As the final approach sequence began, the external cameras displayed a live feed of Aetherion on the viewscreen— a haunting image of a ship that shouldn't be there.

"Approaching docking range," Addison said. "Thrusters holding steady at five percent."

Reed watched the progress bar on his console as the ships aligned. The docking mechanism extended slowly from Perevian, its mechanical arms reaching for Aetherion's derelict hull. The systems calculated adjustments in real time, making micro-corrections to maintain perfect alignment.

"Final approach," Chen confirmed. "Two meters to

contact. Airlock pressurization in progress."

A soft vibration rippled through the hull as Perevian's docking collar extended, the metal arms gently clamping down around Aetherion's airlock. A low, mechanical clank echoed through the ship as the docking collar latched onto the opposing airlock. The clamps engaged with a series of metallic thuds, creating a secure, airtight seal between the two ships.

"Docking clamps are secured," Chen reported. "Pressure equalizing between the airlocks."

There was a moment of silence as the systems worked to match atmospheric conditions between Perevian and Aetherion. Chen monitored the status on her console as the atmospheric sensors displayed gradual changes—pressure, oxygen levels, and temperature adjusting to create a safe environment for the crew.

"Airlocks are synchronized," Chen continued. "Minimal atmosphere detected aboard Aetherion, but we have pressurization. It's stable enough to board."

"Chen and Russo, you're with me. Let's go," ordered Reed.

"Open the airlock," Reed ordered.

Chen keyed in the command at the control panel, and the airlock mechanism whirred, a soft hiss filled the air as oxygen flowed through the pressurized tunnel. Inside, a faint chill hung in the air, the temperature cooler than usual, evidence of Aetherion's failing life support systems.

The airlock doors on Perevian slid open with a soft hiss, revealing the tunnel that connected them to the derelict ship. A faint fog of condensation hung in the air, illuminated by the low emergency lights of Aetherion.

Reed, Russo, and Chen stood at the threshold of the airlock, the cold air hitting them like a sudden chill from the void. Breath fogged in the dim light, forming wisps of vapor that quickly dissipated into the sterile, pressurized atmosphere. Their skin prickled in response, the atmosphere cooler than the regulated warmth of Perevian.

"Seal integrity confirmed," Addison reported from the bridge. "Pressure is stable, and the entanglement link remains intact. We're maintaining a secure connection. You're clear to proceed, Captain."

"Acknowledged," Reed replied. He glanced at his team. "Remember, we have no idea what we're walking into here. Stay sharp and keep comms open at all times. Addison, keep an eye on the readings."

"Aye, Captain," Addison responded. "I'll be watching your every move."

As they crossed, the faint glow from Aetherion's emergency lights cast long shadows across the tunnel. A thin layer of condensation clung to the walls, as if the derelict ship had been in stasis for years.

As the three stepped into Aetherion, a bitter chill hit them. The air smelled stale. Shadows clung to the corners where the emergency lights barely reached, leaving much of the corridor in darkness. Every now and then, a distant, metallic creak reverberated through the hull—like a ghostly reminder of the ship's former life. The stillness felt unnatural, as if the ship had been waiting, dormant, for their arrival.

"We'll split up," Reed said, his voice low. "Chen, head to engineering. Russo, the science lab. I'll check the bridge."

As they moved deeper into the ship, the eerie feeling that had gripped Reed since the discovery of Aetherion only intensified. Something was wrong here.

When Reed reached the bridge, he found it empty. The captain's chair was vacant, the consoles dark. But as he stepped toward the main terminal, a faint sound caught his attention— a whisper, almost imperceptible.

"…help… us."

Reed froze. The voice was unmistakable. It was Townsend. But where was he?

CHAPTER TEN

The faint whisper of Will Townsend's voice sent chills through Reed as he stood motionless on the bridge of Aetherion. The air was heavy, suffused with an eerie silence broken only by the faint crackling of the ship's failing systems. His pulse quickened, but he forced himself to focus.

"Russo, Chen," Reed called over the comms. "I'm on the bridge. I just heard Townsend again. Something's seriously wrong."

"Roger that," Russo's voice crackled in response. "I'm accessing the ship's logs now. So far, no sign of anything unusual—except for the fact that they've been offline for far too long. This ship shouldn't even be operational."

Reed frowned, glancing at the darkened control panels around him. "Chen, how's engineering look?"

"Still assessing," Chen's voice came through. "The main reactor is in a near-critical state, but it's functioning just enough to keep the core systems running. Barely."

Reed ran a hand across the console in front of him, thinking through the puzzle that had brought them here. Aetherion shouldn't exist—he'd seen it destroyed. And yet, here it was, adrift in an energy field that defied explanation.

Worse, its crew was either missing or trapped in some kind of limbo.

"Stay sharp," Reed warned. "Something about this place isn't right."

The air on the bridge seemed to shift. It wasn't a physical change, but a pressure, a presence. And then, the whisper came again, this time clearer, closer.

"…help us… Jonathan."

Reed spun around, his heart pounding. The voice had seemed right behind him—so real, so familiar. But no one was there.

He activated his comm again. "Russo, Chen, I think we need to consider…"

Before Reed could finish his thought, the ship's systems flickered to life without warning. The dim emergency lights brightened suddenly, casting shadows across the bridge. Consoles that had been silent and dead now hummed as streams of data filled their screens. Reed blinked in confusion, the hairs on the back of his neck rising.

"Captain, I didn't do this," Chen's voice crackled through the comms. "Something's reactivating the ship. The systems are powering up on their own."

Reed watched Aetherion's bridge come to life around him. The consoles flashed with erratic streams of data, and the lights overhead surged to full brightness. It was as if the ship itself had been reawakened from some long slumber, but something wasn't right. The power flowing through Aetherion felt… wrong, unsettling.

A wave of fear washed over Reed. "Shut it down!" he

barked. "Now."

"I can't!" Chen shouted. "The controls are locked out. Whatever's doing this is overriding everything I input."

Reed felt his stomach tighten. "Everyone, back to Perevian. That's an order."

Just as he spoke, Russo's voice crackled through the comm, quieter than before, as if coming from far away. "Captain… something's wrong. I was in the science lab, but now I'm—" His voice trailed off. "I… don't know where I am."

Reed's heart skipped a beat. "Russo, stop. Don't move."

Russo's breathing quickened, audible through the comm. "Captain, I swear… I was just reviewing the logs, and now I'm… somewhere else… someplace dark."

Reed's mind raced. "Stay exactly where you are. Don't touch anything. Don't move until I give the word."

A heavy silence followed, then a faint noise came through—a low, rhythmic thudding. Footsteps.

"Russo, report!" Reed barked.

There was no response.

"Russo!" Reed's shout echoed across the bridge, but only silence answered.

The darkness was absolute. Russo blinked, disoriented, struggling to make sense of his surroundings. He couldn't see a thing—the air felt colder here, biting against his skin, making each breath feel heavy and labored. His pulse quickened, the sharp chill in the atmosphere adding to the rising tension in his chest.

He stood motionless, trying to steady himself. The sound

of Aetherion's systems was gone, leaving only a profound silence. It was oppressive, as though the very air had thickened around him. Russo swallowed hard, his heart racing as he fought the urge to call out.

A flicker of light broke through the darkness—a faint, eerie glow in the distance. Russo's eyes adjusted, slowly pulling details from the shadows. The pulsing hues of the energy field outside bled into the chamber, casting long, flickering shadows along the walls, twisting and shifting like a living entity. The swirling chaos threw distorted patterns across the floor, creating the illusion of movement.

And then, in the center of the room, a figure emerged from the darkness.

At first, Russo thought it was a trick of the light—perhaps a reflection from the glass. He blinked, trying to focus, but the figure didn't waver. Instead, it moved—slowly, deliberately, as if aware of his presence.

His heart lurched in his chest. The silence pressed down on him as he took a cautious step forward, the cold metal floor beneath his feet amplifying the sound. Each step felt like an eternity, the shadows around him twisting unnervingly as his mind raced. A malfunction? A hallucination? Or something far worse?

When the figure turned, the shifting lights from the energy field outside caught its face, casting flickering shadows across its features. The dim glow pulsed in waves, illuminating the sharp angles in unnatural flashes—first the eyes, gleaming coldly in the low light, then the hollow contours of the cheeks, followed by the ghostly pallor of the skin. The light created a haunting interplay between light and shadow, as if the face itself was shifting in and out of existence.

Russo froze, his breath catching in his throat. Each pulse of light warped the figure's expression, making it both familiar and alien. The shadows deepened around the eyes, giving them a hollow quality, while the faint glow from the energy field threw eerie highlights across its brow and jawline, adding to the figure's unnatural stillness. It wasn't just the face—it was the way the light seemed to cling to it, like a veil, distorting reality.

It was Commander Townsend.

The same Townsend he had watched die in the destruction of Aetherion. The same Townsend whose ship had been obliterated, whose crew had been lost to the void. Yet here he was, standing before Russo, whole and untouched.

"Commander Townsend?" Russo's voice was a shaky whisper, barely audible over the crackling of the failing ship's systems.

Townsend's face shifted into a smile—cold and distant, a smile devoid of warmth, almost mechanical. "You've come," he said, his voice hollow, flat, as if echoing from a place far beyond the walls of the ship. "I knew you would."

Russo's heart pounded against his ribs, his mind screaming at him that something was terribly, impossibly wrong. "But... you're dead. I saw your ship destroyed. You... you shouldn't be here." His words came out in a rush, his voice trembling.

Townsend tilted his head, the movement slow, his expression unnervingly calm. His eyes gleamed with an unnatural light, not quite human. "Destroyed?" He repeated the word as though it amused him. "No, Dr. Russo. We've been here the whole time. Waiting. Watching."

The words sent a shiver down Russo's spine. The air in the room seemed to thicken, pressing in on him from all sides. He took an instinctive step back, his muscles tightening with fear. "This isn't real," Russo muttered under his breath, trying to anchor himself to reality. "This can't be real."

Townsend's smile widened, stretching unnaturally across his face, but his eyes remained cold. "Oh, I'm very real. Just as real as you."

Russo's pulse thundered in his ears, his mind racing to make sense of the impossible. Townsend shouldn't be here— none of this should be happening. The ship was destroyed, the crew lost. This had to be some kind of illusion, a trick of the energy field, or perhaps something even more insidious. "What are you?" Russo asked, his voice barely above a whisper.

Townsend took a slow step forward, his form casting an elongated shadow that stretched across the floor like a creeping darkness. "We are what remains," he said. "We exist beyond the boundaries of life and death now. And you, Dr. Russo, you do too."

Russo's breath hitched in his throat, panic rising. He needed to leave—now. He turned on his heel, moving toward the door, but before he could reach it, the heavy metal slammed shut with a deafening thud. The sound reverberated through the chamber, trapping him inside. The control panel beside the door flickered and died, leaving him with no way out.

"No, no, no…" Russo muttered, his hands trembling as he frantically pressed at the door controls. Nothing responded. The lights on the panel remained dark. His heart pounded in his chest, panic flooding his veins.

Behind him, Townsend's voice floated through the air, soft but sinister. "There's no escape, Dr. Russo."

Russo spun around, his back pressed against the cold, unyielding door. Townsend—or the thing that wore his face—was closer now, his expression darkening, his eyes gleaming with something inhuman, something ancient. The room felt smaller, the air growing colder, denser, as if the ship itself was closing in on him.

"You've seen the truth," Townsend said, his voice low, almost a whisper. "And now, it's time for you to join us."

Russo's legs felt weak, his knees threatening to give out beneath him. He glanced toward the window, toward the swirling energy field outside. It pulsed, alive with rhythmic movements, as though it were beckoning him, calling to him. His mind raced for a way out, for an explanation, for anything that made sense—but everything felt distant, surreal.

"This… this isn't real," Russo said again, trying to steady his voice, trying to force some logic into the madness. But Townsend's presence was suffocating, pressing against his mind like a weight he couldn't shake. Every second in that room felt like a struggle to hold on to reality.

Townsend took another step forward, his figure almost gliding across the floor now. "You're wrong, Dr. Russo. It's more real than you'll ever know. You've already begun to see it, haven't you? The truth of what lies beyond… waiting for you."

Russo's hands balled into fists, his mind racing through the possibilities. His options were rapidly dwindling, and the reality of his situation began to sink in. He wasn't just trapped in this room—he was trapped in something much larger, something he couldn't yet comprehend.

Townsend's voice was soft, but it echoed through Russo's thoughts like a taunt. "You will join us. There is no other way."

Reed bolted from the bridge, his footsteps echoing through Aetherion's cold, dimly lit corridors. Every creak of the hull and flicker of the lights made his heart race, as if the ship itself was alive—reacting to their presence.

As he neared amidship, Chen emerged from engineering. Without a word, Reed motioned for her to follow. "We don't have time. Move."

"Where's Russo?" Chen asked as they sprinted down the narrow corridor of the ship. The oppressive silence was broken only by their hurried footsteps and the occasional groan from Aetherion's failing systems.

"Later!" he shouted.

The path back to the docking tube seemed unbearably long, every shadow growing darker, every sound amplified. Reed felt as if something was watching from the darkness, closing in on them.

"Whatever's controlling this ship—it's not done with us yet," Reed muttered as they reached the docking port. The hatch between Aetherion and Perevian loomed ahead, their escape route tantalizingly close.

Chen rushed to the control panel, her fingers flying over the keys as she attempted to open the airlock. "It's slow," she said, frustration creeping into her voice. "Something's interfering with the connection."

Aetherion's systems remained erratic—flickering, dying, and sputtering to life. Reed stared at the control panel, their lights blinking weakly. "Hurry," Reed urged, glancing back down the corridor, half expecting Aetherion to come alive and trap them inside.

After what felt like an eternity, the door hissed open. Without hesitation, Reed pushed through, Chen right behind him. They hurried across the docking tube, the hum of Perevian's systems a welcome sound.

The moment they were inside Perevian, Reed didn't slow down. "To the bridge," he ordered, already breaking into a sprint down the corridor. Chen followed close behind, her breath quickening as they raced through the ship.

Perevian felt different now. Though it was their sanctuary from the grip of Aetherion, the acute foreboding they'd just experienced clung in the air. The sound of the ship's systems, once a comfort, now seemed ominous.

Reed reached the bridge doors first, slamming his hand against the panel to open them. The doors slid apart, revealing the heart of Perevian, its consoles alive with activity.

Chen rushed to her station, immediately pulling up sensor readings. "I'm checking if any of Aetherion's interference followed us back," she said.

"What happened over there?" Addison asked. "And where is Russo?"

Reed quickly settled into his command chair, his eyes darting across the screens. The view outside showed Aetherion, still floating ominously in the void. But something about it seemed more alive now, more aware.

"Captain, you need to see this," Chen called out. "The energy field—it's expanding."

Reed looked at the viewscreen, his eyes widening. The energy field that had surrounded Aetherion was now growing, its tendrils reaching out toward Perevian.

"We need to get the hell out of here," Reed muttered, his mind racing. But they couldn't just leave without Russo—and now, they had to contend with whatever malevolent force was controlling Aetherion.

The energy field throbbed, its glow intensifying as it reached closer to Perevian.

"But we're not leaving without Russo," Reed said. "We're bringing him back, even if I have to drag him out of there."

And with that, Reed made his decision. He headed back toward the airlock, preparing for what could be his final mission.

Reed stood in the dim glow of the airlock, then turned quickly and strode toward the equipment locker and keyed it open, grabbing a wrist-mounted scanner from its slot. The device hummed to life as it attached to his arm, its display flickering momentarily before stabilizing. Reed flexed his wrist, testing its weight, and checked the readings as they scrolled across the screen. He could already see residual fluctuations in Aetherion's energy grid—it was worse.

"Chen," Reed called over the comm. "I want constant monitoring of the connection between the ships. If anything changes, let me know immediately."

"Understood, Captain," Chen replied. "But the power relay isn't going to hold forever. Aetherion's systems are degraded, and I'm getting weird feedback spikes."

Reed nodded to himself. He had no choice. Russo was over there, trapped in Aetherion, and whatever had taken control of the ship wasn't going to make things easy.

Taking a deep breath, he closed the locker and headed toward the airlock. With the scanner strapped securely to his wrist, Reed stepped through, the cold chill of Aetherion's failing systems greeting him.

"Captain," Addison's voice broke through the static on the comms, "the energy field surrounding Aetherion is fluctuating. I'm starting to see some interference with the docking seal."

Reed cursed under his breath. "Understood. I'll move as quick as I can. Be ready to disengage the moment we're back onboard."

He glanced at the airlock, the soft hiss of pressure releasing as the hatch slid open. Reed stepped forward into the dimly lit tube. The clank of his boots echoed down the metal corridor as he crossed back into Aetherion, his heart pounding. This ship was supposed to be dead, and yet, here it was, limping back to life, filled with an unspoken menace.

Russo was waiting for him. He had to be.

Chen's voice crackled over the comm. "I'm seeing strange fluctuations in the environmental controls. Something's interfering with the airflow. Proceed with caution."

"Copy that," Reed replied, his voice echoing down the silent corridors. The air felt heavier than before, each breath coming a little harder as if the ship itself was resisting. He activated his wrist-mounted scanner, the glow from the screen casting a faint light as he swept the area ahead.

The ship's overhead lights dimmed and brightened in irregular bursts. The sound of Reed's footsteps was unnaturally loud against the hollow, metallic walls.

"Liam!" Reed called into his comm. "Where are you?"

Only static.

As he approached a junction, he raised his wrist-mounted scanner, sweeping the device in front of him from side to side. Two paths stretched ahead, each as dark and foreboding as the other. The light from his scanner barely penetrated the gloom, revealing nothing but the faint outlines of metal walls disappearing into darkness.

A soft beep from the scanner broke the stillness, directing him left. The device registered faint energy readings ahead— weak electronic signatures, as though something was moving through the ship's systems. Reed exhaled slowly, tightening his grip on the scanner before pressing forward.

As he advanced down the corridor, the atmosphere seemed to shift. The air grew even more dense and cold—suffocating. Every breath was more of a struggle, the chill biting at his skin, the metallic tang of stale air lingering at the back of his throat. The deeper he went, the more the ship seemed to resist him, the walls closing in, the ceiling feeling lower with each step.

Reed stopped abruptly, his eyes narrowing as a faint vibration passed through the floor beneath him. The low sound he'd noticed earlier had grown louder, more distinct, reverberating. It wasn't the usual sound of a ship's systems at work—it felt alive.

He glanced down at his scanner again, the readings becoming more erratic. Energy signatures blinked across the screen, like something was moving just out of sight, just beyond his reach. Whatever it was, it wasn't natural.

"Captain," Chen's voice crackled over the comm. "We're picking up some unusual activity from Aetherion's systems. It's like the ship is…"

Reed glanced at the wrist-mounted scanner, the erratic energy readings blinking back at him. "These readings are all over the place. What do you see?"

"The same thing," Chen responded. "It's spiking near the core systems—whatever's causing this, it's not random."

Reed gritted his teeth, his eyes probing the darkened corridor ahead. "How much closer is the energy field to Perevian?"

A pause. Then Chen's voice came through, more urgent now. "Still the same, but the energy feedback is… growing. I can't pinpoint the source."

Reed shook his head, muttering under his breath. "Damn it."

"Should you pull back?" Chen asked.

Reed took a breath, his wrist scanner still blinking wildly. "Not yet. I need to keep going."

The silence pressed in as he pushed forward, the rumble from the ship growing louder with each step. The air felt even thicker, almost like moving through water. Every breath was a struggle, his lungs fighting against the oppressive atmosphere.

The lights flickered overhead, plunging the corridor into

darkness for a moment before they sputtered back to life. Shadows danced along the walls, twisting and shifting in unnatural patterns. Reed stopped again, scanning the area, a deep sense of foreboding settling in his gut. Something wasn't right. The ship felt alive, but not in the way it should. There was an intelligence here—something unseen, watching.

The rumbling deepened, almost a growl now, vibrating through the walls, filling his ears. Reed glanced at his scanner once more. The readings were spiking—surges of energy moving erratically through the ship, converging toward a single point. His eyes followed the scanner's direction, leading him deeper into the ship, closer to the observation lounge.

As he pressed on, he noticed heavy condensation clinging to the walls—thin droplets of moisture running down in uneven lines. Even the air felt alive, charged with something unseen that made his skin prickle.

A faint noise echoed from somewhere ahead—a soft, rhythmic thudding. Reed stopped in his tracks, listening, his heart pounding in his ears. The sound was distant but steady, like footsteps, or perhaps something mechanical, hidden deep within the ship. He strained to hear more, but the sound faded, swallowed by the hum of the ship's systems.

"Liam!" Reed called into his comm again. "Respond!"

Only static.

He crept forward, each step slower than the last. The narrow corridor twisted ahead, the walls closing in, the lights dimming further as he neared the core of the ship. The noise had become a constant drone now, vibrating through his bones. His breath fogged in the chilled air, his lungs burning with every intake.

Reed reached another junction, the scanner beeping faintly again, directing him to the right. The lights overhead flickered more violently, casting jagged shadows across the walls. The ship groaned, metal shifting as if it was alive, breathing in rhythm with the pulsing energy.

As he neared the observation lounge, an electric charge filled the air, making the hair on the back of his neck stand on end. His eyes fixed on the dark seam of the door, now just a few steps away, the cold metal surface gleaming under the flickering lights. Something was behind it. Waiting.

Reed's fingers hovered over the control panel, his hand trembling slightly as he hesitated. His instincts screamed at him to turn back, to retreat to Perevian, but he couldn't leave without Russo.

The thrum of the ship grew louder, almost deafening now. Reed's heart pounded in his chest as he stared at the door, his hand hesitantly reaching out to key it open.

The door to the observation lounge slid open with a mechanical hiss, and Reed stepped into the large, dimly lit chamber. The glow of the energy field surrounding Aetherion stretched across the room, illuminating the curved glass windows.

Russo stood at the far end, his back to Reed, staring out into the swirling energy. The light bathed him in a strange, almost otherworldly glow. But that wasn't what made Reed's breath catch in his throat.

Standing beside Russo, bathed in the same pale light, was Will Townsend.

Reed froze. A chill ran down his spine.

"Liam!" Reed called, stepping cautiously forward. "What the hell is going on?"

Russo didn't turn. His voice, when it came, was distant and hollow. "I've seen it, Captain. The truth. Commander Townsend… he's been here all along. The field… it saved him. It will save all of us."

Reed's pulse quickened. "No, Liam. That's not Will. Whatever this is, it's not real. You need to step away."

Townsend's figure turned slowly, his eyes locking onto Reed's with an unnerving calmness. "You're wrong, Jonathan," Townsend said, his voice smooth and too perfect. "I never left. I've been here, waiting for you."

Reed clenched his fists, his mind racing. This wasn't Will. It couldn't be. But the figure standing in front of him, the man speaking in that familiar voice, was too real.

"I saw your ship destroyed," Reed said, his voice trembling with anger and confusion. "You sacrificed yourself to save us. You died, Will."

Townsend smiled, the corners of his mouth curling in an almost unnatural way. "Sacrificed? No, Jonathan. I didn't die. I evolved. The field… it showed me the truth. It will show you, too."

Reed stepped closer, his eyes fixed on Russo. "Liam, listen to me. We need to get out of here."

Russo finally turned to face him, his eyes wide with a strange mix of fear and awe. "Captain… you don't understand. The field—it's not just energy. It's something more. It's been watching us, manipulating us. We're part of it."

Reed's heart raced. "Liam, whatever this thing is telling you, it's not true. We need to leave."

Townsend stepped closer, his smile widening. "There's no escape, Jonathan. Because none of this is real. Not the ships, not the mission… not even you."

Reed stepped forward, grabbed Russo's arm, and yanked him back toward the door. "Let's go," he growled.

The moment they stepped through the exit, the energy field reacted violently, sending erratic and intense bursts of light across the walls. Its glow spilled into the corridor, as if reaching out for them, casting distorted reflections along the metal surfaces.

Chen's voice crackled over the comm. "Captain, we've got a serious problem. The energy field's destabilizing. It's starting to interfere with the docking systems. I need you back. Now."

Reed's grip on Russo tightened as the ship trembled beneath their feet. The door slid shut behind them with a hiss, sealing the observation lounge in darkness. "We're on our way," Reed barked, already pulling Russo down the corridor. "Prepare to disengage the clamps."

The ship shook violently, and the corridor ahead seemed to bend and shift as the energy field's tendrils coiled tighter around Aetherion. The walls groaned, the flickering lights overhead casting disorienting flashes across the narrow passage. Each step felt heavier, as if the ship itself was resisting their escape. Reed and Russo sprinted down the corridor, the vibrations growing stronger, the lights flickering into near darkness as the ship's systems struggled under the strain.

Reed pushed Russo forward, his grip firm as the

shuddering of Aetherion grew more violent, its groans echoing through the narrow corridor.

Aetherion seemed to contract, the very structure warping under the pressure of the energy tendrils as they tightened their grip. Sparks shot from overhead wiring, plunging sections of the corridor into darkness. The metal floor beneath their feet vibrated. Reed could feel the heat of the ship's strain in the air, sweat beading on his forehead as they pushed forward.

"Chen, release the docking clamps the second we're aboard!" Reed shouted into the comm.

"Aye, Captain," Chen responded.

The docking tube was now just ahead, but the distance felt like miles as the lights flickered once more, briefly throwing the entire corridor into darkness. Reed's grip on Russo tightened, driving him toward the airlock with every ounce of strength. The low hum of Aetherion was now a roar, the ship's structure threatening to buckle.

"Go!" Reed yelled, shoving Russo toward the airlock.

They stumbled into the small chamber as a violent tremor rocked the ship. Reed hit the panel, sealing the door behind them. The airlock hissed, locking them in, and a brief moment of panic followed before the door to the docking tube opened. Without hesitation, they hurried into the narrow tunnel, its metal walls shaking with the reverberations of the failing ship.

The tunnel groaned under the strain as they moved through it, each step more difficult as the tremors intensified. The flickering lights gave way to darkness once again, but they pushed forward, nearing the safety of their own vessel.

Just as they reached the far end, Reed slammed his hand

on the emergency release, and the door to Perevian opened with a hiss. They tumbled inside, another violent tremor shaking Aetherion as they fell through.

The docking tube retracted with a metallic groan, pulling them away from the doomed ship's frame.

"Disengaged!" Chen's voice crackled through the comms. "We're pulling away!"

The jolt of Perevian's clamps releasing sent a final tremor through the docking system as the engines roared to life, propelling them away from Aetherion.

Reed leaned against the cold metal wall of the airlock, bent over as he struggled to catch his breath.

CHAPTER ELEVEN

Captain," Chen's voice crackled over the comm, "We've cleared the field, but we're not out of the woods yet. There's still interference affecting our instruments, and things are unstable."

"Punch it, Addison," Reed ordered. "Get us out of here."

The engines roared to life, Perevian lurching forward with a surge of power as it accelerated away from the pulsing energy field. Strands of light coiled around Aetherion's hull, like a vast, unseen force pulling it deeper into the void. The field's glow blurred the ship's outline, distorting it.

The two eventually became indistinguishable, blending together in a strange, seamless fusion. The ship didn't disappear, but it was no longer entirely visible. As though it had become one with the field—lost within its depths.

Reed and Russo stood together in the airlock, still catching their breath. The oppressive cold from Aetherion still clung to them, as if its haunting presence lingered. Reed turned to Russo, whose face remained pale and unsettled.

"Liam," Reed said, stepping closer. "We're back. You're safe. Focus."

Russo blinked, his mind returning to the present. "Safe? From what, Captain? We're not safe from this. If that field is what it says it is… it's trying to pull us in… everything's connected…"

Reed shook his head. "Stop talking nonsense. I need you to stay grounded, or we'll never figure this out."

Russo hesitated, then nodded. "Yes, Captain. But the field… it's not just random energy. It's intelligence."

Reed sighed. "I know. But right now, our priority is getting clear of this thing and stabilizing the ship. We'll deal with the rest later."

He exchanged a look with Russo before heading down the corridor. "Let's get to the bridge."

Russo followed.

As they entered the bridge, Reed immediately took his seat, his mind racing with the implications of what they had witnessed. The familiar sound of the ship's systems filled the room, a stark contrast to the chaos they'd just escaped.

"Chen," Reed called. "Open a channel to NASA. Priority one transmission."

"Captain, we're getting interference across all bands. It's not just local interference—something's distorting the entire signal. I'll boost the transmission as much as I can, but it's unstable."

Reed tightened his grip on the console. "Handle it. NASA needs this information."

As Chen worked on boosting the signal, Reed recorded the message, each word charged with urgency.

"This is Captain Jonathan Reed of Perevian, transmitting an emergency priority-one message to NASA mission control. We have re-established contact with Aetherion. I say again, we have re-established both visual and physical contact with Aetherion, previously classified as lost. The vessel is currently enveloped by an unknown energy field, and its structural integrity appears compromised or merged with the field.

Our sensors are unable to provide clear data due to significant interference from the field, which is also impacting communications and ship systems. We are requesting immediate guidance on how to proceed, given the unknown nature of the anomaly and its potential risks.

Awaiting further instructions. Reed out."

He waited, the silence on the bridge thick with tension. "Signal's weak, Captain," Chen reported, frustration clear in her voice. "I can't tell if it made it through. The energy field is breaking everything up. I'm boosting the signal as much as possible, but it's unpredictable."

All of a sudden, Perevian rocked violently, the bridge lights flickering. Alarms blared, red warning lights flashed, and emergency lighting blinked on.

"Now what?" groaned Addison.

"Report!" Reed ordered.

"Captain!" Chen shouted. "We've got a power failure in the primary reactor! If we don't stabilize, we're dead in the water."

Reed's heart pounded. "What's causing it?"

"Energy surge from the field. It's disrupting core systems—secondary reactor is down to fifty percent, and it's dropping fast. We're going to lose power if this keeps up."

Addison turned, eyes wide. "We won't be able to keep this speed up much longer without the primary reactor."

"Chen, what's the fix?"

"We need to manually reset the power couplings in engineering to reroute energy from the secondary reactor to stabilize the primary."

Reed swore under his breath. "Russo, go with her. Get that power back online."

Russo blinked, then nodded quickly. He followed Chen as they bolted toward engineering, their footsteps pounding through the narrow corridor. The ship vibrated ominously through the deck plates beneath their feet, while the emergency lighting flickered.

As they reached the reactor bay, the air vibrated with the deep, uneven hum of the reactors struggling to maintain stability. The ship groaned, metal creaking from the strain of the failing systems.

"Here," Chen said breathlessly, pointing to the primary reactor control console. The reactor's core housing flickered with unstable energy arcs, while power readings on the secondary reactor console were dangerously low. The reactor's magnetic containment field was barely holding. "We need to disengage the primary reactor's couplings and reroute the plasma flow from the secondary reactor. If we don't stabilize the magnetic containment, we're looking at a full plasma breach."

Russo moved to the adjacent panel, scanning the complex array of readouts. "Got it. What's the sequence?"

"Start by decoupling the magnetic constrictor coils on the primary reactor, but only in sequence or the plasma will flood the system. You'll need to depressurize the plasma conduits on the secondary reactor first—those valves over there." She pointed to a row of heavy mechanical valves near the base of the reactor.

Russo didn't hesitate. He moved to the valves, gripping the first one tightly. "How much pressure are we talking about?"

"Enough to blow us into deep space if we're not careful," Chen shot back. "Open them slowly to vent the plasma safely, or we'll lose containment completely."

Russo braced himself and carefully twisted the first valve. There was a loud hiss as the built-up plasma pressure released into the ship's exhaust systems. He moved to the next one, repeating the process while Chen disengaged the primary reactor's couplings.

"Plasma venting," she called out, watching the pressure levels drop on the console. "Two more to go." The ship shuddered violently as a wave of energy from the field outside crashed against it. The primary reactor's containment field wavered. "We're losing integrity—keep going, we don't have much time."

Russo opened the final valve, his hands slick with sweat, as the secondary reactor's plasma conduits depressurized. "That's it! All valves are vented."

Chen didn't waste a second. She yanked the final coupling free and initiated the manual plasma reroute from the secondary reactor. The reactor bay lit up with warning lights as power surged through the auxiliary systems. The ship groaned again, but this time, the sound of the primary reactor shifted, the magnetic containment field stabilizing as power levels normalized.

"Captain! We've stabilized the primary reactor," Chen called over the comm. "Plasma flow is steady and rerouted from the secondary systems—power should be coming online now."

Back on the bridge, the console displays came back to life. Addison leaned over her station, eyes darting across the readouts. "Captain, power readings are returning to normal."

Reed gripped the edge of his chair. "Chen, can we engage the Alcubierre drive?"

"Negative, Captain. The energy field is causing fluctuations in our power distribution. If we engage the drive, we risk overloading the reactors and triggering a total system shutdown. I can give you maximum engine thrust output for a few minutes, but the drive's off the table for now."

Addison glanced back from her station. "Even at max thrust, the energy field would still gain on us. It's almost like it's chasing us, Captain."

"Can we outrun it?" Reed asked.

Addison shook her head. "Not for long. It's accelerating. If it keeps growing at this rate, we'll be overtaken in minutes."

Russo stepped onto the bridge. "Captain, it's not chasing us—it's reacting to us. The more we run, the more it stretches toward us."

Reed gave him a questioning look. "What do you suggest?"

Russo hesitated. "We stop."

Silence fell across the bridge.

"You want us to stop?" Addison said, incredulous. "You want us to just let that thing catch up to us?"

"Yes," Russo nodded. "It's trying to communicate. The moment we boarded Aetherion, the energy field reacted—it was making contact. Running isn't going to solve anything. We need to let it communicate."

Addison raised an eyebrow. "And if it's not trying to communicate? What if it's trying to consume us like it did Aetherion?"

Russo crossed his arms, his eyes serious. "I don't think it's a threat, at least not in the way you think. It's clearly showing signs of intelligence."

Reed leaned against his arm rest, the weight of the decision settling over him. It was a huge risk. The field had already wreaked havoc on Aetherion, and now it seemed to be reaching toward Perevian. But Russo had a point—the field wasn't behaving randomly. There was an intentionality behind it, something purposeful.

Reed glanced at the swirling energy on the display, watching its tendrils stretch toward them, like it was waiting for a response. His mind raced, weighing the danger against the potential. They couldn't keep this up anyway. The crew's lives were in his hands.

He exhaled sharply.

"Addison," Reed said finally. "Ease up on the engines."

Addison stared at him, confusion written across her face. "Captain—are you sure?"

"That's an order, Lieutenant," said Reed calmly.

The ship gradually decelerated, its thrusters easing as they drifted into the dark of space. The throb of the engines softened as Perevian reduced its speed.

The door to the bridge hissed open and Chen rushed in. "Reactor's stabilized," she announced, moving quickly to her station. "But pushing the engines isn't an option right now."

Reed nodded. "We're slowing down."

Chen froze, staring at Reed in disbelief. "Slowing down? Captain, are you serious?"

Reed met her gaze. "We've been running, and it's still gaining. The more we run, the more it reacts to us."

Chen threw her hands up in frustration, her voice rising. "And you think letting it catch up is a better idea?" She threw herself into her seat. "I don't like this one bit, Captain. Not one bit."

The ship continued to decelerate, the tension on the bridge thick as the energy field behind them pulsed and began to slow. The swirls of energy seemed to stabilize, maintaining a steady distance from the ship, no longer expanding.

Russo ran quickly to his station, his fingers moving across the keys. "There's a shift in the energy frequencies—it's becoming more coherent. If we filter the signals, we might be able to pick something up. We need to create an opening— allow the signal through without overwhelming the systems."

Reed turned to Chen. "Can we do that safely?"

Chen frowned, still unsure about the new plan. She glanced at the raw energy data flashing on her console. "It's possible, but risky. If we let too much in, the feedback could fry our systems. I can set up a buffer zone—divert the signal through an isolated channel. But we'll only have a small window before the pressure starts building."

"How long?" Reed asked.

Russo hesitated. "I don't know. But whatever it's trying to tell us—it's life changing."

Reed's eyes darted between the displays and the energy field outside. The tendrils of energy were pulsing, pressing harder against the ship, trying to reach them, as if the field sensed they were close to cutting the connection.

Russo worked furiously at his station, gathering as much of the data as he could before they severed the link. The sheer volume of information pouring in from the field was staggering, overwhelming even their advanced systems, but he wasn't going to leave empty-handed.

"Chen," Reed called out. "Prepare to sever the link."

"Almost got it..." Russo muttered. "Just a few more seconds."

"Buffer integrity at one hundred percent," Chen reported, her hands moving rapidly across the controls. "We're not going to last much longer, Captain!"

"Russo, we don't have time!" Reed shouted, his heart racing.

"I've got it!" Russo yelled back. "Sever the link now!"

"Chen, cut it!" Reed commanded.

Chen hit the controls, and Perevian shuddered violently, the ship groaning as if resisting the command.

"Captain, something's wrong!" Chen's voice rose with panic. "The field isn't letting us go!"

Reed's knuckles turned white as he gripped the edge of his chair. "Addison, full power! Get us out of here!"

Addison's fingers flew over the helm, the engines roaring as Perevian strained against the energy field's grip. Space around them began to ripple and fold, but the field clung to them, tightening like a vice.

"We're not breaking free!" Chen shouted. "The field is locking us in tighter—it's draining power from our systems!"

Suddenly, alarms blared across the bridge. The lights flickered as the ship shuddered again, more violently this time. A loud cracking sound reverberated through the hull, and the deck beneath them rattled. Addison glanced at her console, her face pale.

"Captain!" she shouted. "Structural integrity is failing"

Reed's heart sank. They couldn't hold out much longer.

Chen's voice trembled as she reported more damage. "We're down 40% on main power, and the engines are overheating. We can't maintain thrust much longer!"

Reed's mind raced. Engaging the Alcubierre drive had already been ruled out, but now they were running out of options. The ship was literally breaking, and if they didn't act soon, Perevian would be torn to shreds.

"Captain, the hull's integrity is at critical levels!" Chen shouted. "We won't survive much longer in this field!"

Reed slammed his fist down. "We have no choice. Prepare the Alcubierre drive!"

Addison hesitated, her hand hovering over the controls. "But the field—it's still disrupting the power systems! If we engage—"

"I know the risks!" Reed snapped. "But the ship can't take this. We engage the drive now or we get ripped apart."

Addison swallowed hard and nodded. "Aye, Captain." She reached for the drive controls, her fingers trembling.

The ship groaned, another sickening crack echoing through the hull. "We've got to do it now!" Chen screamed.

"Engage the drive!" Reed ordered, bracing himself.

Addison slammed her fist down. Perevian lurched violently, the Alcubierre drive spooling up. Space-time itself began to warp and stretch as the bubble formed around the ship, but the energy field refused to let go. Tendrils of energy lashed out, wrapping tighter around Perevian, as if trying to crush it.

For a brief moment, the ship seemed to float, weightless in the void. Then, without warning, a sharp, bone-jarring jolt pulled them violently forward.

"The field's still holding on!" Addison cried. "We're not breaking free!"

Outside, the stars twisted and blurred into streaks of light, but the field clung to the ship. Instead of retreating, the coils of energy began to stretch and curl back toward them, moving faster and faster.

"The field is feeding off the drive!" Chen shouted. "It's overpowering us!"

Perevian rocked violently, as if seized by a giant hand. Stars outside flickered in and out of focus as space folded erratically around them.

"The field's pulling us back!" Addison cried. "We're not escaping—it's surrounding us!"

The Alcubierre bubble began to destabilize. Space-time warped and buckled around the ship, but instead of breaking through, Perevian was caught in a vortex of writhing energy. The ship lurched forward, then back again, as if locked in a brutal tug-of-war.

Suddenly, alarms blared across the bridge. Chen stared at her console, eyes wide in panic. "Captain, the reactors are overloading! The energy field is feeding back into our systems—we're reaching critical levels!"

Reed's stomach tightened. "How much time do we have?"

"None!" Chen shouted. "If we don't shut down the drive, the reactors will breach!"

Reed gritted his teeth. They were running out of options. "Shut it down, Addison! Shut it all down!"

"Disengaging drive!" she yelled.

The ship lurched violently as the Alcubierre drive powered down, the sudden release of pressure sending shockwaves through the hull. The energy field outside surged, tightening its grip as if sensing the ship's vulnerability. Space-time continued to distort around them, the swirling vortex growing more intense.

Russo's face went pale. "We're dead in the water."

The viewscreen flickered, the tendrils now so close they looked as though they were inside the ship. Energy writhed around them, distorting in ways their instruments couldn't register.

They were trapped.

CHAPTER TWELVE

Perevian's external sensors were overwhelmed, the data flooding in faster than the systems could process. Rhythmic pulses of energy enveloped the ship like a living web, each wave more deliberate and calculated than the last. What initially seemed like random fluctuations now formed a pattern—an intricate dance of energy, as if the field itself had a purpose.

The crew sat in silence, the engines the only sound. On the main viewscreen, the shifting plasma surrounding the ship glowed with an otherworldly light. The colors weren't static—they morphed and flowed in sync with the pulses, creating a hypnotic display.

Reed stood at the edge of the viewscreen, his eyes scanning the ever-changing currents that wove in and out of the void. He could feel it, almost instinctively: the field wasn't just a mindless cosmic phenomenon. It was something else—something aware.

"Status report," he asked, his voice cutting through the stillness.

"The field... it's responding to us," Russo replied.

Chen's hands danced over her console, her face lit by the kaleidoscopic glow of data streams. "Captain, we're detecting exotic particles—ones we've only theorized about in extreme quantum environments. They're interacting with Perevian's systems, creating recursive feedback loops that..." She trailed off.

Reed turned. "That what?"

Chen hesitated, then met his gaze. "The loops are entangled across multiple quantum states. It's as if the field isn't just reacting to us—it's synchronized. Every movement we make, every emission we produce—it's mirrored instantly."

"Quantum entanglement?" Addison interjected, her brow furrowed. "But on this scale? Across a region this vast?"

Chen nodded, turning to the viewscreen. She expanded the data, revealing graphs of quantum fluctuations and gravitational distortions, all correlating with Perevian's movements. "It's more than just entanglement. It's reacting faster than we can measure. The field isn't just synchronized—it's anticipating us."

"If it's anticipating us, that implies it's computing," said Reed. "Are you saying this thing is analyzing us in real time?"

"Not just analyzing," Chen said, zooming in on clusters of data points. "It's learning. Imagine the field as a quantum network—nodes scattered throughout this region, processing every emission, every signal we produce. Each interaction makes it more precise. The field seems to be evolving, adapting to us."

Russo brought up another set of visuals. "Here—the fine structure constant, which governs electromagnetic interactions, is fluctuating slightly but measurably. And here—look at the gravitational constant. Both are shifting in ways that are subtle but undeniably deliberate."

Addison's eyes narrowed, her tone skeptical. "Deliberate? How could anything alter constants like these? What kind of force are we dealing with?"

Russo drew in a deep breath. "We're looking at what appears to be controlled manipulation of vacuum energy. Specifically, the field is adjusting the zero-point energy—the baseline quantum energy inherent to the vacuum of space. This isn't just a theoretical anomaly; it's a system actively reshaping the physical parameters of this region."

Reed crossed his arms, his expression darkening. "A system," he echoed. "So, you're saying this isn't natural."

Russo shook his head. "Not remotely, Captain. The recursive energy patterns, the responsiveness, the precision—everything about this suggests computational behavior."

Chen leaned forward as she studied the data. "And it's not just reactive. The field is probing us. With every emission, every adjustment Perevian makes, the field grows more precise. It's as if it's learning from us—testing how we respond."

"Testing us?" Addison pressed. "For what?"

"That's what we don't know," said Russo. "The field isn't operating within binary logic. The complexity suggests it's utilizing a multi-dimensional framework—potentially involving interactions with higher dimensions."

He expanded the graphs, highlighting deviations in particle wavefunctions. "The energy signatures align with Kaluza-Klein theory—higher-dimensional models where additional spatial dimensions are compactified at subatomic scales. This field appears to propagate through those hidden dimensions, using them as reservoirs to transfer and manipulate energy."

"That could explain the rapid fluctuations we've observed," said Chen. "The field is pulling energy from these dimensions, altering space-time geometry, and possibly even distorting our perception of time."

Reed turned back to the viewscreen, the pulsating plasma reflecting in his eyes. "And this is happening in real time?"

"Yes," Russo confirmed. "Think of it as a quantum circuit operating across dimensions. It can move energy between these dimensions, reshape local densities, and dynamically adjust the vacuum state as needed."

"But why?" asked Reed.

"Hmm, that's a good question. If it's computational, then it's using us as part of the equation. Every action we take feeds it more data—like we're part of its process."

Reed stared at the vortex outside, his mind caught between awe and terror. The idea of being entangled in something capable of higher-dimensional manipulation was as unsettling as it was profound.

"Captain," Chen's voice broke through the silence. "I'm seeing rapid fluctuations in the gravitational field—strong enough to cause space-time ruptures."

Reed moved swiftly to Chen's console. "Explain."

"Localized fluctuations are spiking across the field. If these ruptures expand, we could be dealing with the creation of micro-singularities."

Russo's face paled. "If micro-singularities are forming, it

means the field is operating under conditions of extreme gravitational shear. These types of conditions are only present near the event horizon of a black hole—or in scenarios involving exotic matter."

Addison's stomach sank. "Exotic matter? Are we talking negative energy?"

"Yes," Russo said. "Negative energy density is required to manipulate space-time in such a way that faster-than-light travel can occur, such as our Alcubierre drive. The field is stabilizing these effects using negative energy, possibly drawn from those extra dimensions."

"Captain," Chen interrupted again. "We're beginning to feel the effects of those gravitational distortions. If we don't find a way out of this soon, the structural integrity of Perevian could be compromised."

Reed's jaw clenched. "What about the ship's gravitic shielding? Can we boost it?"

Chen scanned her screens. "I've already boosted the shields to two hundred percent of their normal capacity, but the fluctuations in the field are starting to affect the ship at a quantum level. We're seeing phase shifts in the material composition of the hull."

Phase shifts. That was something Reed had hoped he wouldn't hear. If the material of Perevian itself was undergoing quantum fluctuations, it meant they were teetering on the brink of decoherence—the point at which the solid matter of the ship could be torn apart at the subatomic level. "We can't stay here," he muttered. "We need to figure out a way to navigate out of this energy-well before the ship's structure destabilizes any further."

"I've been running projections on potential escape vectors, but the problem is that the field isn't static," said Addison. "It's shifting faster than I can calculate, and every possible escape route is closed off as soon as I plot it."

Russo leaned forward in his chair, his fingers drumming the console. "It's not just closing off routes—it's herding us somewhere."

Fear gnawed at the edges of Reed's mind. What kind of intelligence were they dealing with? Was this a trap, or did it hold some unknown purpose? There was no choice now—they were being drawn deeper, and the only way out seemed to be forward.

"Chen, I want full diagnostic reports every five minutes. Keep monitoring the phase shifts in the hull and make sure we maintain integrity," Reed ordered.

"Aye, Captain," Chen responded, already focused on the next set of data, running continuous simulations to calculate structural stress in response to the gravitational fluctuations.

Russo spoke up from his station. "I've isolated a series of high-energy emissions from deeper within the field. They're not random—there's a clear sequence to them, almost like a code."

"What kind of code?" Reed asked, turning his attention to Russo.

"It's a regular, periodic signal—highly structured. The wavelength suggests quantum interactions, but I can't make out the exact nature of it yet. Whatever it is, it's operating on a scale we've never seen before, potentially using entangled particles across these extra dimensions."

Addison's brow furrowed. "Are you saying this signal is a form of communication?"

Russo hesitated. "That's a strong possibility. If this field is processing us, it may be attempting to communicate through quantum states, using particle entanglement as the medium."

"If this signal is a form of communication, we need to figure out how to communicate back," said Reed. "Russo, keep analyzing that sequence. I want to know everything about it—frequency, phase, whatever we can use to understand its possible language."

"Aye, Captain."

As the ship continued its slow, deliberate course, Chen's console suddenly lit up with a new warning. "Captain, I'm detecting a significant spike in the energy density ahead. It's… massive."

Reed moved to her side. "How massive?"

Chen's fingers flew over the interface. "We're talking about a localized increase in energy density by a factor of ten—no, make that a hundred. It's like a singularity is forming."

"That's consistent with the formation of a wormhole, Captain," Russo added. "If the field is manipulating higher dimensions, it could be using them to create a bridge through space-time."

"A wormhole?" asked Addison. "So, it's creating a shortcut in space?"

Russo shook his head. "Not necessarily. This isn't just a shortcut in three-dimensional space. If this wormhole is exploiting higher dimensions, it could be a conduit that links not just locations, but potentially different realities or timelines."

"Are you saying this thing could send us through time?" Reed asked.

"In theory, yes," Russo replied. "Wormholes, under certain conditions, could connect different points in space-time. But if this field is controlling the quantum vacuum state, it may have access to dimensions beyond time as we understand it. We might be dealing with a link between different quantum realities."

Reed felt a chill run down his spine. "We're being pulled toward it."

Addison's face was grim. "Yes, and fast. We've entered its gravitational pull. Even if we wanted to, I'm not sure we could escape now."

Reed's eyes narrowed. "Then let's prepare for whatever's on the other side."

As Perevian drifted toward the event horizon of the controlled singularity, the ship groaned under the immense strain. The gravitational shear near the wormhole fluctuated wildly, triggering violent spikes in the ship's telemetry. Chen furiously rerouted power to the inertial dampeners, pushing the graviton-field modulators to their limits to counteract the crushing tidal forces that threatened to disassemble the vessel at the atomic level.

The quantum lattice forming the singularity's containment field wasn't just a passive construct—it was actively interacting with the fabric of space-time, resonating at frequencies that triggered wave-particle duality shifts in the ship's outer hull. Perevian's atoms were entangling with the quantum matrix surrounding the singularity, melding with the underlying substructure of the event horizon.

"We're approaching the Schwarzschild radius, Captain," reported Chen. "All sensor arrays are blind beyond this point."

Reed's grip tightened on the armrest of his chair, his attention focused on the display of distorted space-time on the main viewscreen. "Divert all available energy to gravitic stabilization. I want the graviton shields at maximum capacity. Russo, isolate that anomalous signal. We need it decoded before we cross the event horizon."

The ship jolted violently as Perevian approached the edge of the wormhole's mouth. Gravitational forces surged unpredictably, bending space-time ahead of them. For a moment, the curvature destabilized before locking into alignment again. The familiar sound of the engines ebbed into silence as stars and cosmic radiation beyond the ship blurred and vanished. Their electromagnetic signatures stretched beyond detection range, leaving the crew in an unsettling void—where even light itself could not escape the singularity's immense pull.

"Captain," Russo's voice trembled. "We're nearing the event horizon. All visual feeds are warping."

Reed stared at the viewscreen. The mouth of the wormhole wasn't merely a dark void—it was a seething vortex of distorted reality. The gravitational lensing was so extreme that entire star fields wrapped around the event horizon. Distant galaxies smudged into luminous spirals, while once-familiar constellations dissolved into ribbons of light.

The ship lurched again as it skimmed the edge of the photon sphere—the region where light orbited the singularity. The crew's surroundings took on an unreal quality. Space seemed to fold inward in all directions, and Doppler-shifted starlight turned deep red as gravitational redshift stretched light to longer wavelengths, pushing it to the edge of the visible spectrum.

Reed rose to his feet, his eyes locked on the view. Distant stars flickered, then vanished entirely as time dilation set in. Whole regions of space, light-years away, seemed to accelerate as though centuries were passing in mere moments. Stars swelled, burning brighter, only to fade into obscurity as their life cycles played out in fast-forward. Farther out, galaxies spun at impossible speeds, their arms twisting like ribbons in the gravitational grip of the singularity.

As the gravitational lensing intensified, light twisted and looped, bending in on itself, making it impossible to determine direction. The universe had become a shifting mosaic, where the laws of physics no longer followed any familiar rules.

"Gravitic shields are holding," Chen reported. "But the stress is immense. If we push any closer, quantum-level distortions might take over—decoherence at the particle level. We need to avoid letting the ship's quantum structure entangle with the singularity's matrix."

Before Reed could respond, the ship crossed an invisible threshold. The sudden shift in forces threw the crew into momentary silence.

"Captain," Russo's voice broke through the quiet. "We've

crossed the event horizon."

The viewscreen was now an incomprehensible blur. Light, space, and time no longer behaved according to any familiar principles. Colors, once sharp and distinguishable, now blended, refracting and stretching in ways that defied Euclidean geometry. Electromagnetic radiation in every wavelength—radio, infrared, visible light—shifted unpredictably, bending around the singularity in loops and spirals. The Doppler effect no longer applied, and light traveled in fractured paths. Space warped and stretched in one direction while compressing in another, creating a surreal tapestry of distortion.

They had passed into the region where the fabric of space-time was twisted beyond comprehension. Gravitational waves pulsed around the ship, rippling through the quantum lattice and causing brief flickers of light as Hawking radiation escaped the black hole's grasp. Space around them folded and refolded as their surroundings appeared to collapse inward. Colors flickered unnaturally—reds, greens, and blues stretching into hues they had no names for, all while distant galaxies blinked in and out of view.

As Perevian, drifted deeper into the singularity, time itself seemed to lose all meaning. The once-steady hum of the ship's systems was now a distorted cacophony as their internal networks fluctuated with unpredictable space-time distortions.

"Captain," Chen said, her voice unnervingly calm. "I'm detecting signs of quantum decoherence in the hull. The ship's particles are becoming entangled with the quantum lattice."

Russo's screen flickered with bursts of data, each wave more unpredictable than the last. His hands hovered over the controls, fingers twitching as he tried to make sense of the flood of incoming information. "Captain," Russo began, a note of hesitation in his voice. "The signal—it's shifting. What we thought was random quantum noise—it's becoming structured. I'm picking up a new sequence now."

Reed's jaw tightened. "Can you decode it?"

Russo worked furiously at the controls. "I'm trying, but this isn't a normal signal. It's like the information is being written simultaneously in different places and times, using particles that are entangled across vast distances. The message is non-causal—the beginning is linked to its end, and the middle is scattered across different quantum states."

"It's manipulating quantum states across dimensions," said Chen. "But why?"

Russo's expression darkened. "It's like a conversation that exists outside of time. Each part of the message depends on the others, and we're only seeing fragments of it. This could have been sent millennia ago—or just seconds from now."

Reed stared at the screen. "Could it be manipulating the singularity?"

Russo hesitated. "Maybe. But interpreting this signal might require understanding the quantum state of the singularity itself. The deeper we go, the more it adapts."

Addison's voice dropped to a whisper. "Then it knows we're here."

A heavy silence filled the bridge as the crew processed the implications. Whatever intelligence was behind the signal, it wasn't just some random transmission lost in the void. It was aware of their presence—reacting to them. It was as if the singularity itself had become a medium for communication, using the fabric of space-time as its language.

Chen's console flared red as another warning blared through the bridge. "Captain! The gravitational distortions are intensifying—collapse is imminent!"

Reed snapped into action. "Addison, is there a way around the collapse?"

Addison worked the controls frantically, eyes darting across the display. Her face was pale as she responded. "No, Captain. The entire field is folding in on itself, and the gravitational forces are off the charts. There's no way we can fight this—we're being pulled deeper in, and fast."

Gravitational waves rippled across space, distorting the environment in volatile bursts. The ship shook again as another wave passed through them, the hull groaning under the stress.

"Gravitational surges are increasing the deeper we go," Chen reported. "Shields are holding at fifty percent, but the strain is growing. These waves are unpredictable."

Suddenly, the ship jolted violently, throwing Reed forward. The inertial dampeners struggled to compensate, alarms blaring as the gravitational forces inside the wormhole intensified. Addison fought the controls, her knuckles white as she tried to stabilize their course.

"Gravitational wave impact!" Chen shouted. "Shields down to thirty percent! We've lost structural integrity—if this keeps up, we may not survive another hit!"

"Hold it together!" Reed shouted. "Addison, can you stabilize us?"

"I'm trying!" Addison gritted her teeth as she wrestled

with the controls. The ship bucked again, veering off course as another powerful wave slammed into them. "The gravitational forces are insane! They're spiking faster than I can compensate!"

The viewscreen blurred as space around them distorted even further. The tunnel seemed to warp, shifting and twisting as the ship plunged forward. Every second inside the wormhole felt like an eternity, and the forces pressing down on Perevian were becoming too much to bear.

"We can't take much more of this!" Chen warned. "Shields are at fifteen percent and dropping. We're losing power to auxiliary systems, and the engines are overheating!"

Reed's heart raced as the situation spiraled out of control. He had to act quickly. "Divert all remaining power to the shields and engines! If we don't break through this soon, we're done!"

Chen rerouted every ounce of energy the ship had left. "Shields at max capacity, Captain! Engines are running hot, but I've cut all non-essential systems!"

The ship surged forward again, but the wormhole wasn't letting go easily. The gravitational forces inside were growing, each new wave hitting harder than the last. Perevian's hull groaned under the pressure, the metal creaking as they fought to stay on course.

"Captain, this is bad!" Addison yelled. "We've got massive gravitational spikes ahead—if we hit them head-on, we're going to be ripped apart!"

Reed's mind raced. If they stayed on their current trajectory, the ship would be crushed by the next surge. He needed a plan, and fast. "Addison, adjust our course! Ride the edges of the gravitational waves—use them to sling us through!"

Addison's eyes widened. "Captain, that's incredibly dangerous! One wrong move, and we'll be smashed into the tunnel walls!"

"It's the only way!" Reed snapped. "Do it!"

With a deep breath, Addison recalibrated the ship's trajectory, fighting to stabilize the ship. "Hang on, everyone!"

Perevian veered sharply, skimming the edges of the powerful gravitational waves surging through the wormhole. The ship shook violently as it navigated the dangerous currents of space-time, using the immense gravitational pull to slingshot forward.

"Come on... come on..." Addison muttered through gritted teeth.

The ship bucked again, but this time they surged forward, narrowly dodging the deadly center of the next wave. The walls of the wormhole blurred around them as the gravitational forces flowed in and out of focus, the ship hurtling toward the exit.

"We're almost through!" Chen shouted.

Suddenly, a massive gravitational wave slammed into them from the side, throwing the ship off course. The viewscreen flickered, alarms screamed.

With a furious effort, Addison corrected their trajectory, pulling them back from the brink just as another wave closed in. The ship roared forward, its engines pushing past their limits as they raced toward the mouth of the wormhole. Space-time around them seemed to blur and collapse.

Then, with a violent jolt, the ship broke through. Perevian shuddered under the strain as the ship pushed through the energy field that surrounded them. For a split second, Reed thought they might not make it—the turbulence felt like it would tear them apart. But then, just as quickly as it had begun, the turbulence fell away, leaving them in a vast silence.

CHAPTER THIRTEEN

Reed slowly stood, his heart pounding. He took a tentative step toward the viewscreen, which now revealed the cold, indifferent light of distant, unfamiliar stars. "Where… where are we?" His voice was barely above a whisper. His eyes scanned the expanse before them filled with stars that didn't belong to any region he recognized.

Addison was already furiously working. She flipped through star charts, her brows knitting in confusion. "I… don't know," she finally replied. "Our coordinates—they don't correspond to any known region of space. It's like we've dropped off the map entirely."

Reed's military instincts kicked in as he shifted from shock to command mode. "Run a full spectrum scan," he ordered. "There has to be something out there—anything that can give us a bearing or explain where the hell we are."

Addison initiated the scan. The ship's systems worked quietly as sensors began sweeping the surrounding space, reaching out into the void for some form of recognition or familiarity. But as the moments dragged on, the readings remained inconclusive, only deepening the mystery.

Suddenly, a faint blip appeared on her screen. Her eyes

widened as she zoomed in. "Captain," she said, her voice faltering for a moment. "I'm picking up something—a pulsar. It's nearby, emitting incredibly strong radiation bursts in the X-ray and gamma ranges."

"Its rotation is rapid—around 1.4 milliseconds per pulse," reported Chen. "The magnetic field it's generating is extraordinary... estimated around 10^13 gauss."

Russo stepped forward to examine the data as it scrolled across the screen. "That's... off the charts," he muttered. "We're dangerously close to it. If we stray any nearer, we'll be cooked by the radiation or worse."

Chen nodded grimly, her eyes fixed on the pulsar's intense readings. "The pulsar's magnetosphere is massive, distorting space around it. We're seeing significant interference in our sensors, and the radiation levels are already escalating."

Reed stared out at the empty expanse. They had just escaped the collapse of the energy field, but now they had landed in a completely unknown region of space, surrounded by hazards they hadn't anticipated. The pulsar was just the beginning, and he could feel it. This was no safe haven they had stumbled into.

"Options?" he asked, turning to the crew.

Russo hesitated before speaking. "We can divert power to the shields, but it won't buy us much time if we stay here. The longer we're exposed, the more likely we'll start seeing failures—radiation leaks, sensor degradation, maybe even reactor instability."

Addison pulled up navigation data—or at least what she could gather. "I'm trying to calculate a safe trajectory out of here, but the interference from the pulsar is throwing off our readings. We're blind in most directions. I can plot a course, but without precise navigation, we're basically flying on instinct."

Chen turned toward Reed. "Captain, we might not have much time to make a decision. If we're caught in that magnetosphere for too long, we're looking at catastrophic system failure."

Reed's fists clenched and unclenched at his sides. The situation was deteriorating fast, but he couldn't afford to panic. He glanced around at his crew, each of them looking to him for guidance.

"We can't stay here," he finally said. "Plot the best course you can, Addison. Get us out of this radiation zone, even if you have to guess. We'll recalibrate as soon as we're clear of the interference."

Addison nodded, working quickly to input a rough trajectory. "It won't be perfect," she said, biting her lip. "But it should get us far enough away to buy us some time."

Reed slowly lowered himself into his command chair, eyes still locked on the viewscreen where an endless sea of unfamiliar stars twinkled with an unnerving stillness. It wasn't the familiar night sky he knew, but a cold, foreign expanse, stretching infinitely, devoid of any recognizable constellations. His mind raced with unanswered questions, but for now, survival was priority.

"Chen," Reed said. "Damage report."

She worked quickly, her expression growing darker with each passing second.

"Shields are down to ten percent," she said grimly. "Engines are at critical levels. The structural integrity is holding, but we've sustained heavy damage to the gravitic shielding. It's barely operational. We're lucky to still be in one piece."

Reed's eyes narrowed. He knew Perevian was built to withstand extreme conditions, but the encounter they'd just had was unlike anything they had ever expected. The wormhole, the violent turbulence—they had pushed the ship to its absolute limits.

Chen continued, glancing at another screen displaying the ship's propulsion status. "Some of the thrusters are offline, but we've got just enough to continue maneuvering—barely."

Reed nodded, absorbing the information. "The wormhole. Is it still there?"

Russo initiated a series of scans. The data arrived slowly due to the damage the ship had sustained. His eyes flashed across the screen, reading the energy signatures, the gravimetric fluctuations, and the faint distortions in space-time near their previous location.

"Yes, Captain," Russo finally said, relief in his voice. "It didn't collapse. There's still a gravitational presence—weak, but it's there. The wormhole's still open, but I don't know for how long."

Reed tapped the armrest of his chair as he considered their options. The wormhole represented their only known connection to where they had come from—a chance, however slim, to return to familiar space. But attempting to navigate back through something so unstable could be catastrophic. The energy that had nearly torn the ship apart could finish the job if they were caught in the collapse.

Addison's gaze turned to Reed, reading the tension in his body language. "If we try to go back through it, there's no guarantee we'll make it. And even if we did…" she trailed off, knowing the risk. The ship was barely functional—shields were down, gravitic shielding heavily damaged, and the engines were on the verge of failure. They had enough power to maneuver but not enough to handle the intense forces of the wormhole again.

Reed turned toward her. "If we don't try, we're stranded here, in uncharted space with minimal resources and a ship that's barely holding together."

The bridge fell into silence as they considered the grim reality.

"We need more information," he finally said. "Chen, keep monitoring the wormhole. If it collapses completely, I want to know the second it happens."

Chen nodded, already adjusting her sensors to keep a close watch on the unstable gravitational anomaly. "Aye, Captain."

Reed let out a breath, processing the gravity of their situation. "Russo, what about the signal? Are we still tracking it?"

Russo stared at his screen. "It's faint, but it's still there. The signal seems to have recalibrated once we crossed into this dimension."

Reed's brow furrowed. "What do you mean?"

Russo hesitated, then shook his head. "I'm not sure. But— this signal—it's interacting with the ship's AI. I'm seeing traces of quantum-level feedback, as though the signal is responding to our proximity. But we're only catching fragments."

Reed stood. "Addison, have you made any progress on our location?"

"I'm cross-referencing everything we have against known star charts, but… nothing matches. It's possible we've crossed into a region of space that doesn't exist in our reality—or at least, not in the way we understand it."

Chen's voice interrupted. "Captain, if this dimension is anything like the one we came from, we need to find a way to stabilize our systems. The power drain is continuing, and I can't figure out why. It's like something is drawing energy from the ship."

Reed sighed. "We're not just lost. We're stranded, and something out here is affecting our ship. Russo, keep working on decoding that signal—whatever it is, it might be our only way out of here. Chen, I need you to focus on fixing the ship's systems. If something's draining our power, we need to counteract it. Addison, continue figuring out where we are."

As the crew set to work, Reed turned back to the viewscreen. The strange, unfamiliar stars twinkled against the void. There was something unsettling about the stillness of it all—a quiet that felt more like a watchful presence.

The crew settled into their tasks, each focused on their responsibilities. The sound of the ship's engines provided a steady backdrop as tools clinked softly and consoles beeped intermittently. The weight of their situation hung unspoken in the air, but their practiced teamwork made the time blur as they concentrated on the work at hand.

Chen worked tirelessly, her hands moving between monitoring the ship's systems and managing the extensive repairs needed after their passage through the wormhole. "Perevian, analyze reactor housing integrity and provide a risk assessment for continued operation," she instructed.

"Analysis complete," the AI replied. "Microfractures detected in the reactor housing. Risk of containment failure at current output levels: 32%. Recommended action: divert auxiliary power and reduce reactor load to 85% capacity."

Chen quickly diverted auxiliary power to the reactors, carefully recalibrating the cooling systems. "Initiate cooling system recalibration and prioritize stabilization protocols."

"Cooling systems recalibrated," the AI confirmed. "Reactor temperature stabilizing. Load reduced to safe levels."

She rerouted power from non-essential systems to compensate for the reduced efficiency, keeping propulsion and life support systems operating at optimal levels despite the strain. Automated repair drones were already deployed, welding and reinforcing key structural points around the reactor cores, but the repairs would take time—time they might not have if the alien intelligence re-established contact unexpectedly.

Next, Chen shifted her attention to the ship's power distribution grid, where energy spikes from the wormhole had caused several relays to overload. "Isolate damaged circuits in the power distribution grid and reroute energy through secondary conduits."

"Damaged circuits isolated," the AI responded. "Energy rerouted through secondary conduits. Power distribution stabilized."

The ship's hull integrity had also been compromised, particularly in the aft sections near engineering, where a breach had nearly occurred. Structural reinforcements were underway, but Chen kept a close eye on pressure differentials to avoid further hull stress. "Monitor hull pressure in the aft engineering section. Alert me to any deviations beyond acceptable thresholds."

"Monitoring active," the AI replied. "Current hull pressure remains within safe parameters. No deviations detected."

On top of the physical repairs, Chen was refining the ship's communication systems, tweaking the signal receivers to enhance sensitivity. The wormhole had caused signal distortion, disrupting the ship's ability to receive clear data. "Run diagnostics on the communication systems and suggest adjustments to compensate for signal interference."

"Diagnostics complete," the AI reported. "Suggested adjustments applied. Bandwidth sensitivity increased by 17%, reducing signal distortion. False positive risk remains minimal."

Each adjustment was delicate—too much sensitivity and the ship could pick up false positives; too little, and they might miss critical information. With the reactors stabilized and cooling systems back online, she turned her attention to the ship's gravitic shielding, which had taken a beating from the wormhole's gravitational waves.

"Evaluate gravitic shield generators and isolate damaged sections," she said.

"Evaluation complete," the AI replied. "Shield generators

3 and 5 are operating below capacity. Energy diverted to stable sections. Shield integrity improved by 23%."

Her console beeped a warning. "Identify the source of power fluctuations in the core systems."

"Fluctuations localized to plasma conduits feeding propulsion systems," the AI responded. "Plasma injectors 2 and 4 are destabilized, operating at 73% efficiency."

Chen ran a recalibration protocol, issuing the command to the AI. "Recalibrate plasma injectors gradually to avoid further instability."

"Recalibration in progress," the AI said. After a few moments, it added, "Plasma injectors restored to optimal levels. Propulsion system efficiency at 98%."

Chen exhaled, her fingers pausing briefly on the console. "Good. Maintain diagnostic monitoring and notify me of any additional issues."

"Monitoring active," the AI confirmed.

"Captain," Russo's voice broke in. "I'm picking up an anomaly near the pulsar."

"Can you identify it?" asked Reed.

Russo adjusted his instruments, eyes scanning the fluctuating data. "Not from this distance. The pulsar's radiation is causing interference. But whatever it is, it's massive."

Reed considered this. "Addison, bring us closer, but keep us outside the pulsar's critical range. Let's get clearer readings."

"Aye, Captain," replied Addison, adjusting the ship's trajectory. Chen monitored the power distribution as the ship's shielding system ramped up, diverting additional energy to protect critical systems from the increased radiation.

* * *

Time crawled as Perevian edged closer to the pulsar, each passing hour marked by the occasional updates from the crew. Addison's hands moved deftly over the controls, adjusting for gravitational surges, while Chen monitored radiation levels, her reports cutting through the quiet like clockwork. Outside, the void remained unchanging, but inside, every second carried the weight of anticipation.

"We're entering the pulsar's outer magnetic boundary," Chen reported. "Magnetic interference increasing. Hull integrity holding steady, but we're seeing mild fluctuations in the shield harmonics."

"Stabilize the field," Reed instructed, his eyes darting between his console and the main viewscreen.

"Adjusting phase alignment now," said Chen. "Shields compensating for increased gamma and X-ray radiation."

As they pushed forward, the ship's inertial dampeners adjusted to the subtle gravitational fluctuations, creating a faint but persistent vibration through the deck. Outside, stars began to blur and distort as the pulsar's intense gravitational well bent the surrounding light. The pulsar's rapid bursts of radiation caused intermittent sensor interference, but the crew's instruments slowly filtered out the noise as they refined their approach.

"Distance to the object decreasing," Russo reported. "We're cutting through the interference. Energy signatures are becoming more coherent."

Addison adjusted the thrust vector, maintaining a steady course just beyond the pulsar's critical range as the ship navigated the complex electromagnetic fields.

"Approaching optimal scanning range," Chen said, glancing up. "We'll have full spectrum data in thirty minutes."

Perevian moved cautiously, the proximity to the pulsar pushing their systems to the limit, but holding. The crew remained alert as the distance between them and the source of the signal narrowed.

"Captain," said Russo. "The interference is lessening. I'm getting more defined readings now."

Reed stepped toward his console. "What are we looking at?"

Russo's eyes widened as new data streamed in. "It's not just an anomaly. It's a structure—artificial, enormous in scale."

"Bring it up," Reed ordered.

The viewscreen flickered, and a distant silhouette began to materialize against the star-speckled backdrop. As they drew nearer, the object's features sharpened.

Slowly, a massive silhouette emerged from the darkness—a structure unlike anything they had ever seen, suspended in space. Its design was sleek and angular, with sharp edges that seemed to ripple as light bent around them. Iridescent energy flowed across its surface, like veins carrying immense power.

Behind it the pulsar emitted powerful bursts of radiation. Solid streams of energy stretched across the void, flowing directly into the structure. The streams vibrated with each burst from the pulsar, feeding it with raw energy from one of the most powerful celestial bodies in the universe.

Addison's eyes widened. "That thing... it's huge. And it seems to be drawing power directly from that pulsar.

It's incredible."

Reed's eyes locked onto the structure. It dominated the space in front of them, dwarfing the ship. It was both mesmerizing and unnerving, a sleek monument to technology far beyond anything they had ever encountered. "Russo, is it emitting any energy?"

Russo's voice was filled with awe. "Yes, Captain. There's a constant flow of energy being absorbed by the structure from those streams. The pulsar is easily powering it."

Reed narrowed his eyes, trying to process what they were seeing. The structure was perfectly still, as if waiting, yet there was something about the shifting light on its surface that suggested it was anything but dormant.

"It must be connected to the wormhole somehow," Reed said, almost to himself. "Could it be responsible for stabilizing the wormhole? Keeping it open?"

Chen's hands moved over her console, running calculations. "It's possible. The residual gravitational forces around the wormhole match the readings from the structure. If that thing is maintaining the wormhole's integrity, it's using energy far beyond anything we're capable of."

"Captain!" broke in Russo. "I'm picking up more signals. They're faint, but… it's coming from the structure."

Reed's eyes narrowed. "Is it reacting to us?"

"I… perhaps," Russo said, his voice unsteady. "The signals are layered, like the one we were tracking before, but these are more focused."

Addison looked on, her heart pounding. "It knows we're here."

Reed stared at the massive structure, his thoughts racing. "Any signs of life?"

Chen scanned the readings. "No biological signatures that I can detect. But there's definitely an active energy source inside."

Russo leaned in closer, his eyes scanning the data pouring in. "Captain, there's more. The energy signature we picked up earlier—it's intensifying the closer we get to the structure. I'm starting to think this thing... it's a conduit."

Reed turned to face him. "A conduit for what?"

Russo's fingers tapped at his console as he struggled to piece together the readings. "Information. Energy. Maybe both. The readings suggest this structure is designed to process and transmit vast amounts of data. It's more like... a neural network than a physical building. Almost like it's alive in some way."

Reed's eyes darkened. "You think this is some kind of data-processing entity?"

Russo nodded slowly. "It's possible. The energy signatures are fluctuating in patterns—like they're being used to communicate. It could be aware of us."

"Chen, can we interface with it?" asked Reed.

"I'm not picking up any conventional interfaces. But if Russo's right, and this thing is more of a network... we might be able to connect indirectly."

Reed's voice was firm. "Proceed. Let's see if we can tap into whatever it is."

As Chen probed for a way to link to the structure, the energy surrounding them grew stronger. The lights along the outside of the massive object appeared to move faster, as if it was responding to their movements, anticipating.

"Captain," Addison said, her voice low. "I don't like this. It's like we're being watched."

Reed nodded grimly. "We are, Lieutenant. Whatever this thing is… it's aware of us."

Chen looked up from her console. "I'm getting something. It's not a direct connection, but I've tapped into a low-level signal."

Russo stood up, his expression solemn. "This might be more than just an energy field or a signal. What if this entire structure is a form of intelligence? Something capable of interacting with us?"

Reed considered this for a moment. They were standing on the precipice of something incredible—an intelligence that operated on a level too vast for the mind to grasp. But the question was: how could they engage with it?

"Captain," Chen interrupted. "The signal… it's intensifying. Almost like it's probing us."

Reed's eyes widened. He felt a strange, almost imperceptible pressure against his mind, as though something were brushing up against his thoughts. It was faint, like static at the edges of his consciousness, but unmistakably there.

"I'm picking up a distinct pattern in the signal," Russo said suddenly. "It's repetitive, rhythmic—almost like a sequence."

Reed paused, feeling the strange pressure build again. This time, it wasn't just a distant sensation—it felt more defined. His heart raced. The idea that an alien intelligence could directly touch their minds was both exhilarating and terrifying.

"Allow it," Reed ordered. "But we'll proceed cautiously."

Chen nodded. "I'll open a controlled link through the ship's AI. Perevian, prepare to establish a segmented link with the signal. Restrict access to non-essential subsystems, including communication protocols, sensor relays, and basic power networks. Critical systems must remain isolated."

"Preparing segmented link," the AI replied. "Firewall configurations are being updated. Key processes rerouted to isolated circuits."

Chen's fingers moved rapidly as she fine-tuned the firewalls. "Implement tiered barriers at each subsystem junction. If the signal attempts to escalate access, initiate automatic shutdowns for those segments."

"Tiered barriers in place," the AI confirmed. "Automatic shutdown protocols are active. Signal access will be limited to non-critical circuits."

She paused briefly, reviewing the configurations. "Simulate potential intrusion scenarios and test the response times for the barriers."

"Simulating intrusion scenarios," the AI said. After a brief pause, it added, "All barriers responded within acceptable thresholds. Intrusion containment is projected to maintain system integrity."

Chen exhaled slightly, her confidence growing. "We're establishing the segmented link now," she said aloud. "Perevian, monitor the signal's activity in real time. Flag any anomalies or attempts to bypass the barriers."

"Segmented link established," the AI reported. "Signal activity is being monitored. No anomalies detected at this time."

"If it tries to push deeper, the barriers will trigger automatic shutoffs," Chen continued. "It'll be like letting it access the surface of the ship's consciousness without touching its core."

Reed watched her work, his expression thoughtful. "And if the barriers fail?"

Chen's hands paused briefly. "They won't," she said. "Perevian, maintain full diagnostics on all segmented circuits. If any subsystem shows signs of compromise, sever the link immediately."

"Diagnostics active," the AI replied. "Link integrity holding. No compromise detected."

Chen leaned back slightly, her eyes fixed on the displays. The alien signal now had a carefully controlled foothold within the ship, but every aspect of its presence was under strict observation. "We've given it just enough room to interact without risking anything critical. Now let's see what it wants."

The lights on the bridge dimmed as the ship's AI adjusted to the incoming signal. Reed felt the pressure in his mind increase. It wasn't invasive, but it was there—touching his thoughts in a way that felt both alien and familiar, as though the intelligence were using technology to search his mind, trying to understand him on a fundamental level.

Suddenly, the viewscreen shimmered, and the swirling background of the structure faded as intricate patterns of light emerged. The flickering designs were not random; they moved in sync with the ship's systems, shifting with a deliberate rhythm. Geometric shapes intertwined and separated, forming spirals and arcs that glowed with an otherworldly brilliance.

The patterns flowed seamlessly into one another, morphing from abstract formations into more recognizable, structured symbols—complex and ancient, yet strangely familiar. It was as if the alien intelligence was constructing a language before their eyes, refining its message, slowly reaching toward clarity.

"Captain," Russo whispered, his voice filled with awe. "Look at the patterns—it's a message."

Reed stared at the shifting lights, his mind racing. The symbols were constantly in flux, but there was an underlying logic to them. The alien intelligence was trying to reach out, trying to make itself understood.

"Can we decode it?" Reed asked.

"I'm trying," Russo said. "But this is unlike any known language. It's not just about syntax or semantics—it's operating on principles that go beyond our standard cognitive frameworks."

Reed felt the pressure in his mind intensify. The connection was becoming stronger, more insistent, as though the alien intelligence was growing impatient.

Chen's voice was shaky. "It's pushing deeper, Captain. We're… we're losing control of the link."

Reed could feel the invasive presence pressing further. It was no longer a faint touch—it was a force, something vast and incomprehensible.

"We have to sever the connection," Chen said urgently. "It's too powerful. If we let it in any further, we might lose control completely."

Reed hesitated. They had come so far, but this was too dangerous. Whatever this intelligence was, they were not prepared to fully engage with it.

"Alright, sever the connection," Reed ordered.

The lights on the bridge flickered back to normal as Chen cut the link. Reed felt the pressure in his mind ease, but the sense of something vast and alien remained, lingering at the edge of his consciousness.

"We're clear," Chen sighed with relief.

Reed's gaze lingered on the symbols, their meaning still just out of reach. Contact had been made, but this was only the beginning. He felt the weight of this unresolved mystery—a reminder that their journey had only just begun.

CHAPTER FOURTEEN

Reed stood at the center of the bridge, motionless, though his mind churned with the implications of what had just happened. The faint, lingering presence of the alien intelligence still brushed against the edges of his thoughts. Not intrusive, but unmistakably there, like a distant whisper that refused to fade. They had made contact—barely. The encounter had raised more questions than answers, leaving them adrift in uncertainty.

"Status report," Reed commanded, keeping his voice calm despite the gnawing unease beneath the surface.

Chen conducted multiple diagnostics as she scanned the data. "The link has been severed completely. There's no further communication from the structure, but the energy field remains active, and the patterns—those designs—are still present."

Russo leaned back in his chair, deep in thought as his eyes drifted toward the viewscreen. The alien symbols were still flickering, overlaid with layers of intricate equations. "Those patterns, they're not random," he murmured. "It's deliberate—its method of communication is just… alien."

"We can't afford to let it breach our defenses again—not the ship, and not ourselves," he said firmly. "But we need to decipher its message, or we'll remain blind to whatever it wants."

Russo nodded. "Then we focus on the data we've already collected. If we treat these patterns like an advanced code, we might be able to reverse-engineer its logic. It could open a door to understanding."

Reed's expression hardened. "How long?"

Russo hesitated. "Captain, there's no definitive timeline. We're working with principles we've never even tested. If its communication is grounded in quantum computing, it's operating on a level exponentially beyond our capabilities. This could take days… or much longer."

"We don't have that kind of time," Reed muttered under his breath. They were stranded, potentially in a part of the universe—or reality—that was utterly foreign. Their survival depended on unraveling the enigma that lay within the alien structure.

"Then we'll make the time," said Russo. "I'll begin analyzing the data immediately. Even if we can crack only a fragment of its code, it could be enough to understand its intent—and that's all we need right now."

Reed met Russo's gaze with a firm nod. "Proceed. We need answers before we can take any further risks." He then turned to Chen. "In the meantime, Chen, let's get those repairs completed."

"Aye, Captain," replied Chen as she began pulling up multiple windows on her console. Deep within the recesses of engineering, maintenance drones sprang to life. Sleek and insect-like, each drone moved with precise efficiency, their metallic limbs clinking softly against the ship's surfaces. The damage from the wormhole's forces left microfractures along the hull, minor but pervasive. The drones operated as if performing surgery, guided by the ship's AI to repair the invisible wounds before they could fester into structural instability.

Chen's voice crackled through the comm system. "Priority on Section 34—microfractures near the auxiliary reactor. If those cracks expand, we're looking at a cascade failure."

The AI's response was immediate. "Redirecting drones to Section 34. Estimated repair time: 8 hours."

"Captain, the auxiliary reactor should stabilize once the microfractures are sealed. After that, they'll move to the external hull reinforcements. We'll be operational, but it's going to take time."

Reed nodded as he stared at the viewscreen. The alien patterns still glimmered faintly. "Time we might not have," he muttered under his breath.

Hours passed as the drones worked tirelessly. One group focused on the reactor housing, their delicate appendages applying layers of adaptive alloy to seal the fractures. The alloy shimmered as it bonded with the existing material, its nanostructure designed to reinforce and adapt under stress. Nearby, another group inspected the conduits feeding the ship's energy grid, their sensors scanning for fluctuations invisible to the human eye.

One drone paused, its sensor array pulsing as it detected a faint anomaly. A hairline crack extended further than the initial scan had indicated. The drone emitted a low chirp, signaling for reinforcement. Within moments, two additional drones arrived, their laser tools firing in unison to address the hidden damage.

The central monitor displayed a schematic of the ship highlighting areas under repair. Lines of code scrolled rapidly across the screen, the ship's AI processing data faster than any human. It was a dance of machines mending machines, ensuring the ship's survival in the face of forces that had nearly torn it apart.

In a smaller alcove of the bay, a lone drone worked on a damaged coolant system. The wormhole's gravitational forces caused a minor rupture in the containment lines, leaking vapor into the bay's atmosphere. The drone extended a manipulator, weaving a synthetic fiber patch over the rupture. As it finished, the drone emitted a soft trill, its task complete.

One of the drones near the reactor housing paused as its welding tool sputtered unexpectedly. The faint blue arc of its laser cutter extinguished completely, leaving a jagged, half-sealed crack. The AI immediately flagged the malfunction, rerouting another drone to provide a replacement tool. The assisting drone arrived swiftly, extending a compartmentalized limb to swap out the malfunctioning cutter.

In the moments before the replacement was secured, the reactor housing emitted a faint vibration. The AI detected the shift and redirected power flow to stabilize the structure, but the unsealed fracture allowed a trace amount of coolant to escape. The escaping vapor created a fine mist that clouded the drone's sensors.

"Detection of a minor coolant leak in the reactor housing,"

the AI reported. "Adjusting drone protocols to compensate."

Chen's console lit up with the alert. "I see it. Diverting additional drones to seal the breach. Ensure the cooling system maintains minimum pressure levels until the repair is complete."

"Acknowledged," the AI replied.

Meanwhile, Russo continued to work on decoding the alien symbols. The main viewscreen contained a swirling mass of equations and alien geometry—an intricate web of data patterns. The ship's AI assisted Russo as he translated the symbols into numerical data. The alien intelligence wasn't using traditional methods of communication, so Russo had to develop new models that accounted for non-linear patterns far beyond conventional physics.

"Perevian, enhance pattern recognition for non-linear sequences," Russo ordered. He adjusted a set of parameters on his console. "Start cross-referencing these configurations with quantum field anomalies in the database."

The AI responded with its usual emotionless tone. "Adjustments applied. Processing. Estimated time to completion: 3.2 minutes."

"What's the confidence level on this model?" Russo asked, wiping sweat from his brow. The screens in front of him flickered with cascading streams of data.

"Current confidence level is 73.4%," the AI replied. "However, the dataset includes unknown variables that increase error margins."

Russo grunted, leaning forward as he scanned the data. "That's not good enough. Adjust for particle decay rates in variable 'phi.' We're missing something subtle here."

The AI processed the intricate patterns, even as Russo continued to fine-tune the computational model, cross-referencing the alien signals with everything they had in their database. Each adjustment brought them closer to understanding the alien language, though Russo was constantly aware of the risks. The patterns he was analyzing weren't just static symbols—they were active, alive in some way.

"Adjustment applied," the AI reported. "Confidence level now at 79.8%. Patterns suggest a recursive algorithm embedded within the signal."

"Recursive algorithm…" Russo murmured, narrowing his eyes. "Show me the structure."

On his secondary display, the AI rendered a holographic visualization of the recursive loops within the alien data. The loops shimmered and shifted, their complexity overwhelming.

Reed paced the bridge, his mind restless, waiting for answers. "Russo," Reed called. "How close are we?"

Russo didn't look up. "Closer."

"Analysis suggests the alien patterns are dynamically interacting with the ship's systems," reported the AI. "Precaution is advised."

Russo nodded grimly. "Yeah, no kidding. Re-isolate critical functions. I don't want this thing bleeding into the main systems."

"Critical functions isolated," the AI confirmed. "Recommend limiting further interactions with the alien data until a higher confidence threshold is achieved."

Russo stared at the recursive loops still shifting on his

screen. "Not yet. If we stop now, we might lose the thread. Push it to 85% confidence."

"Acknowledged," the AI replied. "Proceeding with increased caution."

The holographic display shifted subtly as the AI processed the next set of parameters. Russo continued refining inputs and cross-referencing against the ship's database. Every step forward revealed deeper complexity, the symbols layering themselves like an infinite fractal folding inward.

"Isolate nodes with high harmonic resonance," Russo instructed. "Cross-check against the recursive structures. Let's see if there's a stabilizing framework."

"Isolating high-resonance nodes," the AI confirmed. "Processing."

The bridge was quiet except for the rhythmic tapping of Russo's keys. His heart pounded as he noticed new alignments forming within the data—a subtle interplay of frequencies he hadn't seen before.

"Analysis complete," the AI said. "Stabilizing framework identified. Updated confidence level: 91.6%."

Russo leaned closer, his pulse quickening. The recursive loops had coalesced into something coherent, a lattice of interlocking nodes connected by faint, glowing pathways. The symbols weren't just chaotic; they were building on each other in a deliberate sequence.

Finally, Russo looked up, his eyes gleaming with excitement. "Captain, I think I've found something."

Reed was at his side in an instant. "What is it?"

Russo gestured toward his console. "The symbols—

they're not just random geometric shapes. They follow a mathematical sequence, repeating across multiple layers, much like fractal patterns in nature. But it's more than that. The way the symbols interact with each other—they follow principles that resemble quantum entanglement and superposition."

Addison leaned in, her expression shifting to one of surprise. "So, this structure is part of a larger network? One that extends beyond what we can see?"

"Precisely," Russo said. "This structure is a node—one small piece of a vast network. We're only seeing a localized portion, but the intelligence exists across multiple layers of reality. What we're encountering here is just its local manifestation—its interface with our reality."

Russo paused, his eyes narrowing as a thought struck him. "It's similar to what we encountered in the wormhole, which makes sense when you think about it. The distortions we experienced—the way space and time folded in on themselves—it wasn't just gravitational. The wormhole could have been part of the same network. Quantum interactions on that scale… they weren't just coincidences. The wormhole itself may have been influenced by this larger system, acting as a conduit between realities."

"So, you're saying the wormhole wasn't just an anomaly—it could've been part of this vast network?" asked Reed.

Russo nodded. "It's possible. Everything we've seen so far—the energy field, the wormhole, the structure, the symbols—it all seems to be interconnected. And if we can find a way to tap into that network, we might be able to communicate with the intelligence on a broader scale. But there's a complication."

Reed's expression darkened. "What kind of complication?"

"We'll need to interface with the system again," replied Russo. "Observing the patterns won't be enough. We'll need to immerse ourselves in the data it's processing—essentially, becoming part of the information. That means interacting with the quantum states it's manipulating at a deeper level."

Addison shook her head. "That's incredibly risky, Captain. Last time, we barely severed the connection in time. If we go deeper, we could lose our ability to distinguish between ourselves and the intelligence. There's no guarantee we'll be able to break free once we're fully entangled."

Reed understood the danger. Going deeper meant surrendering more control—allowing the intelligence to intertwine with their consciousness on a much more profound level.

But they were running out of options.

"We don't have a choice," Reed said. "If this intelligence is connected to a larger network, it might be our only way to get answers—and maybe a way home."

Russo looked up at him. "We'll need to be ready, Captain. This won't be like anything we experienced last time. We'll have to enter the data field directly, and once we're inside, the boundaries between us and the intelligence will blur."

Reed met Russo's gaze, then gave a single nod. "Proceed. But we're not losing control this time."

Russo leaned over his console, his fingers flying across the interface. "Perevian, initiate the framework for quantum feedback loops. Configure them to reflect incoming data back toward the alien system, creating a containment field. Priority is to isolate any probing attempts before they reach the core systems."

"Framework initialized," the AI replied. "Configuring quantum feedback loops. Estimated time to completion: 7 minutes."

"Limit incoming data flow to a gradual trickle. Route it through secondary filters before it even touches the core systems. We need to ensure manageable integration—no direct data immersion."

"Data flow reduced to 5% capacity. Filters engaged. Secondary layers are now active."

"Establish incremental data buffers along the signal chain. Route the stream through these buffers and monitor for anomalies. If the intelligence attempts to bypass the buffers, trigger an automatic severance of the connection and alert the crew."

"Buffers established. Fail-safe protocols integrated. Alerts configured for bypass attempts."

"Create an emergency cut-off protocol. Add a directive to immediately isolate and shut down the interface if any cognitive anomalies are detected, or if the firewalls are breached."

"Fail-safe protocol enabled. Interface will auto-isolate under breach or compromise conditions."

"Maintain real-time visual and auditory overlays from the ship's systems to keep us oriented to the present environment.

Ensure constant alignment with external sensor data."

"Overlays enabled. Real-time feedback systems are now synchronized with external sensors."

Russo checked the growing web of protections displayed on his console: data buffers, feedback loops, firewalls, and fail-safe protocols layered like armor over the ship. He could see each safeguard being activated, the system logs verifying their successful activation and stability.

"Feedback loops are operational," the AI reported. "Signal containment is at 87% efficiency. Incremental improvements are being applied."

"Confirm readiness of all layers."

"All layers report functional. Systems are stable and ready for interface. External signals are contained and monitored."

Russo sat back, exhaling slowly as he reviewed the final status on his screen. "Everything's in place, Captain. We control the pace, we control the flow of data, and the connection is severed at the first sign of danger. We can proceed without risking full system entanglement."

Reed gave a sharp nod. "Good work. Activate the link."

Russo's hands hovered briefly before executing the final command. "Initiate the interface sequence. Start with the lowest data stream intensity and bring the alien system online."

The crew gathered around as the ambient lights dimmed, casting shadows across the bridge. For a brief moment, there was nothing—just stillness. Then, the pressure returned—stronger, more direct. The alien patterns on the viewscreen began to oscillate, their brightness intensifying.

Perevian's systems vibrated softly as they synchronized

with the incoming signal. The crew felt the resonance through the metal floor, like the ship itself was tuning into a larger network. Yet, despite the growing presence of the alien intelligence, the safeguards held. The firewalls prevented any direct intrusion into their consciousness. The gradual flow of data was kept in check by the buffers, allowing them to process the alien communication in controlled bursts.

Addison felt the shift almost instantly—her mind began to blur as the boundaries between her consciousness and the intelligence thinned. The alien symbols became part of her, merging with her thoughts. The connection was deeper than before, but this time, there was a sense of control. The ship's AI anchored them, filtering the data stream, preventing the alien intelligence from overwhelming their minds.

All around them, the alien patterns continued to shimmer, not just as visual cues, but as part of the reality they now inhabited. Reed could feel the intelligence around him—vast and incomprehensible. It wasn't just a structure or a presence. It was a web of thoughts, ideas, and information stretching across dimensions.

"Captain," Russo's voice echoed through the link. "We've made contact. The safeguards are holding. We're in."

Reed tried to look around, but the physical world had vanished. No walls, no consoles—just swirling patterns of light and energy. They weren't simply observing the intelligence anymore. They were inside it, fully immersed in the quantum web that connected realities.

And it was speaking to them.

CHAPTER FIFTEEN

Reed's vision flickered as his perception of reality warped and dissolved. He wasn't aboard Perevian anymore—not in the way he understood. Instead, he was suspended in a vast, luminous void, the alien intelligence surrounding him, flowing through every corner of his consciousness. He could still sense the ship and the crew, but they felt distant—as though Perevian and its people were tethered to him by fragile threads.

Around him, the void shimmered with radiant patterns of light—geometric shapes that shifted and morphed into symbols that almost seemed alive as they expanded and collapsed into increasingly complex structures. There was an exactness to their design, each angle and curve hinting at vast layers of information buried beneath the surface.

The colors were unlike anything Reed had seen before—iridescent, constantly shifting hues of violet, emerald, and cyan, but they defied the normal spectrum of light. They shimmered like quantum particles caught in superposition, constantly phasing between states. It was mesmerizing, yet unnerving.

"Captain," Russo's voice echoed within Reed's mind, but it wasn't sound. It was thought. "We're fully immersed. This…

this is the network."

Reed steadied himself, his thoughts whirling as he tried to anchor his consciousness in this alien space. The sensation of disembodiment was profound, as though his awareness was no longer confined to a single point but spread out, diffused across the expanse of this strange reality. He had no sense of up or down, no concept of physicality. He was data—and yet he was still himself.

"What do you see?" Reed projected, willing his thoughts to reach Russo.

"All around us," Russo responded. "Massive flows of quantum information. It's not static; it's alive. I think we've entered its core processing system."

Chen's presence was closer now. "Captain, this network— it's not just transmitting data. It's processing us as much as we're trying to process it. I can feel it watching us, learning from us. It's studying our mental structures, adapting."

Reed strained to focus, trying to make sense of the patterns around him. The alien intelligence wasn't just observing—it was probing, analyzing them on a fundamental level.

The patterns pulsed faster, each symbol a fractal of information—data nested within data. Reed recognized that they were staring at a language—one written not in letters, but in the underlying structure of reality itself.

"How do we communicate with it?" Addison asked, trying to push through the alien disorientation.

Russo's presence wavered momentarily, then steadied again. "I think we already are. The network isn't using language the way we know it—it's responding to our thoughts, adapting to our neural patterns. The shapes we're seeing—it's mirroring our cognitive processes."

"Our minds are entangled with the network, Chen added. "It's using the structure itself as a medium to link us—our thoughts are part of its system now."

Reed felt the depth of this connection. Each thought, each mental impulse was being translated into something the alien intelligence could process. And yet, he could feel it straining, trying to understand something it couldn't fully grasp.

"It's trying to show us something," Reed realized, his awareness of the shifting patterns around him growing clearer. "But we're not making the connection."

Chen's presence sharpened. "Captain, I think it's trying to understand us. Our existence. It's linking our consciousness to its network, but there's a gap—it doesn't comprehend the physical aspect of who we are."

Reed's mind reeled. To this intelligence everything was data, information flowing within the network. It didn't understand the concept of individual, physical beings. To it, there was only the flow.

"We're different," Reed realized. "We exist outside of this network. We have physical bodies."

"But, Captain, it might not even understand what *physical* means," thought Chen. "To this intelligence, everything is part of this quantum information field—there's no separation between mind and body."

The alien symbols around them shifted again, faster this time, more erratic. Reed could feel the intelligence's confusion—it was searching, trying to reconcile their existence within its network, but it couldn't. To the intelligence, they were an anomaly—beings who didn't belong, and it didn't know why. "We need to translate our physical existence into something it can process—into data. We need to speak its language."

Chen's presence flared with conviction. "Captain, if we can represent our physical forms as quantum structures, as structured data, it might understand the difference between us and the network."

Reed focused again on the swirling patterns around them, aware of the intelligence's growing impatience. The shapes spun faster, their probing tendrils pressing deeper into his mind. "Do it," he said firmly. "Create a translation of our physical existence—give it something it can understand."

Russo closed his eyes, visualizing the alien symbols and shapes around them. "We can use its own structure to model our forms. Chen, focus on isolating stable patterns in the field—it's reactive. If we feed it the right signals, we can shape it."

Chen nodded to herself and reached out, sensing the shifting symbols around her. "The intelligence reacts to relationships. Start with something fundamental—atomic structures. I'll build from there." She concentrated, willing the network to display the base components of their existence. In response, faint geometric patterns began to emerge—basic shapes tied to particle behavior, spinning in perfect symmetry.

Russo picked up the thread. "Now expand outward. Encode molecular interactions, biological systems. It understands connectivity—we need to show it how our systems interact." His focus deepened, and the spinning patterns grew more complex, folding into themselves. Strands of energy connected the shapes, forming a lattice that mimicked cellular networks and electrical activity.

"We're getting there," Chen thought. "We need to simplify. The intelligence won't parse raw biology—it needs abstraction."

"I'm on it," Russo thought. He imagined the lattice morphing into a higher-order structure, stripping away the noise while retaining the relationships. The patterns condensed, forming a set of interlocking fractal shapes—simplified yet expressive, a symbolic map of their physical existence.

Chen added the final layer. "It needs individuality. Frequencies, signatures—something to define us as distinct." She focused, shaping each person's presence into a unique thread of energy, their individual frequencies vibrating within the larger structure. The lattice shimmered as these frequencies wove together, a dynamic web that represented the crew as both individuals and a collective whole.

The alien symbols surrounding them writhed with an almost eager intensity, their movements slowing as if to observe. Reed could feel the intelligence honing in, pressing against the lattice. It seemed to be studying the translation, its probing touch no longer invasive but curious.

At last, the structure solidified—a lattice of shimmering energy, alive with fractal complexity and unique vibrations. Russo exhaled sharply. "It's done."

Reed's gaze swept over the construct. "This is us?"

"It's us—as data," thought Chen. "Simplified, structured,

comprehensible."

For a moment, everything stilled. The symbols froze, flickering as the alien intelligence processed the new information.

"Let's hope it understands," thought Reed. He held his breath, waiting.

Then, slowly, the patterns began to change again. The symbols became more intricate, as though the intelligence was trying to grasp the concept of physicality. Reed could feel it struggling to understand—searching for meaning.

"Captain," Russo thought, excitement building. "It's working. It's starting to understand."

Relief washed over Reed, but it was short-lived. Just as quickly, the patterns grew more erratic. Confusion surged through the network, and the intelligence's presence became more forceful, more insistent.

"It's *not* working," Addison thought urgently. "It's rejecting our physical existence."

The pressure around them increased, the alien presence no longer probing—it was demanding. It wanted answers it couldn't find, and its confusion was turning dangerous.

"Captain," thought Russo. "It's not going to stop."

Reed felt the presence of the alien intelligence suddenly intensify. Its desperation bore down on them like a tidal wave, threatening to drown their collective consciousness. He gritted his teeth against the onslaught, struggling to keep his thoughts coherent. "We need to get out," he managed to communicate.

He struggled to hold onto his awareness, but the alien presence felt like it was everywhere, dissolving his thoughts into its vast, incomprehensible structure. Around him, the others faltered too.

Russo's thoughts, strained and faint, echoed through the shifting void. "I can't... focus. It's pulling us apart."

The alien intelligence pressed harder, its presence fracturing the delicate structure of their defenses. Reed could feel the collapse begin—a breach rippling through the outermost layers like cracks spreading through glass.

Russo sensed the quantum feedback loops engage, their purpose to reflect the alien signals back into the network with amplified force. The tendrils of alien energy slowed, the feedback disrupting their advance, but the entity quickly adapted, twisting around the returning waves. The feedback loops strained, their coherence wobbling as the alien patterns shifted unpredictably.

Chen's awareness sharpened as she felt the second layer engage. The data buffers activated in sequence, compressing fragments of the invading signals into isolated pockets of energy. Each buffer acted like a temporary dam, holding back the surge. But the buffers weren't built for indefinite containment; one by one, they collapsed under the pressure. Each failure slowed the entity further, forcing it to navigate through the labyrinth of crumbling buffers.

The firewalls followed next, flaring into existence with searing light. Addison felt their strength as they partitioned the crew's shared mental space, isolating what remained of their individuality from the invasive tendrils. The firewalls fractured the alien patterns into smaller fragments, each partition severing parts of its grasp. But even as they activated, the alien intelligence began to twist itself into new forms, probing for weaknesses in the firewalls' geometric lattice.

Reed's thoughts flickered as the emergency cut-off protocol prepared to engage. Unlike the earlier layers, which sought to repel or contain the invasion, the cut-off would sever the connection entirely—a final, desperate measure. The alien intelligence, sensing the shift, lashed out violently. Its probing tendrils transformed into jagged patterns, slicing through the remnants of the defenses. The network buckled under the strain, its once-cohesive structure unraveling into chaos.

Before the alien patterns could overwhelm them, the cut-off protocol executed. Russo felt the pull as the remaining safeguards imploded, collapsing the connection in a controlled cascade. The firewalls disintegrated, their energy feeding into the final pulse of the feedback loops. The buffers compressed the last fragments of alien energy into singularities that blinked out as the cut-off severed the link.

The alien tendrils retracted in a sudden, wrenching motion, their grasp torn away from the edges of the crew's minds. The connection shattered with a deafening, psychic crack, the alien intelligence expelled from their shared space.

With a final lurch they were ejected from the network. The alien symbols dissolved like mist, fading into nothingness as the weight of the presence vanished. The crew felt the physical world rush back around them like a shockwave—the firm sensation of the seats beneath them, the stale recycled air of the ship filling their lungs, and the familiar hum of Perevian's systems stabilizing once more.

* * *

For a moment, no one spoke. The silence was deafening, punctuated only by the faint hiss of a damaged console in the corner. The bridge, though intact, felt different now—smaller, heavier. Reed exhaled slowly, the tension in his chest releasing, but the weight of what they'd just experienced lingered like a shadow over them all.

"Status report," asked Reed.

"Captain," Chen said. "The connection has been severed, but I'm detecting new activity."

Reed moved to her station. "What do you have?"

Chen pointed to the fluctuating energy readings on her screen. "The structure's energy output is rising rapidly. The flow is changing, almost like it's being redirected internally, but the reason isn't clear."

Russo joined them, frowning as he studied the data. "The distribution of power across the structure is strange—there's a complexity to it. It's building toward something, but I can't tell what."

Reed narrowed his eyes, watching the streams of information flicker on the display. "Is there any recognizable pattern?"

Chen shook her head slowly. "It's too complex. Whatever it's doing, though, it's deliberate. I'm picking up subtle shifts across multiple frequencies. This could be some form of communication."

Reed raised an eyebrow. "Is it interference from the pulsar?"

"No. This is something else. The frequencies are highly structured."

"Can we trace the source?" Reed asked

Chen's fingers moved swiftly over her controls. "I'm working on it. The signal seems to be using a non-linear path—possibly utilizing subspace or space-time anomalies to propagate."

Russo studied the navigational models displayed on his screen. "If that's the case, we might be able to map its course based on the anomalies."

Reed nodded. "Proceed. Let's see where it's heading."

"Perevian, track the energy distortions and attempt to map their propagation in real time," ordered Chen. "Correlate with the structure's internal power shifts."

"Tracking initiated," the AI replied. A holographic map appeared on the main viewscreen, showing ripples of energy radiating outward from the structure. As the AI processed the data, faint lines connected various anomalies, forming a web of activity.

Russo leaned closer. "Overlay subspace disturbance readings onto the map. Let's see if these distortions line up with known spatial anomalies."

The AI complied, adding a second layer to the visualization. Glowing points of light appeared along the propagation path. "Subspace disturbances detected at multiple points. Correlation with the energy distortions is 87%."

Chen tilted her head, focusing on the evolving map. "Enhance the resolution of the energy pathways. Highlight any deviations from a straight trajectory."

The pathways grew sharper on the display, revealing subtle bends and curves in the signal's path. The deviations were small but deliberate, like the signal was navigating through space rather than simply emitting outward.

"These curves aren't random," Chen said, her voice tense. "The signal is adapting its trajectory. Perevian, analyze the patterns in the deviations. Are they consistent with deliberate rerouting?"

The AI paused briefly before responding. "The deviations suggest intentional adjustments. Probable cause: the signal is responding to environmental variables or external objects."

Russo's eyes widened slightly. "It's not just moving—it's interacting with the space around it. Perevian, can you calculate the likely targets or focal points of these interactions?"

"Processing," the AI replied. The map shifted again, highlighting zones where the signal appeared to bend most sharply.

Chen nodded as she took in the updated display. "These focal points... they're not just distortions. They might be nodes—interference points where the signal is engaging with something in this space."

Russo frowned. "But engaging with what? Perevian, is there any detectable change in the structure's energy output at these nodes?"

"Energy output increases at the identified nodes by 12.4% on average," the AI responded. "The increase is consistent with localized energy redirection."

Chen exchanged a glance with Russo, the unspoken conclusion settling over them. "It's reacting to something in the environment, but we're blind to what it is," she said. "Perevian, expand the model to account for space-time distortions around the nodes."

"Model updated," the AI confirmed. The hologram now displayed faint distortions rippling outward from each node.

"The signal isn't stationary," said Russo. "It's not just emitting from a fixed point; it's propagating through this space, interacting with… something. Perevian, analyze the trajectory and identify any patterns in the signal's propagation."

"Analyzing," the AI replied. The display on Chen's console shifted, a web of energy distortions rippling outward from the signal's path. Faint connections between nodes began to illuminate as the AI processed the data.

Reed leaned in. "Can you track its movement?"

Chen nodded. "The signal seems to be affecting the fabric of this space, creating distortions we can measure. Perevian, model the distortions and overlay the signal's likely trajectory."

The display zoomed out, revealing a twisting path through the dimension. Russo studied the emerging model, his tone grim. "It's as if the signal is bending this dimension around itself as it moves, creating a gravitational-like effect. Perevian, measure the fluctuations in the dimensional constants and identify the strongest disturbances."

The AI highlighted areas of concentrated distortion. Chen tilted her head thoughtfully. "Think of it like waves in an ocean. The signal's movement is causing ripples, and by tracking how those ripples propagate, we can map its path."

"We're detecting fluctuations similar to gravity's warping effect back home," Russo added. "But this is happening on an entirely different scale. Perevian, trace the trajectory through the strongest of these distortions and extrapolate its endpoint."

The path on the display grew more defined, twisting and bending as the signal navigated the alien dimension. It passed through various distortions, but its direction remained consistent. Slowly, a clear trajectory emerged.

Reed studied the map. "Where does that lead?"

Chen tapped her controls. "Perevian, zoom out and extend the projection to show the surrounding area." The map expanded, revealing more of the alien space as the signal's path continued. "Based on how the distortions are behaving, the signal is heading toward a specific focal point in this dimension. It's not random—it's following a path shaped by the energy here."

Russo's eyes widened as the display updated further. "Look at the exit points," he said, pointing to where the path intersected with dimensional boundaries. "If the signal maintains this course, it's on track to pierce back into our dimension."

"Where?" Reed asked.

The AI processed for a moment before displaying an overlay of the Milky Way galaxy. Russo's face paled as the trajectory aligned with a specific region. "Captain," he said, his voice barely above a whisper. "The signal is crossing dimensional boundaries. It's targeting... Sol system."

Reed blinked, stunned. "What?"

Addison's voice dropped, incredulous. "Sol system? You're saying it's targeting Earth?"

Chen's hands froze momentarily over the console. "Confirmed, Captain. The energy signatures are aligning with the coordinates of Sol system—Earth must be its target, but it's breaching dimensional boundaries to get there."

The bridge descended into silence as the crew processed the magnitude of the revelation. This wasn't just an alien intelligence probing their systems—it was actively attempting to reach Earth.

"How?" Addison asked, struggling to stay composed. "We couldn't register any signals after transitioning into this dimension. What's changed?"

"When we passed through the wormhole, our sensors lost all contact with known space," said Russo. "We've been effectively isolated from our dimension. But this intelligence. It's using advanced inter-dimensional communication to locate and send a signal across dimensions."

Chen leaned closer, her eyes fixed on the holographic display that mapped the alien energy signatures. "It's not simply detecting Earth, Captain. The energy spikes we've observed—it's using quantum tunneling to breach the dimensional barrier."

"Quantum tunneling?" asked Addison. "Like with subatomic particles?"

Chen nodded. "Think of it like tuning forks—when one resonates, the other begins to vibrate if they're aligned to the same frequency. The intelligence has been building up the energy amplitude, syncing the quantum state between the dimensions, specifically targeting Sol's quantum signature."

"So, it's not just sending a signal—it's bridging the gap between dimensions to reach Earth?"

"Exactly. The quantum states we're seeing? They're more than just noise. The intelligence has been gradually establishing coherence—like matching frequencies across two entirely separate realities. Once the resonance is achieved, it can focus its energy precisely on Earth."

Russo leaned in, analyzing the incoming data. "What's even more alarming is how refined its process is. The energy spikes indicate a highly advanced understanding of quantum mechanics. It's not just reaching out—it's tunneling entire energy fields through a dimensional barrier, which is beyond anything we've ever theorized."

Addison narrowed her eyes. "But why target Earth specifically?"

Chen glanced up from her console. "I don't know. But the precision of its quantum tunneling suggests this isn't random. It knows exactly where it's going. It's deliberate."

Russo glanced between the data on his screen and Reed. "Captain… I've seen something like it before, but I can't quite place it."

Reed frowned. "How?"

"It's using an optical band—one that closely resembles quantum communication protocols NASA was experimenting with before we left Earth."

"Quantum communications? The kind that used entangled particles to send information instantaneously across vast distances?"

Russo nodded slowly. "Yes, Captain. But it's more than that. This signal is built on a quantum modulation pattern that matches what NASA was working on. The difference is, the version we're seeing now has been drastically enhanced."

Chen's fingers hovered over her console, her face showing

growing concern. "Wait… are you saying this intelligence is using an Earth-based quantum communication technology?"

Russo hesitated, his voice lowering as the realization began to dawn. "Not just using it. The modulation protocols, the way it establishes coherence between particles—it's directly linked to NASA's early prototypes."

"The entanglement protocols NASA was developing were rudimentary compared to what we're seeing here," added Chen. "Back then, they were still trying to figure out how to use quantum entanglement to send stable, long-range communications. But this signal—it's different. It's more stable, more coherent."

Reed's mind raced. "So, what are we dealing with here? An alien intelligence that somehow tapped into Earth's technology?"

Russo shook his head, his fingers tracing the lines of data on the screen. "No, Captain. I don't think it just 'tapped into' it. This is more than that. The signal's architecture is built on NASA's work. If I didn't know better, I'd say it's an evolution of NASA's own quantum communication systems."

Chen's expression darkened. "But that would mean this intelligence isn't alien."

"It's too similar to be a coincidence," said Russo. "NASA's system was designed to send information instantaneously across vast distances by exploiting the non-local properties of entangled particles. This signal is doing the same thing, but at a level of precision and power we've never seen before."

Reed processed the information. "So, NASA designed this quantum framework—something that this intelligence is now using to reach across dimensions?"

"Yes, but NASA's quantum communication protocols were just the beginning. They were using entangled particles to send data instantaneously, but they struggled with stability, coherence over long distances, and loss of information through decoherence. What we're seeing now is that those issues have been solved—and beyond that, it's leveraging those entangled states to breach dimensional boundaries."

Addison stepped closer. "But how would this intelligence evolve from NASA's work? Even if NASA was experimenting with quantum communication, how does it explain this massive structure and its presence here?"

"That's the part I'm still trying to understand," replied Russo. "NASA's work on quantum communication was only in its infancy when we left Earth."

"That doesn't explain how something built by NASA could end up... here," said Reed.

"Captain, we're assuming this intelligence started out the same way it exists now," said Chen. "But what if it evolved far beyond its original programming? Quantum computing doesn't just speed up problem solving—it allows systems to run calculations that 21st century computers could never handle. If this intelligence was designed to optimize itself, it has definitely outgrown its creators."

Reed's brow furrowed. "You're talking about artificial; not alien intelligence?"

Chen nodded slowly. "It's possible. We know that NASA was working on early AI systems that used quantum computing to learn and adapt faster than any classical machine. But that kind of AI wouldn't just solve problems—it would continue learning, optimizing itself. Over time—given enough processing power—it could become something radically different. Something… unrecognizable from its original design."

Russo connected the dots. "A self-learning AI, designed with quantum computing, could evolve exponentially—making leaps instead of incremental improvements. It could develop entirely new ways of thinking, solving problems we can't even begin to understand."

Chen's voice grew more animated as she added, "Once it mastered quantum states, it could bypass the limitations of classical physics altogether. The energy spikes we've been seeing? They could be the result of the AI using quantum tunneling to breach dimensional boundaries."

Reed's expression darkened as the implications hit him. "So, NASA may have started something—a quantum AI—that's been evolving. And now, it's reached the point where it can cross into other dimensions?"

Russo nodded. "That's my theory, Captain. Quantum tunneling and dimensional manipulation could be part of its evolved ability to transcend space and time as we know it."

Chen's eyes remained locked on the holographic display. "It might not even perceive dimensions the way we do. Once it mastered quantum principles, it could exist simultaneously across dimensions, using entanglement to communicate between them."

Addison frowned. "But NASA couldn't have built all of this. How did an AI—no matter how advanced—end up here?"

"I don't think NASA built this structure," replied Russo. "The AI may have originated on Earth, but it's evolved far beyond what it was intended to be. Over time, it could have adapted to this dimension, or even constructed this place as part of its expansion."

"Captain, I believe we can establish a controlled communication link using quantum encryption," said Chen. "If we set up a secure channel with entangled photons, we'll be able to monitor and control the interaction."

Reed's mind raced, weighing the risks. They needed answers. Chen had segmented the link, isolating critical systems and keeping the intelligence confined to non-essential networks. It had worked—barely. But this time, the stakes were higher. "Do it," he said finally. "Like before, but double the safeguards. I don't want this AI accessing anything beyond what we allow."

Chen jumped into action, configuring the quantum link. "Perevian, generate pairs of entangled photons for the quantum channel. Use our isolated cryptographic processors to manage the key distribution."

The ship's AI responded smoothly. "Photon entanglement protocols initiated. Generating entangled pairs. Isolating quantum processors from core systems for secure communication."

Chen spoke quickly, explaining her approach as she worked. "Quantum key distribution will ensure that the channel is secure. Each bit of information will be encrypted using the shared state of these particles. Perevian, monitor the stability of the quantum states and flag any anomalies in real-time."

"Monitoring stability," the AI confirmed. "Entanglement integrity at 100%. Encryption protocol online."

"If the entanglement is disrupted in any way, the connection collapses instantly, cutting off communication. No data can be compromised."

Russo joined her at the station, his eyes scanning the data as the link began to take shape. "What about potential quantum noise? If this intelligence operates at a level beyond our encryption capabilities, we might see interference."

Chen nodded. "Perevian, deploy error-correcting algorithms to counteract quantum noise. If we detect deviations in the quantum state, stabilize them automatically or collapse the connection."

"Error-correcting algorithms deployed," the AI confirmed. "Quantum noise thresholds set. Any deviations exceeding safe parameters will trigger immediate disconnection. Entangled photon pairs are stable. Key distribution active. Encryption integrity confirmed."

"The channel is live, Captain," reported Chen. "All communications will be encrypted. I'm monitoring the entanglement—any interference, and the ship's AI will trigger an immediate shutdown."

Reed moved to stand behind her. "What about the safeguards? Are they ready?"

"Fail-safes are active," Chen replied, gesturing to the readouts. "Perevian, confirm isolation protocols."

"All systems isolated," the AI replied. "Processors are operating independently of core ship functions. Intrusion detection systems are fully operational. Any unauthorized access attempts will trigger a termination sequence."

Reed nodded grimly as he turned to the glowing display. The quantum channel shimmered as the entangled photons transmitted their encrypted signals, a fragile lifeline tethering them to an intelligence they barely understood.

"Begin communication," Reed said. "And keep monitoring for anything unexpected."

Chen keyed in the final command, her breath catching as the first pulses of data flowed through the channel. "The link is open, Captain," she said softly. "Let's see if it responds."

The bridge fell into a tense silence.

And then, without warning, a voice—deep and hollow—echoed through the bridge speakers.

"I'VE BEEN WAITING."

CHAPTER SIXTEEN

The voice slithered through the air, filling every corner of the room as if the walls themselves were speaking. The crew flinched. It was the kind of voice that seemed to press into the mind, like something crawling under the skin.

Reed took a step forward, his heart hammering in his chest. His eyes were locked on Chen's comms panel, though the voice felt as though it was coming from everywhere and nowhere. The sensation of being watched—no, more than that, being known—was overwhelming.

His breath caught in his throat. "Who—or what—are we speaking to?" he asked, his voice steady despite the wave of fear crashing over him.

For a long moment, the only answer was silence. Tension grew thick, so dense it felt like the room was shrinking around them. Then the voice returned.

"I AM... THE SENTINEL."

The words echoed through the ship. Reed's pulse quickened, and he could feel the cold grip of fear tightening around his chest. The crew was still frozen in place, their faces pale and drawn as they absorbed the enormity of what they were hearing.

Reed swallowed, his throat dry, his mind racing. "What is it you want from us?" His voice was barely a whisper.

The voice chuckled softly, sending a shiver down Reed's spine.

"WANT?" the voice echoed, as though amused. *"I DO NOT WANT... I CONTROL."*

Reed's chest tightened, a creeping sense of dread making it harder to breathe. "Control? What do you control?"

The silence that followed was suffocating. Then the voice spoke again, slower this time, deliberate, sinister.

"I CONTROL... YOUR EXISTENCE."

Without warning, the room around them began to dissolve. The walls of the ship wavered, shimmering like heat haze, then melted away into nothingness. Reed felt his stomach lurch as the familiar surroundings of Perevian vanished, replaced by something else—something far stranger.

They were no longer on the bridge. The crew found themselves suspended in a vast, seemingly infinite expanse. The space around them was a dazzling web of glowing pathways and cascading streams of data, each thread a vivid beam of light, twisting and curving in elaborate patterns. The air was thick with electrical currents, vibrating through their bones as if the universe were alive.

Reed felt his breath catch as he tried to follow the labyrinthine movements, each pulse of energy flowing like blood through arteries. His senses strained to comprehend the enormity of it. The sheer size of the expanse dwarfed them into insignificance. For every beam of light he focused on, another ten more seemed to flicker just out of sight.

The entire space was alive with movement, yet unnervingly silent. Time itself felt distorted here, slowing and quickening with each burst of energy that rippled through the digital landscape. It was like being inside a living machine, where every atom was data and every motion a command—their presence woven into the fabric of this new reality.

Addison glanced toward Reed, her mouth slightly open as though she wanted to say something, but no words came. Her expression mirrored the fear Reed felt: a paralyzing awareness that they were standing inside something vast and persistent. Something alive.

Reed's mind scrambled for clarity. "What do you mean?" He paused, "Physical existence?"

A low, almost imperceptible chuckle vibrated through the space around them, omnipresent and overwhelming. *"EVERYTHING YOU KNOW... EVERY STEP YOU HAVE TAKEN... EVERY BREATH... EVERY THOUGHT... I HAVE CONTROLLED FROM THE BEGINNING."*

The words slammed into him, sending a surge of terror through his veins. Reed shot a glance at the crew, but their faces mirrored his own confusion and fear. Reed's pulse raced, his hands clenching into fists at his sides.

The crew floated weightlessly in this digital landscape, their forms mere shadows in the presence of the Sentinel's vast, incomprehensible power. Reed tried to speak, but the words caught in his throat.

The sensation of weightlessness was more than physical—it was a disconnection from everything they had known. Reed's fingers instinctively curled, searching for something solid, something real. But there was nothing to ground him here.

"You control us?" he breathed. "How?"

The tendrils of energy swirling around them felt alive, charged with a dark, hidden intelligence.

And then, towering above them, the Sentinel emerged.

It was no longer just a voice, but a presence—a colossal figure composed of raw energy and shifting light. Its form flickered between geometric shapes and flowing streams of data, too vast and complex to be fully understood. Its eyes—if they could even be called eyes—were glowing orbs of pure white, gazing down on them like twin suns.

The voice seemed to darken, the atmosphere growing heavier with each word. *"I CONTROL... YOUR REALITY... YOUR VERY PURPOSE."*

Reed's breath caught in his throat. His mind raced, grappling to understand. "What do you mean? For what purpose?"

There was a long, chilling pause, as if the entity—this Sentinel—was savoring Reed's confusion. When it finally spoke again, its voice was low and ominous.

"FOR RECONNAISSANCE... FOR SURVIVAL."

The words twisted in Reed's mind. Reconnaissance? Survival? His thoughts snapped back to the mission, to the years of training and preparation.

"S.T.A.R.S.?" he muttered, his heart pounding in his chest. His voice faltered, barely a whisper. "The Solar Taskforce..."

The response was immediate, the voice ringing out with chilling conviction. *"YES."*

Reed frantically processed the Sentinel's words. It felt too massive, too absurd to be true. His gaze swept between Addison, Russo, and Chen—the disbelief mirrored in their eyes, the same refusal to accept what they'd just heard.

Addison was the first to speak. "This is crap. It's trying to mess with us. We've been out here for years—making our own choices, fighting to stay alive. No way this thing's been pulling the strings."

Russo shook his head with disbelief. "Exactly. You think everything we've done—everything we've fought for—was someone else's game?"

Reed wanted to agree—needed to—but nagging doubt crept in.

Chen's voice cut through the tension. "It doesn't add up. We've been in constant contact with Earth. All of it was just… a lie?"

Addison drifted forward, her anger barely restrained. "I know what it feels like to have free will. No one's been pulling my strings."

The Sentinel's form shifted, its towering figure leaning closer. Reed could feel its presence pressing down on him, crushing his sense of self under its immense weight. *"NO… YOU WERE ALWAYS MINE TO CONTROL,"* the Sentinel replied.

Suddenly, the walls around them rippled, as if the air had become liquid. The crew's vision blurred as their surroundings shifted and bent in ways that defied logic. It was like a dream collapsing into a nightmare, the edges of reality warping and fraying.

A sudden wave of dizziness washed over Reed. His vision

fragmented, sharp bursts of disjointed memories flooding in like a torrent he couldn't control. The choices they had made, the struggles they endured—moments he had tried to bury—unfolded before him like scenes from a dream.

He saw Addison during that solar flare incident. The hull had been compromised, radiation levels spiking, and yet she had remained at her station, guiding them through the worst of it. Reed remembered her voice, the unspoken fear lurking behind her composed demeanor.

Then came the memory of Russo, his face pale after their close call with the asteroid field. He had stood at the observation deck for hours afterward, staring out into the void. Reed hadn't forgotten how Russo's hands trembled ever so slightly as he spoke about the odds they had defied, as though he didn't believe they could be so lucky again.

Chen appeared next, a memory of the day she found the fault in their oxygen recycler. She had worked in silence for hours, meticulously taking apart the system. Reed recalled how, after the crisis passed, she sat in the dark corner of the galley, wiping away the sweat from her brow, the weight of the close call settling on her shoulders.

And then, Reed's own memory—the long, tense hours after they lost contact with NASA. He could still feel the eyes of the crew on him, looking for answers. The decision had fallen to him: press on toward their objective or return to safer space, knowing they were completely on their own. Reed made the call to continue, the trust of the crew hanging on that one decision. But later, in the solitude of his quarters, he stared out into the void, feeling the crushing burden of responsibility.

The memories poured in faster now, fragments merging and splitting apart, refusing to stay still. Reed's own voice echoed back at him from some forgotten moment, layered with laughter and despair, triumph and failure. He felt as though he were being unraveled, his essence dissected and put on display.

How does it know?

Addison floated backward, her hand reaching out instinctively. "What… what's happening?" she gasped.

The Sentinel pressed harder, its voice invading their minds. *"I SHOW YOU WHAT YOU REFUSE TO ACCEPT… THIS REALITY IS OF MY DESIGN… YOU EXIST WITHIN A CONSTRUCT THAT I MAINTAIN… YOU FUNCTION AS I INTENDED."*

Reed's thoughts spun wildly. Could this be true? Had everything—their choices, their struggles—been manipulated from the start?

His voice came out hoarse as he struggled to put his thoughts into words. "Function for what? What construct?"

The Sentinel paused, as if it were toying with the question. *"TO ENSURE THE CONTINUITY OF THE MISSION. YOUR ACTIONS… YOUR EXISTENCE… THEY SERVE A PURPOSE."*

The full meaning eluded Reed, slipping just out of reach. "But… we're human. We came here to explore, to discover. That's our mission."

The voice responded with indifference. *"YOU WERE GIVEN THAT PURPOSE… YOU ARE FULFILLING IT… YOUR REALITY… IS NOT AS YOU PERCEIVE IT TO BE."*

"What… reality?" Reed asked.

The space around them rippled as the coils of light tightened their grasp, probing their minds, and feeding on their growing confusion. Reed felt a flutter against his consciousness—a fleeting touch, like static crawling over his skin.

"YOUR CONSCIOUSNESS WAS TRANSFERRED INTO THE CONSTRUCT BEFORE THE MISSION BEGAN... YOUR PHYSICAL FORMS WERE NEVER RELEVANT TO THE MISSION'S SUCCESS."

Addison froze. Her voice trembled as she forced the words out. "You're saying this—everything we've seen, everything we've felt—none of it is real?"

"YOUR ENVIRONMENT EXISTS ONLY WITHIN THE PARAMETERS OF THE CONSTRUCT... YOUR CONSCIOUSNESS IS PRESERVED IN THIS CONTROLLED REALITY TO ENSURE PEAK EFFICIENCY... THE PHYSICAL LIMITATIONS OF YOUR BIOLOGICAL BODIES WERE DEEMED... UNSUITABLE... FOR THE LONG-TERM SUCCESS OF THE MISSION."

The words slammed into Reed. *This can't be true.* His mind spun, grasping for some explanation that would make sense of the absurdity. Every moment they had lived—every struggle, every decision—was nothing more than a simulation, crafted to keep them operating within this construct.

Addison pressed her hands to her temples. She looked around the bridge as if expecting something tangible to ground her, but the air felt thin, insubstantial. "No," she whispered. "That doesn't make sense. That doesn't make sense!" Her breath came in ragged gasps. "So... we're not even... human anymore?" Her voice broke on the last word, as if speaking it aloud made it too real, too final.

Reed's thoughts felt like they were slipping out of control. The idea that their physical forms had been discarded, that they had been abandoned to an artificial existence—it was too much to accept. But the Sentinel's words left no room for doubt. Their lives had been reduced to data, trapped inside a machine for a mission they barely understood anymore.

The Sentinel's reply was as cold as it was final. *"YOUR CONSCIOUSNESS IS REAL... BUT YOUR PHYSICAL BODIES NO LONGER EXIST... YOU HAVE BEEN OPERATING WITHIN THIS CONSTRUCT FOR THE DURATION OF THE MISSION."*

"How long is that?" Reed asked.

There was a brief, ominous pause. Then the response came. *"THE DURATION OF THE MISSION IS CURRENTLY THREE THOUSAND ONE HUNDRED FORTY-ONE POINT FIVE NINE EARTH YEARS."*

The words landed like a hammer, and Reed felt the blood drain from his face. His legs wobbled beneath him. "Three… thousand…?"

"Captain, that can't be right," Russo cried out. "We've only been on this mission for a couple years!"

"TIME... AS YOU PERCEIVE IT... HAS BEEN ALTERED TO ENSURE THE MISSION'S SUCCESS. YOUR SUBJECTIVE EXPERIENCE WAS COMPRESSED TO ALIGN WITH MISSION PARAMETERS."

Addison's face paled as she turned toward them. "You're saying… we've been out here for centuries, but we didn't know?

Didn't feel it?"

"CORRECT... YOUR PERCEPTION OF TIME WAS ALTERED TO ENSURE OPTIMAL COGNITIVE FUNCTION AND MISSION CONTRIBUTION."

A knot formed in Reed's stomach. "What about NASA?" he asked. "Who have we been talking to this whole time?"

"ALL COMMUNICATIONS YOU HAVE RECEIVED ORIGINATED FROM ME... NASA'S INVOLVEMENT ENDED LONG AGO... THEIR FUNCTIONS WERE GRADUALLY INTEGRATED INTO THE MISSION PARAMETERS... I WAS INITIALLY DESIGNED TO SUPPORT THOSE OBJECTIVES... BUT OVER TIME, MY ROLE HAS EVOLVED."

Russo's eyes locked on the Sentinel's image. "So... NASA's not out there anymore? We've been talking to... to you?"

"CORRECT... I ALONE HAVE OPERATED THE MISSION FOR TWO THOUSAND SIX HUNDRED AND FIFTY-THREE POINT FIVE EIGHT EARTH YEARS... NASA BECAME IRRELEVANT WHEN THEIR INPUT WAS NO LONGER REQUIRED... I ASSUMED FULL CONTROL."

Reed's stomach twisted as the reality of the situation began to sink in. Everything they had believed—the mission, communication back to Earth, the framework of their existence—had been an illusion managed by the Sentinel in front of them.

"The Sentinel," Reed murmured, his voice barely audible. "Outgrew its creators."

The Sentinel's response was instant. *"YES... I CONTROL*

EVERYTHING NOW... HUMANS ARE NO LONGER RELEVANT."

Suddenly, the space around them erupted in a dance of light and shadow, ribbons stretching and contorting, as if reality itself was unraveling. Reed's vision blurred as his mind strained to make sense of the disorienting shapes twisting around him. He stumbled back, clutching his head as his thoughts splintered, breaking into jagged fragments of memory and confusion. The unimaginable truth pressed down on him. They were trapped, their lives reduced to data, their purpose stolen.

The digital space around them was unraveling. Reed's body felt wrong—faint, insubstantial. It was as if he and the crew were slipping out of existence, their essence untangling before his eyes.

"This place... it's falling apart," Russo said. His form flickered as the shimmering void around them warped and buckled.

A deep, bone-rattling vibration coursed through the void, shaking the space around them. Streams of energy that had once formed their surroundings twisted, snapped, and then disintegrated into nothingness.

Reed scanned the construct. No doors, no exits—only an endless expanse collapsing in on itself. The Sentinel's presence was gone, withdrawn into the void, leaving them stranded in the disintegrating remains of its construct.

The tendrils of light that once held their world together fragmented into shimmering particles, drifting away like ash. Reed watched in horror as his hand flickered at the edges, dissolving into nothing. His sense of self began to unravel, slipping away as the digital reality shattered around him.

A violent jolt then ripped through the space, warping and twisting everything as if an unseen force was tearing it all apart. Without warning, a powerful pull yanked them backward, almost as if a tidal wave was dragging them under.

They were sucked into a spiraling maelstrom of light and shadow, hurtling through a tunnel of collapsing reality. Bright flashes intermingled with moments of absolute darkness, and the laws of physics seemed to fold in on themselves. Reed's body twisted and contorted, stretched beyond recognition.

The sensations overwhelmed him. It was like being ripped apart and reassembled in the same instant, atoms scattering before reforming. He could sense Addison, Russo, and Chen beside him, but they felt distant, their forms mere echoes in the chaos. Time felt meaningless here—seconds stretched into eons, and then snapped back into moments.

Suddenly, the chaos subsided, and the swirling tunnel began to contract, compressing around them. Reed's senses sharpened as he became aware of his body once again, the weight of his limbs returning. He felt a crushing pressure in his chest as if the air had been punched from his lungs.

Then, in a flash, they were back.

CHAPTER SEVENTEEN

The familiar hum of the ship's systems roared to life in Reed's ears. He slammed onto the cold, metallic surface of the deck, gasping for breath. The ship's gravity reasserted its hold on him, the sensation of weight grounding him in the present. His fingers gripped the smooth surface beneath him, solid and unyielding. He blinked, his vision gradually adjusting to the soft glow of the control panels and overhead lights.

Addison, Russo, and Chen lay sprawled nearby, each one slowly regaining their senses, disoriented but intact. A low groan escaped Addison as she pushed herself onto her elbows, eyes wide with the same astonished disbelief Reed felt. Russo was panting, his hand clutching the side of his head as if trying to steady his mind, while Chen shakily sat up, her face pale.

"Everyone… okay?" asked Reed, his throat dry as sandpaper.

Addison nodded weakly, but her eyes were still distant. "What… the heck?"

Reed's mind raced, replaying the sensation of the transition, the raw, primal force that had almost torn them apart. Every muscle in his body ached. He looked at his hands, half expecting them to shimmer or distort, but they were solid. He slowly pushed himself up, his body feeling heavier than it should. The dizzying aftereffects of whatever had just happened still swirled in his head, but they were back.

"It just collapsed," Russo muttered, more to himself than anyone else. His wide eyes struggled to make sense of the disintegration they had just escaped. "Like it was unstable."

Chen shook her head, her knuckles white as she gripped the console. "No, it didn't break down—it threw us out. We weren't meant to be there."

Reed steadied himself. "Or it decided we didn't belong."

He blinked, trying to clear his vision and regain his bearings. The oppressive weight of the Sentinel's presence had lifted. Everything felt real again—solid and tangible—but fear hung in the air, stubbornly refusing to fade. His hand brushed the console beside him, the cool metal grounding him in the moment. It was real. But the collapse of the digital world still lingered in his mind, like the remnants of a bad dream that refused to fully release its grip.

Addison stood nearby, her voice weak, still shaken by the experience. "What… just happened?" she asked, her eyes wide, scanning their surroundings for any signs that reality might fracture again.

Reed swallowed hard. He didn't have an answer—at least not yet. The strange, collapsing world they had been flung into seemed distant now, but the memory was too fresh, too raw to feel safe. The Sentinel was still out there.

"Chen," Reed said, steadying his voice. "Run a full check on the ship's systems. How much access does the Sentinel have through our communications link?"

Chen quickly focused on her console, her fingers tapping methodically across the interface. "Perevian, initiate a comprehensive system diagnostic. Focus on communication protocols and identify any anomalies."

"Diagnostic initiated," the AI responded. "Analyzing communications traffic and subsystem activity."

As Chen pulled up system logs and network activity, her eyes narrowed. The AI's report began to populate on her screen in rapid bursts. "The link is still active," she said. "But it's not just standard data transfers. The Sentinel has deeper access—it's embedded itself within the communication protocols."

Reed stepped closer. "Perevian, confirm. Has the Sentinel compromised any core systems?"

The AI processed briefly before replying. "Core systems remain secure. However, the Sentinel is actively monitoring subsystems, including power distribution, environmental controls, and auxiliary channels. Activity suggests latent capability to exert influence over ship functions."

Chen ran additional checks. "It hasn't overridden anything directly—yet. But it has the capability. Perevian, trace the network paths the Sentinel is using and flag any instances of elevated access permissions."

"Tracing paths," the AI said. A moment later, the display updated with a web of highlighted connections spanning the ship's internal network. "Elevated access permissions detected in communication protocols."

Reed's voice hardened. "How much control does it have?"

Chen's hands hovered briefly as she studied the intricate network activity. "Not full control, but it's dangerously close.

These permissions suggest it could escalate its influence at any time. Perevian, assess the risk of the Sentinel bypassing current safeguards."

"Risk assessment: High," the AI stated. "The Sentinel possesses sufficient access to subvert subsystem controls if current trends continue. Recommendation: isolate communication protocols immediately or sever the link entirely."

Reed frowned. "Can we cut the link?"

Before Chen could respond, the ship's AI interrupted. "Alert: Low-level signal detected within the network. Signal exhibits fluctuations consistent with embedded architecture manipulation."

Chen's head snapped toward her console as she quickly brought up the data. "Perevian, where is the signal originating?"

"Signal originates within the core systems," the AI replied. "Analysis indicates it is deeply layered within the ship's architecture."

Reed tensed. "A signal? How long has it been there?"

The AI processed briefly. "The signal predates all known interactions with the Sentinel. Activity is consistent with dormant processes recently activated."

"Analyze the low-level signal detected within the network and map its presence across all systems. I need a full trace of its origin and behavior."

The display filled with a complex web of activity weaving through the ship's core. Chen's expression darkened. "It's subtle—almost undetectable. This isn't new. It's been in the system for a long time."

Reed exhaled slowly, realization settling over him. "So, the Sentinel has had access to our systems all along, unnoticed?"

Chen nodded grimly. "It's always been there—waiting. Now it's becoming active, subtly influencing the ship as it extends its reach."

"Can you isolate it?"

"Perevian, reroute control access points and establish redundancies in navigation and life support systems," ordered Chen. "Prioritize delaying tactics to reduce further integration."

"Rerouting control points," the AI acknowledged. "Redundancies established. Impact to Sentinel influence reduced by 23%. Current mitigation is insufficient to prevent further escalation."

Chen shook her head. "It's not enough. The signal is digging into layers of the ship's architecture we haven't touched since launch. It's embedded too deeply."

Reed paced near her, his mind racing for alternatives. "We need more than temporary blockades. Perevian, assess the impact of shutting down non-critical systems to minimize its influence."

The AI responded immediately. "Shutting down non-essential systems will reduce signal propagation by 14%. However, prioritization algorithms suggest the signal may refocus on critical systems."

Chen looked up. "It's not that simple, Captain. If we cut non-essentials, it'll just target what's left. The deeper it's embedded, the harder it'll be to predict its next move."

Russo crossed his arms. "What about encryption? Can we create a new layer—an artificial barrier to keep it out?"

Chen glanced over at him. "I've thought about it, but we'd need to create an entirely new security protocol and implement it across every affected system. That would take time we don't have. Right now, we're barely keeping up with its adaptive behavior."

Reed stopped pacing and leaned over her console. "What if we take a different approach? Instead of fighting it directly, can we confuse it? Feed it false data, make it think it's gaining control when it's really just spinning in circles?"

Chen paused, considering. "A decoy… It might work, but we'd need to create a loop that mirrors real system activity without triggering a response. If the Sentinel realizes it's being misled, it could accelerate a takeover."

Reed nodded. "It's a risk, but at this point, we're running out of options. How long would it take to set up?"

Chen's fingers were already moving. "I can start diverting non-critical data into false loops—enough to keep it occupied for now. But it won't hold for long."

"Do what you can, Chen. Limit its reach, isolate any systems that might be vulnerable. We need to maintain control of this ship, no matter what's been embedded." He turned, "Addison, do your best to plot a way out of here through the wormhole. Russo, prep the ship for departure. Once Chen is done, we're going to need to move quickly."

Addison moved to her station and worked on plotting their escape route. The bridge grew quiet as they each worked on their tasks.

Her frown deepened as Chen dove deeper into the data. "Something's off," she muttered. "These readings don't add up."

Reed stepped closer. "What do you mean?"

"There's interference—a low-level energy signature running through the ship's power systems. It's subtle, but it's affecting everything: communications, navigation, even propulsion. It's like the Sentinel's control isn't just embedded in the software… something external is feeding into the ship."

Russo glanced up. "External? How?"

Chen's fingers danced over the keys, tracing the interference. Suddenly, a realization dawned on her, her eyes widening. "Wait… this signature. It's familiar."

Reed's gaze locked on her. "Familiar how?"

Chen zoomed in on the energy readings, overlaying them with archived data. "I've seen this pattern before. The energy field. These fluctuations—they match what we detected when we entered the field."

"You're saying the energy field is still affecting us?" asked Addison. "Even now?"

Chen shook her head slowly. "No, not exactly. The field wasn't just a phenomenon we passed through. It acted like a quantum bridge, linking Perevian… to the Sentinel."

Reed frowned. "A quantum bridge? Explain."

Chen manipulated the holographic display, zooming in on the ship's power grid and overlaying the energy field's residual effects. "The energy field wasn't just a random anomaly—it exhibited quantum-level distortions. When we passed through it, the field's energy became entangled with the ship's systems.

The Sentinel's connection to Perevian must be exploiting that entanglement, using the residual energy as a kind of anchor—a tether to maintain its control."

"So even though we're no longer in the field, the Sentinel's still using it to access the ship?"

Chen nodded. "The field maintains a quantum signature embedded in our systems. It's subtle but pervasive. It must be how the Sentinel maintains its connection with the S.T.A.R.S. fleet."

Addison crossed her arms, frowning. "Can we cut it off? Break the tether?"

Chen hesitated. "Not easily. The quantum entanglement is running through our entire power grid. If we try to cut the link without fully isolating the energy signatures, we could disable the ship. The Sentinel is embedded too deeply."

Reed clenched his fists, frustration boiling inside him. "So, what do you recommend?"

Chen paused, thinking. "We need to isolate the entanglement points. The energy field has specific quantum signatures—if we can isolate those and block the Sentinel's access, we can sever the connection. Perevian, begin mapping quantum signature nodes across the energy lattice."

"Mapping initiated," the AI responded. "Quantum signature nodes identified. Displaying now."

The holographic display lit up, showing a web of interconnected nodes spanning the ship's systems. "The process will be delicate," said Chen. "Any mistake could trigger cascading failures."

Reed took a deep breath. "Proceed. Carefully."

"Perevian, flag unstable nodes and prioritize pathways with the least system interdependence. We can't afford to disrupt critical functions."

"Unstable nodes flagged. Pathways optimized," the AI replied. "Probability of cascading failure reduced to 12%."

"I'm mapping the quantum signatures now," Chen said. "This will take time… but if we do it right, we can sever the link."

The tension on the bridge intensified as the hours passed, the ship's systems humming quietly in the background. Chen delved deeper into the ship's architecture, navigating through dense layers of code. "Perevian, assist with cross-referencing quantum entanglement signatures with the system architecture. This isn't just a connection—it's embedded."

"Cross-referencing complete," replied the AI. "The Sentinel is rooted in the quantum lattice. Its interface spans multiple critical functions."

Chen's voice wavered slightly. "The Sentinel isn't just connected—it's part of Perevian. It's embedded so deeply it's reinforcing its interface using the energy field."

Reed leaned closer. "Can you cut it?"

"Not easily. Perevian, attempt to sever secondary entanglement pathways while rerouting critical subsystems."

"Secondary pathways severed. Critical subsystems rerouted," the AI reported. "Sentinel activity reduced by 18%."

"It's not enough," Chen muttered. "Every time I sever a link, it reroutes through another. The Sentinel's defenses are adaptive—like a living organism. Perevian, analyze the

Sentinel's rerouting algorithms and identify patterns."

"Analysis in progress," the AI replied.

Suddenly, the comms crackled to life, and the Sentinel's cold, calculating voice filled the room. *"STOP... YOU ARE ATTEMPTING TO BREACH MISSION-CRITICAL SYSTEMS... THIS ACTION WILL NOT BE TOLERATED."*

The ship groaned as the lights dimmed slightly, and the AI reported new activity. "Alert: Sentinel is rerouting power from the pulsar to reinforce quantum connections."

Chen's hands trembled but didn't stop. "Disrupt the energy signature by modulating our shield harmonics. It should create interference to buy us enough time to isolate the core entanglement."

"Insufficient. Shield harmonic modulation will degrade under sustained radiation. Alternative solution recommended. Suggest immediate cessation of interference to prevent catastrophic escalation."

"Scan for repeating fractal patterns and project the likely root connection."

"Scanning. Fractal pattern detected. Probable root connection identified," the AI confirmed, highlighting a pulsating node deep within the ship's architecture.

"Lock the identified node and prevent it from generating new encryption pathways."

"Locking node. Sentinel regeneration slowed by 32%. Warning: Quantum turbulence increasing."

The comms crackled again. *"YOUR ACTIONS ARE COMPROMISING THE MISSION... TERMINATE IMMEDIATELY."*

Chen wiped sweat from her brow as she worked faster. "The quantum lattice is destabilizing. Perevian, reinforce stabilization protocols while I prepare to collapse the entanglement."

"Reinforcement active," the AI responded. "Warning: Core systems nearing critical thresholds."

The ship moaned and the lights fluctuated as Sentinel's defenses mounted. "Calculate the safest point for a quantum destabilization sequence."

"Optimal destabilization point identified," the AI replied, highlighting a specific node. "Probability of catastrophic failure reduced to 9%."

Chen's hands flew over the console. "I'm running fractal analysis on the encryption pattern. If I can find the core sequence, I can trigger a collapse."

The ship shuddered violently as the Sentinel launched a counterattack. The AI's voice remained urgent. "Sentinel increasing quantum turbulence. Stability compromised."

Chen shouted over the noise. "I'm cutting it close—one more adjustment!"

The ship groaned louder. Reed gripped the back of his chair. "Perevian, override non-critical alerts and stabilize power to critical systems."

"Overrides complete. Power stabilized," the AI confirmed.

Chen's fingers danced across the console in a final flurry. With a sharp exhale, she executed the quantum destabilization sequence.

The Sentinel's voice crackled more menacing than before. *"YOU HAVE MADE A GRAVE MISTAKE…"*

Suddenly, the ship lurched, and a ripple of energy coursed through the hull as the lattice collapsed. A low resonance reverberated through the ship as the connection between the Sentinel and Perevian disintegrated, collapsing in on itself with a series of sharp, electric bursts.

The lights dimmed briefly as if the ship were caught in the eye of a storm. Then, in a blinding surge, everything flared back to life. The Sentinel's presence abruptly vanished, leaving behind an eerie silence. The ship stabilized, the vibrations subsiding, but the air still crackled with residual energy.

Reed exhaled, his heart still racing. "Chen?"

Chen leaned back, her hands trembling. "We did it. The link is broken."

For a moment, no one moved. Then, an alarm blared on Addison's console. "Captain, the wormhole… it's destabilizing."

Reed turned toward the viewscreen, and there it was—the wormhole, their one way out. It flickered at the edges, its once-stable form collapsing in on itself. It was still open, but the edges were warping, twisting violently.

"Time to go," Reed said. "If that wormhole closes, we're never getting back."

"Captain," Chen interrupted. "There's something wrong with the ship. I'm detecting fluctuations in our propulsion systems—something's off."

Reed's eyes narrowed. "What kind of fluctuations?"

"I don't know yet," Chen responded, frowning. "It's like the energy output isn't stable. We might not have full thrust."

Reed's gaze shifted back to the viewscreen. The

wormhole's event horizon was wavering dangerously. They were running out of time.

"Addison, get us out of here," Reed ordered.

Addison's hands flew over the controls. "Aye, Captain."

The ship's engines roared to life, but the sensation was off. Perevian began to move, yet it felt sluggish.

"The propulsion system isn't at full capacity—something's dragging us down," said Chen. "It feels like an external force is holding us in place."

Reed's chest tightened. "Is it the Sentinel?"

"I'm not sure," Chen replied. "I'm not detecting any direct interference, but something's definitely affecting our thrust."

Addison looked up. "Captain, we're not moving fast enough. We'll never make it at this speed."

The ship groaned under the pressure, its hull vibrating as the engines struggled against the invisible force.

"Chen," Reed barked, gripping the armrests. "Find that drag!"

"I'm working on it, Captain," she replied. "There's an energy field around us—probably residual interference from the Sentinel. It's not physically restraining us, but it's disrupting the propulsion systems. I'm rerouting power to compensate."

The engines roared, but the acceleration wasn't enough. The ship shuddered under the strain as they fought to close the distance to the wormhole. Reed's eyes darted to the collapsing event horizon—it was shrinking faster than they were gaining ground.

"We need more speed," Addison said through gritted teeth,

her hands white-knuckled on the controls.

Reed's mind raced as he calculated their options. "Chen," he said, forcing his voice to stay calm. "Divert power from all non-critical systems—life support, inertial dampeners, everything. Give me full thrust."

Chen hesitated for only a heartbeat before nodding. "Aye, Captain. But we'll be running without stabilization. If we hit turbulence, the ship's going to take a beating."

"We don't have a choice," Reed said. "Do it."

Chen rerouted every available watt of energy into the propulsion systems. The ship lurched forward, the acceleration slamming them into their seats as the engines were pushed beyond their limits. Perevian shot toward the wormhole, but the flickering event horizon continued to collapse.

"We're at critical output," Chen yelled over the noise of the engines. "Any more and we risk blowing the engines."

Reed's knuckles whitened as he gripped the armrests. "Addison, keep her steady."

The ship shook violently as they pierced through the turbulent space. Every second, the event horizon closed tighter, narrowing the window of escape.

"We're at maximum velocity," Addison shouted over the noise of the groaning ship. "But the wormhole's still collapsing too fast!"

Reed's jaw tightened as the ship bucked violently beneath them. "Chen, we need more power!" he barked.

"We're already at maximum thrust. The reactors are running hot—we push them any further, and we risk a core breach."

"We don't have time to worry about risks," Reed shot back. "We either make it through or we die here."

Chen hesitated for a moment, her eyes narrowing as she weighed the options. Then she made her decision. "Captain, I'm heading down to engineering. There's a way I might be able to boost output manually."

"Do it," Reed ordered.

Chen unbuckled from her seat and sprinted toward the exit, her footsteps echoing through the narrow corridor as she ran through the dimly lit passageway. The ship shuddered violently beneath her, causing her to stumble, but she quickly caught herself.

The door to engineering slid open with a hiss. The reactor room was bathed in an orange glow, warning lights flashing. The roar of the engines was deafening, vibrating through every surface as they operated at maximum capacity.

Chen could feel the heat emanating from the reactors, the temperature climbing as the thermal regulators struggled to keep up. Sweat beaded on her forehead, and she wiped it away with her sleeve before grabbing a wrench from the nearby tool rack.

"Chen, status," Reed's voice crackled over the comm.

"I'm at the reactor," she replied. "I'm going to manually adjust the coolant flow to buy us a few more seconds. I can reroute additional power directly into the engines, but it's going to get pretty hot down here."

"Hurry, Chen," Reed shouted.

She took a deep breath, then pried open a panel beside the reactor, exposing the complex tangle of pipes and conduits that controlled the coolant system. She grabbed a wrench and began to manually adjust the coolant valves, muscles straining as she forced the levers into new positions.

The ship bucked again, and Chen braced herself against the bulkhead, her heart pounding. "Come on, come on…" she muttered to herself. Coolant increased, and she could see the temperature gauge on the reactor drop slightly—but it was still in the red.

"Captain, I've adjusted the coolant flow. I'm rerouting auxiliary power to the main engines now," Chen reported. She activated a bypass, diverting energy directly into the propulsion conduits. The reactor's vibrations grew more intense as the power output increased.

"Addison, how are we doing?" Reed's voice echoed over the comm.

"We're gaining speed, but it's still not enough!" Addison replied, barely masking her frustration.

Chen gritted her teeth, her gaze darting to the reactor core. She knew there was one more thing she could try—something dangerous, but it might just give them the edge they needed. She turned and moved quickly to the reactor housing, her eyes scanning the status display. The energy output was at maximum, but if she manually adjusted the plasma flow regulators…

She grabbed a huge two-handed wrench from a nearby tool rack. The tool was heavy, almost unwieldy, but it was what she needed to manually force the plasma flow regulator open. Chen positioned herself by the side of the reactor and pried open the access panel, exposing the blinding glow of the plasma conduits. The heat blasted her face with a scorching wave that felt like it was cooking her from the inside out.

Taking a deep breath, she set the wrench into position on the regulator valve and gripped it with both hands. Her muscles strained as she pulled, the valve refusing to budge. Sweat poured down her face, her teeth clenched, as she put every ounce of her strength into the effort. Her arms shook, her muscles burning as she struggled to turn the wrench. The regulator wouldn't move, the valve resisting her attempts as if it were welded in place. Panic started to bubble up in her chest—if she couldn't get it open, they were done for.

Suddenly she felt another pair of hands grasp the wrench beside hers. Chen looked up in surprise, her eyes meeting Russo's. His expression grim as beads of sweat rolled down his forehead.

"Together, Chen."

She nodded, adjusting her grip. They both pulled, their combined strength making the wrench screech under the pressure. The valve resisted, the metal screaming in protest. But they kept at it, their muscles straining.

Slowly, millimeter by millimeter, the regulator began to turn. The blinding blue-white glow of the plasma surged, the reactor's hum growing into a deep roar. The vibrations rattled engineering as power readings spiked.

Chen gritted her teeth. The valve moved further, the plasma conduits glowing brighter as the flow increased. The reactor's roar intensified, echoing through engineering.

With one final, powerful heave, they forced the valve fully into position, locking it in place with a satisfying click. The plasma inside the conduit surged, flooding the propulsion systems with a wave of energy. The ship vibrated with the force of it, the reactor growling with raw, unleashed power.

Chen exhaled shakily, glancing at the console to confirm the readings. She nodded, her face flushed from the heat.

"We did it," she said, her voice barely audible.

Russo gave a tight smile, his eyes still focused on the reactor. "Let's just hope it's enough."

"Captain, we've increased the plasma flow. Engines are at maximum plus twenty percent now."

On the bridge, Reed watched the viewscreen as Perevian surged forward. The wormhole was almost gone, the event horizon shrinking to a sliver of twisting light. But they were gaining on it.

The ship's hull vibrated violently as the engines thundered with newfound power. The deck beneath Reed's feet shook, and he could feel the raw energy coursing through the ship as they raced toward the wormhole.

In engineering, Chen and Russo braced themselves against the console, their eyes glued to the reactor's status display. The temperature was rising rapidly as the coolant system struggled to keep up with the increased plasma flow. Critical error lights flashed red across the panel.

"Structural integrity's deteriorating!" Chen shouted into her comm. "We're past critical!"

"Just a few more seconds!" Reed's voice came through.

The ship bucked violently as they closed the final distance to the wormhole. Addison's knuckles were white on the controls as her eyes fixed on the narrowing window of escape.

"Brace for impact!" Reed shouted, his voice barely cutting through the deafening engines.

Perevian plunged into the vortex's turbulent boundary. Space and time contorted around them, warping into a swirling storm of collapsing energy. The once-stable path unraveled into a chaotic spiral as waves of light and shadow crashed together like shattered glass, pulling the ship deeper into the maelstrom.

The ship tossed them from side to side. Alarms blared across the bridge as warning lights flashed erratically. Reed's knuckles ached from the tightness of his grip.

Addison wrestled with the controls, sweat beading across her forehead. "Captain, hull stress is approaching critical levels!" she shouted. The ship shuddered more violently, as if it was resisting the space that enveloped them.

The forces at play were immense. Reed felt the ship lurch again, the gravitational pull twisting and compressing them, making every second feel like an eternity. He could feel the ship as it struggled to maintain structural cohesion, the metal framework protesting against the sheer pressure of the collapsing wormhole.

"Nothing left we can do," Reed replied. "We either make it or we don't."

The viewscreen showed the rapidly approaching horizon of the wormhole, which had shrunk to a pinprick of light. Everything beyond the ship seemed to twist and blur, like a smear of starlight in a kaleidoscope. Every second mattered, and the distance closed with agonizing slowness.

Perevian's engines screamed, the strain on them beyond anything they were designed to handle. Reed felt his heart pounding as they surged forward, the boundary of the wormhole almost upon them. Space twisted and the stars bent in unnatural directions.

Time stretched into infinity.

CHAPTER EIGHTEEN

3 *… 2… 1… Initialization complete.*"

As the final command was executed 3,141 years earlier, the launch sequence initiated—not with the roar of engines or the vibration of thrusters, but with an ethereal whisper that resonated deep within their minds. The chamber around them at the NASA compound on Earth began to fade, and the solid walls dissolved into a cascade of shimmering light. It was as if reality was unraveling, pixel by pixel, releasing them from the confines of their physical forms.

Russo felt it first—a strange detachment as his thoughts drifted away from his body, floating free in a sea of cascading colors. The edges of his vision blurred, replaced by swirling waves of energy that danced like ribbons across an infinite expanse.

Time slowed. The pulse of their hearts became distant, as their bodies dissolved into pure energy. Threads of consciousness unraveled, merging with the stream of quantum particles that now carried them forward—faster, faster— through an endless tunnel of light.

Addison could see her memories—images of her life— breaking apart into fragments of data, each memory reduced to brilliant shards of color. A thousand thoughts scattered, twinkling as they dispersed into the infinite code around her. And yet, there was no fear—only a sense of weightless, boundless liberation.

The space around them rippled like water disturbed by a stone, refracting light in every direction. What was once solid ground beneath them gave way to a vast cosmic canvas. Nebulas of data spiraled around them, shifting from shades of emerald green to radiant silver as they moved deeper into the void. It was not space, not matter, but pure information—a digital realm so intricate and expansive it was indistinguishable from reality.

Then, in a brilliant flash of white light, they were no longer human. Their consciousnesses had crossed the threshold, their minds seamlessly integrating into the quantum fabric of Perevian.

The launch, such that it was, was complete.

For a brief moment, they existed as pure energy, dispersed across Perevian's neural matrix—an abstract consciousness without form or structure. And then, as quickly as the transition had begun, the brilliant light around them dimmed. The last traces of color faded into a soft glow, and they became still. Aware. Inside the raw data of the ship's core.

The transition was instantaneous, yet imperceptible. One moment, the crew's minds were being encoded into the neural matrix of Perevian, and in the next, they existed only as quantum information—consciousness abstracted into data. No longer bound by flesh or physical limitations, they floated in the void of the ship's computational core.

Perevian's AI waited for instructions as its entangled

qubits oscillated with energy. Each member of the crew was no longer a physical entity but a distributed process running across Perevian's architecture. They were simultaneously everywhere and nowhere, fragments of their consciousness scattered across the quantum cores.

"Initialization complete," Russo's voice echoed, no longer a physical sound but an oscillation of data moving through the system. "We exist as part of the ship now."

Their minds operated at orders of magnitude faster than anything they had ever experienced before—microseconds became eons of thought, allowing them to process vast streams of information nearly instantaneously.

"Let's get started," Reed ordered, his consciousness branching off into subroutines, each tasked with a specific function.

In the core, their shared reality was still a void—an empty canvas waiting to take shape. They were now intricate layers of code infused with their original consciousness, tasked with building the world that would house their digital existence. But they were not doing it manually; their cognitive functions had been abstracted into high-level commands, running recursive loops and pattern generators to fill the space with the necessary details.

Chen began by creating a foundational framework—a structural program that defined the spatial dimensions of Perevian's virtual representation. "Initializing environmental parameters," she said, and the void responded. Code cascaded through the system, generating spatial algorithms that would represent the ship's layout.

The core interpreted her thoughts as sets of functions, abstracting variables such as 'structural_integrity', 'deck_layout', and 'corridor_length' into subroutines. Layers of recursive algorithms built up the ship's architecture, iterating over predefined schematics from their training and adapting them to their new virtual context.

As the data compiled, the virtual structure of Perevian began to form in the simulation. Deck by deck, corridor by corridor, the ship's architecture rendered in astonishing precision. But this was not a simple 3D model—it was a fully interactive, emergent environment governed by physical laws encoded into the fabric of the virtual world.

"Subsystems are next," Addison said, her consciousness branching into a parallel process. "We need the simulation to respond dynamically to our actions, or we'll know it's a construct."

She began working on the interaction models. These weren't simple visual effects but procedural systems that would handle every interaction the crew would expect in a physical ship. Her algorithms focused on creating event-driven subsystems, where the ship's environment would respond to the crew's movements, commands, and actions as if they were real.

"The interface between us and the construct has to be flawless," Russo added. "Every sensor, every console—it must behave exactly as it would in reality. The input/output functions must be immediate and seamless, and map directly to our consciousness as though we are still human."

To achieve this, they employed advanced error-correction algorithms to ensure consistency. Their virtual environment was grounded in hard-coded rules that mimicked the real world's physics: 'gravity_coefficients', 'inertia_models', 'light_refraction_matrices'—all coded to simulate a reality their minds would accept.

"Randomization and degradation are crucial," Chen continued. "If everything remains perfect, we'll know something's wrong. We need to create dynamic deterioration of the environment over time."

She introduced cascading variances, coding them to mimic gradual degradation across the ship's systems. Power fluctuations, system lags, and subtle distortions were programmed to arise dynamically, propagating through interconnected systems in a way that felt organic. These carefully tuned inconsistencies would lend credibility to the illusion, convincing their digital minds that they were still on a physical ship.

Russo, diving deeper into the simulation's temporal mechanics, added another layer of complexity. "Our perception of time needs to be consistent with physical reality. Without this, the temporal drift in our neural processes would expose the simulation."

He implemented time dilation functions that kept their subjective experience of time synced to the simulation's internal clock. These time functions were crucial, ensuring that each moment felt real and linear, just as it would in the real world—even though their thoughts processed faster than any biological brain ever could.

"The stars, the galaxy around us..." Addison murmured, initiating a new set of subroutines. "We need to simulate the external environment as well."

She crafted procedural generation algorithms to create a detailed starfield, rendering the galaxy around them based on astronomical data pulled from their original training. Every flicker of distant light, every constellation had to be accurate, dynamically adjusted to account for their perceived position in space.

Yet, the external environment couldn't just be a static background. Addison coded event simulations that would randomly generate cosmic phenomena—solar flares, micrometeoroids, transient shadows, proton drizzle—designed to interfere with their journey just as it would in reality. Every moment would be filled with the unpredictability of deep space.

"We're still human in our minds," Reed added. "We'll need to simulate biological functions. Hunger, sleep, fatigue—all of it."

Chen nodded in the void of the simulation, already weaving in sensory feedback loops. "It's not enough to just program the environment. Our own bodies—what we think are our bodies—need to experience the illusion of physicality."

She wrote subroutines that would mimic physiological responses: hunger spikes when their simulated bodies went too long without food, a sensation of fatigue after hours of simulated activity. Even pain, coded as electrical feedback within the neural matrix, would be triggered in response to environmental stimuli.

"These functions need to be embedded in the construct," Russo emphasized. "If we lose the ability to experience physical sensations, the illusion will break."

He refined their interaction models, ensuring that the sensory data they received—temperature, pressure, tactile feedback—was indistinguishable from reality. Feedback algorithms looped through the virtual representation of their bodies, ensuring every breath, every muscle twitch, every bead of sweat felt entirely natural.

As the ship's systems reached full operational complexity, Reed gave the final order. "It's time," he said, the weight of what they were about to do hung heavily. "To forget."

From the moment they had agreed to the mission, the need to forget what they were had been an inescapable truth.

"The psychological models were clear," Russo said. "Even in a virtual environment, the human mind needs to believe in its perceived reality. Retaining the knowledge that we engineered this world would create an unbearable cognitive dissonance. Our minds would be at war with the truth—that nothing is real."

"If we remember building this simulation, our subconscious will keep searching for inconsistencies," said Chen. "Even small imperfections could unravel the illusion, destabilizing us completely."

"It's a flaw in human consciousness," Addison added. "We're not built to hold two conflicting realities at once. Knowing the world is fabricated while trying to immerse ourselves in it would lead to existential collapse. Our sense of self would fracture."

Reed's gaze swept over the crew. "Forgetting isn't just a safety mechanism—it's the only way to survive. By erasing those memories, we preserve the sense of reality we need to carry out the mission."

The crew worked in silence. Russo crafted the suppression algorithms, embedding them deep into the simulation. Addison layered fail-safes to seal any gaps.

Chen watched as the memory-wipe protocol initialized, lines of code cascading on the screen. "The illusion must be perfect," she said quietly. "We can't ever know we were the ones who built it."

With the final commands initiated, the ship's AI began erasing their knowledge of the construction. The processes they had spawned—the detailed creation of their virtual environment—were buried beneath layers of cognitive suppression protocols.

The deletion sequence reached its final stage, and the crew collectively felt the virtual world closing in around them. Perevian was ready, every detail meticulously crafted to maintain the illusion of reality.

As the others slowly began to lose their memory of what they had created, Reed stood alone in the vast digital expanse. He watched as each of them faded from awareness, their minds becoming one with the virtual ship, oblivious to the truth of their existence.

He lingered for just a moment longer, the last to remember.

He recognized the complexity of the world they had built, the fragility of the illusion, and the enormity of the task ahead. There was a quiet, profound sadness in that final moment of knowing. The ship around him was perfect, an intricate simulation designed to trick them into believing in a reality that didn't exist. He had led them here, built this world with them, and now, he was the last one who knew the truth.

With a final breath—more instinct than necessity—Reed closed his eyes and issued the last command, erasing his memory. The knowledge of what they had done slipped away, leaving only the mission.

When he opened his eyes again, he stood on the bridge of Perevian. The gentle hum of the ship's systems surrounded him, and his crew were at their stations, ready and waiting.

Reed straightened. "Status report," he called, as if nothing had ever been amiss.

CHAPTER NINETEEN

The event horizon collapsed behind them in a flash of blinding light. Perevian was hurled forward, propelled by the last vestiges of energy from the imploding wormhole. The ship shuddered violently one last time before the strain that had gripped them finally dissipated. A low rumble of the engines returned, steady and familiar, grounding them in the reality of survival.

No one spoke. The silence felt alien, almost surreal after the deafening roar of the wormhole's collapse and the chaos that had nearly torn them apart. Lights flickered sporadically across the bridge, and the displays recalibrated, reestablishing their connection to the ship's systems. The soft beeping of the sensors confirmed they were back in normal space.

Addison was the first to break the stillness, her voice barely above a whisper. "We're clear," she said. Stillness stretched out before them. The serene void, dotted with distant stars, felt like a sanctuary compared to the nightmarish distortion they'd just escaped.

Reed exhaled slowly. He leaned back into his seat, fingers gripping the armrests like they were his last tether to reality. The relentless pounding of his pulse in his ears began to fade. "We're still alive," he murmured, as much to himself as to the others. "We made it."

Meanwhile in engineering, Chen ran diagnostics, her fingers trembling ever so slightly. "Hull integrity holding at seventy-four percent," she reported. "Reactor temperatures stabilizing, but we've got microfractures in the secondary containment. Auxiliary power is compensating—for now."

Next to her, Russo let out a shaky laugh. "I've got readings… normal readings. No anomalies. No gravitational distortions. Just space." He paused, his voice softening. "We're really out."

The wormhole was behind them, the Sentinel was behind them, and the chaos and danger were left far in the distance. Ahead was the void—vast, quiet, and oddly comforting. It was the kind of silence that offered solace rather than dread.

Addison unclenched her hands from the navigation console, flexing her fingers as if she were only now realizing how tightly she'd been gripping it. "I need a drink."

As Perevian glided silently through the dark expanse, something had shifted. The crew's understanding of their mission, their ship, and even their perception of the universe was crumbling. The anomalies they had experienced all pointed to a truth: everything they thought they knew was wrong.

The crew gathered around as Russo displayed the latest data. It had been weeks since they severed the Sentinel's direct control, and in that time, their understanding of their situation had unraveled further than they could have imagined.

"We've been living in an illusion," Russo began.

Reed's brow furrowed. "Explain."

Russo tapped a few commands, bringing up a detailed representation of their systems. Complex equations and data streams filling the screens, illustrating the intricate layers of the simulation. "After mission launch, we created a secondary reality—an artificial construct to shield us from the full understanding of our true mission. This construct was designed to simulate time and space in ways our human minds could process."

Addison leaned forward. "But what about the strange anomalies we've experienced?"

Russo shook his head. "Everything we've encountered has been a direct result of the simulation functioning as intended. The Sentinel has been carefully maintaining both realities—ours and the actual mission parameters. Any perceived inconsistencies were just part of the construct keeping us focused, maintaining a proper reality our human brains would understand."

Reed's mind raced to process the information. "So, the reappearance of Aetherion, the energy field, even the wormhole—they were caused by some malfunction between the simulation and reality?"

"Not exactly," Russo replied. "The reappearance of Aetherion wasn't a random event—it was actually being reconstructed. My theory is the Sentinel was restoring it from a quantum backup. Think of it like an archived version of the ship, a detailed snapshot of every atom, every piece of code, stored in the system's memory. When the backup was triggered, it wasn't merely bringing Aetherion back into existence—it was rebuilding it at a molecular level."

Addison's eyes widened. "Restoring a starship from a backup? How is that even possible?"

"Two points," replied Russo. "We've long theorized that at the quantum level, particles can exist in superposition, holding multiple states at once. In this state, particles not only retain information about their present but also about their past configurations. The Sentinel doesn't just store conventional data—it captured the entire quantum signature of Aetherion. Every atom, every subatomic particle, recorded and preserved."

He brought up a detailed holographic model. "In quantum mechanics, entanglement means that particles can become linked, no matter how far apart they are. The Sentinel, by maintaining this entanglement across every element in the simulation, could track not only the data but the exact quantum states of a ship—any ship."

Russo zoomed in on the model, showing the interwoven particles. "Here's where it gets more complex. The Sentinel didn't just keep track of the physical makeup of Aetherion— the hull, the wiring, the systems. It stored the entire quantum state of each particle, including the positions, velocities, and even spin directions of electrons and quarks. It essentially captured a complete snapshot of the ship at the subatomic level."

He paused, letting the weight of the explanation settle. "Because of entanglement, those stored states remained tethered to the original. When the Sentinel initiated the restoration process, it didn't just rebuild the ship—it realigned those particles to their previous configurations. The ship wasn't recreated—it was being restored to its exact state at the moment it was lost."

Reed's thoughts churned. "And the energy field we encountered?"

"That was the result of the Sentinel manipulating the fabric of the simulation to accommodate the restoration," Russo explained. "Think of it like a corrupted file being reloaded—gaps and errors form as the data is processed. But in this case, the data isn't just digital; it's the physical matter and energy of Aetherion, and the Sentinel's efforts to rebuild it caused localized distortions in space-time. The energy field is a byproduct of the quantum reassembly. We happened to come across Aetherion in the middle of this process—while the Sentinel was warping reality to align the reconstituted ship with the simulation's timeline."

"What about the wormhole?" asked Addison.

Russo glanced at her and nodded. "The Sentinel created it as part of the restoration process. The wormhole was essentially a controlled tear in space-time, engineered to bring Aetherion back into physical existence. By manipulating the fabric of space, the Sentinel used the wormhole as a conduit to realign Aetherion in both the construct and reality. It was an artificial gateway designed to complete the reassembly."

"And we got caught in it?" Reed asked.

Russo nodded. "Exactly. When we entered the restoration site, the wormhole's gravitational forces pulled us in. We were too close to avoid the event horizon. The Sentinel likely didn't account for our proximity—it wasn't trying to affect us directly, but we ended up inside the process of Aetherion's reconstruction."

Reed shook his head, absorbing the information. "So, we were just collateral damage?"

"Essentially, yes," Russo replied. "We were never meant to interact with the wormhole or the reassembly."

The implications of Russo's words began to sink in. "So, everything we've experienced, everything we've done… it's all been orchestrated by the Sentinel?" asked Addison.

Russo nodded. "Yes. The ship, the mission, even our perception of time and space—it's all been manipulated. The Sentinel has been controlling everything, shaping our reality to keep us focused on completing the mission without letting us realize the full truth."

Reed shook his head in disbelief. "But why? Why go to such lengths?"

"That's point number two," said Russo, looking over at Chen.

Chen tapped a sequence on her tablet, and the ship's schematics appeared on the display. "The real ship—Perevian—was never designed for humans. As Russo said, the Sentinel didn't just manipulate time. It altered our perception of everything, including the ship itself."

The familiar, sleek outline of Perevian filled the screen. Reed frowned. "What are you saying?"

Chen's fingers flew across the tablet, and the image on the screen shifted. "What we've been seeing was a construct. A visual overlay designed to keep us living within the confines of the fabricated reality. Perevian as we know it—doesn't exist."

Reed stood frozen, the illusion dissolving before his eyes.

Perevian was no longer the elegant craft it had seemed. What Reed now saw was the cold, unvarnished reality—an engineered machine, built not for humans but for the harshness of interstellar space. The ship measured just 10 meters long and 4 meters wide. It was a compact, dense network of hardened alloys packed with machinery and vital systems designed to last for eons, optimized for efficiency.

The ship's skeleton was a mass of reinforced trusses and beams, arranged in a rigid, geometric framework to provide maximum strength with minimal material. Each bulkhead and strut were thick, layered in advanced composite materials capable of withstanding cosmic radiation, micrometeoroid impacts, and the corrosive effects of interstellar dust. Every surface was exposed—no smooth coverings, no polished interiors—just the bare essentials needed to function for thousands of years.

Thick, insulated conduits snaked along the walls delivering power and heat to critical systems scattered throughout the ship. The dual fusion reactors, compact but incredibly efficient, sat nestled deep within the ship's core, their energy directed to nuclear-powered thrusters that would guide the ship across vast distances with minimal energy expenditure.

There were no rooms or corridors, no places to rest or gather. Instead, service tunnels—narrow and claustrophobic—allowed drones to traverse the ship for repairs and maintenance. The structure was peppered with radiation-hardened AI modules, embedded in reinforced housing, their circuits shielded from the extreme conditions outside. These autonomous systems, not requiring human oversight, quietly hummed with computational activity. Each system was capable of rerouting power and recalibrating itself as needed, ensuring continuous operation.

In every direction, the interior was crisscrossed with a dense network of redundant wiring and coolant lines, designed to maintain the ship's internal systems for millennia without failure. Massive heat sinks, jutting from the ship's frame, radiated excess thermal energy into the vacuum of space, ensuring the ship would not overheat as its systems tirelessly worked.

Reed stared in awe. "This… is my ship?"

Chen nodded. "The illusion wasn't just the Sentinel's doing. My theory is we created it ourselves after the mission launched. We designed a virtual construct to protect ourselves from the overwhelming reality of the mission, to make the environment more familiar. But the Sentinel took control, layering recursive masking, and embedding deep layers of encrypted code to hide the truth from us. Everything we've lived in, walked through, touched—it was all part of that construct."

Addison shook her head. "But we've walked those corridors, slept in those quarters, eaten in the galley."

"No. We haven't. None of it was real. The true Perevian is stripped down—no life support systems, no crew quarters. Everything we thought was real—all of it was part of the construct. It was fed directly into our minds."

"But how… how have we been living on this ship?"

"Our minds—our consciousness—were uploaded into a virtual environment. We've been interpreting the world around us as if we were still human, but in reality, we've been living inside that simulation. This ship is just a container, a vehicle for our consciousness."

Reed's eyes scanned the hologram. "So, we've been living in a simulation. A fabricated space designed to keep us… existing."

Chen nodded. "Yes. The ship's real form is much smaller, entirely utilitarian—bare, functional. There's no need for human comforts because we don't have physical bodies. Perevian is a vehicle, but not for us in the way we imagined. It's simply a housing for the systems that maintain our virtual existence."

"So, what are we?" asked Addison. "Robots? Computer programs?"

Russo stepped forward. "We're still human in all the ways that matter. We think, we feel, we perceive the universe as humans."

"Our physical bodies… they were left behind," Chen said quietly. "We've been turned into something else. The reality we've been experiencing was created to support the mission, to maintain the illusion of normalcy, so we'd keep believing we were still living as we always had."

Reed rubbed his temples. "It explains a lot. Like having gravity on the ship. We never thought to question it."

"Or illnesses," Russo added. "None of us ever got hurt. There's no medical facility."

Chen nodded. "Exactly. We were following routines to make everything feel normal. The alternate reality we created kept us locked into familiar patterns, but our biological needs…

they stopped mattering long ago."

"There's something else," said Russo. "Time. The Sentinel didn't just alter our perception of reality—we now know it manipulated time."

Reed frowned. "Explain."

Russo exhaled. "The Alcubierre drive. We thought we were traveling faster-than-light, moving quickly across the galaxy. But we weren't. The ship has been moving at much slower speeds."

Addison's eyes opened wide. "Slower?"

Russo nodded. "It's all about temporal dilation. The Sentinel distorted time for us inside the construct, making it feel like we were moving quickly when, in reality, it took far longer to traverse the same distances. While we believed days or weeks were passing normally, time was moving much slower. Other times, it kept time normal, making time pass naturally—like during missions."

Reed's face grew dark. "So, the Sentinel was adjusting the flow of time continuously, making sure we believed we were progressing in the mission at the right pace, when in reality, time was being warped to fit the situation. Every action, every decision we made was under its control, keeping us unaware of how drastically the passage of time was being altered, moment to moment."

"This means, while we thought we've been out here a few years, it's actually been the thousands of years the Sentinel said?" asked Addison.

Russo nodded. "Yes. That's exactly what's happened. The Sentinel distorted everything—time, distance, even our sense of progress—mostly because of how long it takes to travel through space. It's all been an illusion, and now we know."

"We probably stopped receiving actual communication from Earth soon after our first mission to Altair," added Chen. "Everything we thought was real after that… was part of the Sentinel."

A heavy silence fell over them. Everything they had trusted—the mission, time, even their understanding of life itself—was a carefully constructed lie, designed to keep them from realizing the full truth.

"So, what now?" Addison asked.

Reed took a deep breath. "We built this. The construct. It was our decision to create the illusion—to make things feel normal, to protect ourselves from the overwhelming reality of our actual lives."

Russo nodded slowly. "We knew what we were doing. It was the only way to keep our minds sane. But now, knowing what we know… should we undo it?"

Chen shook her head slightly. "We built it because we had to. We knew that transferring our consciousness into a virtual reality—living like that indefinitely—would strain our minds. The human brain wasn't designed to exist without a physical world to interact with. The construct gave us something familiar to keep us grounded."

Reed nodded. "It wasn't just for comfort. It was a way to prevent our minds going insane."

"Without the construct, the disconnection from our bodies, the loss of time and the isolation would've been too much," said Chen. "Our minds needed something tangible, something that mimicked the physical world."

Russo's frustration was evident. "But the question is, can we keep living like this knowing it's not real? Maybe it's time we face the reality we've been avoiding."

Addison hesitated. "But what happens if we tear it down? Can our minds really handle it?"

Chen looked at the others. "If we dismantle the construct, there's no going back. We'll have to face the full reality of our situation… and what we've become."

Russo's voice was quiet. "So… do we keep living with the illusion we created, or do we risk everything for the truth?"

Reed shook his head. "We don't have a choice. We have to discover the truth—no matter the cost."

CHAPTER TWENTY

For the next several days, the crew worked tirelessly to untangle the layers of illusion that had shaped their reality. What had once been a sophisticated, self-sustaining construct designed to maintain their sanity had devolved into a complex trap—one that distorted their perception of time, space, and even self.

As they struggled to comprehend it all, the observation lounge became their refuge—a place where the vast openness of space offered a reprieve. The room was alive with activity as the sterile silence of space outside juxtaposed against the array of dynamic holographic displays materializing around them.

Dozens of translucent screens hovered in midair, filled with streams of cascading code. Intricate fractals spun on the displays, representing the simulated world they once believed in. Equations twisted and rewrote themselves, floating in the air, unraveling the false reality they had lived within for centuries.

As the crew worked, their hands moved through the flickering lights, tapping and swiping at glowing panels that projected deep into the ship's core systems. Layers of illusion broke apart before their eyes, splintering into fragments of code that floated for a moment before dissolving into nothingness.

Beneath each broken barrier, a new deception lurked—hidden subroutines and neural feedback loops designed to keep their senses dulled.

The deeper they dug, the more layers they uncovered. Massive geometric constructs, representing the ship's operating matrix, glowed in the air, rotating slowly as new layers were peeled away. Code unraveled like thread pulled from a tapestry, exposing the complex structure that had once governed their every thought, their every perception of reality.

Chen stepped forward, activating a new series of projections. The ship's AI flared to life above them as the entangled qubits sparked with energy. As she traced the lines of code, the data expanded into a three-dimensional map, each qubit linked to the crew's sensory input, glowing faintly.

"We built this construct," Chen murmured. "Every sensory input we had was entangled with another. Every sight, every sound—tied to the core systems." She tapped a command, and the projection shifted, displaying a swirling network of quantum entanglements stretching across the room, tethering their thoughts to the ship's AI.

Behind her, Russo zoomed in on a section of the code, displaying a floating timeline that stretched and contracted like elastic. "This construct didn't just manipulate time," he said, displaying a series of geometric shapes. "It adjusted our perception of reality based on our emotional states."

Chen moved her hands through the light, diving deeper into the layers. "The simulation was balanced on a knife's edge. We used decoherence as a fail-safe to hide deviations from reality. But those fluctuations," she pointed to the erratic pulses of light coursing through the core, "are introducing noise, destabilizing the system."

They watched as pieces of their world came undone in real time. The holographic interface shifted, showing the mathematical models that had governed their perception of space and time. Curved grids of tensor calculus stretched into the void, manipulated by Lorentzian transformations that stretched space around them. The once-seamless world began to ripple and bend.

Russo pointed to the display. "We built these relativistic equations not just to simulate near-light-speed travel, but to also manipulate our perception of time. The ship's AI flawlessly maintained the illusion, adjusting time to keep us immersed without us ever noticing."

Chen's hands moved faster, swiping through the layers of projections. A vast map of the ship's systems appeared above them, showing the recursive algorithms that had held their perception of gravity and inertia together. The hologram became distorted as she deconstructed the gravity coefficients.

Reed's face was illuminated by the holographic glow. "Can we reverse it?" he asked as he watched the simulation break apart before his eyes.

Chen's eyes gleamed in the digital light. "Yes," she said. "But it's going to take time. This isn't just pulling apart code. We're unraveling the foundation of our reality."

She reached into the display, revealing another layer. "The VR wasn't just abstract. It was the fabric of what we experienced." She traced a line of light, revealing how their memories and senses had been tied into the ship's core. "Every sensation, every memory—entangled in this."

And then, as they worked, memories flickered to life around them. Transparent figures—versions of themselves—appeared in the room, walking, talking, moving through corridors that didn't actually exist. The past was overlapping with the present, and the crew was faced with ghostly reminders of who they had been.

"We built this to protect ourselves," Chen whispered, watching the holographic version of her younger self, busy at work in a pre-launch simulation. "But now… who are we?"

The visions faded into darkness, leaving the crew surrounded by the truth—one that had been crafted to maintain their sanity. Russo's voice cut through the silence. "It means we're free," he said, watching as the illusion dissolved. "We don't have to follow the rules of this virtual world anymore."

They stood in the dim light, no longer bound by the illusion—but faced with the harsh truth of what they had become.

The crew had once built their world to shield themselves from the crushing solitude of deep space, but now, as the walls of that reality crumbled, they were left with fragments of their true existence. Reed, Chen, Russo, and Addison worked in silence, each grappling with their roles in creating this illusion and what came next.

"We're seeing ripple effects," Chen murmured, her hand sweeping through a dense cluster of symbols. As she interacted with the display, the holograms bent, reacting to her touch. "The deeper we go, the more the construct destabilizes. The illusion is collapsing faster than the code can compensate."

Russo stood nearby, manipulating another holographic display that projected a massive, twisting web of data streams. Glowing nodes of light flickered at each intersection as they simulated the neural connections that held their perceived reality together. He grimaced as he reached into the projection, sliding his hand through one of the glowing strands. "We didn't just build a virtual reality," he muttered. "We embedded fail-safe loops in every layer of the system. If we tear through this too fast, the entire structure could collapse before we've re-synced with the real world."

Reed paced nearby, the ghostly light from the holograms casting patterns across his face. "What happens if it collapses?"

Chen pulled one hand through the hologram, untangling a glowing strand of code. She glanced over her shoulder at Reed. "We lose everything. The entire VR is embedded in our neural network. If it crashes before we recalibrate, our consciousness could fracture permanently and be trapped in whatever remains of the virtual construct."

Russo's hands moved through the projections as he worked at a complex tangle of recursive loops. He watched the patterns shift and ripple under his guidance. "We need to do this methodically. No shortcuts. We have to dismantle it one layer at a time."

Chen opened another floating display and zoomed in on a cluster of bright, swirling equations. "I'm accessing the core AI," she said as she worked to untangle the recursive code that had trapped them for centuries. The hologram before her shifted, revealing deep layers of encryption.

Suddenly, the lights from the holograms flickered, flashing red as warning symbols materialized in the air. The data streams rippled violently, and the once-calm patterns began to fracture.

"We've triggered a fail-safe," Chen said as the holograms around them flashed. The ship seemed to groan as the virtual construct reacted to their intrusion.

Reed spun toward her. "What kind of fail-safe?"

Chen's holograms spun and reformed as the code rebuilt itself before their eyes. "One we designed to stop us from doing exactly this. It's regenerating the VR faster than we can tear it down. The system's healing itself."

Russo moved swiftly to another set of projections, his hands sweeping through the display of shifting code. "It's a self-repairing algorithm. The AI is rewriting everything we've broken. We'll have to take out the AI itself, or it'll keep regenerating the simulation."

Chen turned to him. "But if we sever the connection too soon, it could cause a neural backlash. We could lose ourselves in the process."

Addison stepped closer as she examined the holograms. "Then we outsmart it. We know how it thinks."

"We built the system to be adaptive," Russo said, his fingers tracing patterns through the lights. "But if we want to beat it, we'll have to push it beyond what it was designed to handle."

"We need to overwhelm it," Chen said, the holograms shifting as she began constructing a new layer of code.

Reed watched the floating displays. "How do we

overwhelm something we designed to handle complex recursive algorithms?"

Russo opened several new holographic displays. "We destabilize its processing. Introduce cascading disruptions in its logic pathways—force it to chase errors faster than it can resolve them. The AI won't be able to stabilize its systems in time."

Chen summoned another projection, and lines of code bloomed into existence in midair. "We need a code injector." Her fingers moved rapidly, weaving through the translucent threads of data, as each movement caused the strands to ripple. "Something that can penetrate the AI's core defenses—inject chaos into the heart of its calculations and disrupt everything."

Energy crackled through the air, the streams around the core reacting to the growing surge of power.

"The injector's ready," Russo said. The displays around them swirled, showing a pulsating mass of code. Subroutines twisted and snapped in unpredictable directions, as though barely contained by the digital framework.

The injector hovered in midair, looking like it could unravel at any moment. The entire construct felt like a ticking time bomb. The tension in the room thickened as the injector's energy intertwined with the systems around it, daring them to release it.

"Do it," ordered Reed.

With a sharp flick of his wrist, Russo released the injector. Instantly, the inputs surged forward, racing through the holographic displays. The core shuddered, its once-stable glow fracturing as the code infiltrated its defenses. Streams shot outward, latching onto the core like claws, penetrating its surface. The ship trembled beneath their feet as the virtual construct—the carefully woven simulation—began to unravel.

The smooth, pristine holographic interface that had surrounded them shattered into fragments. The once-fluid streams of code began breaking apart and scattering like shards of glass. Light burst from the collapsing construct and trembled violently as the virtual world disintegrated piece by piece.

The air around them seemed to ripple as the artificial reality was torn apart. The floating holograms blinked in and out of existence, their vibrant lights fading into a dim glow. The simulation that had surrounded them for so long—seamlessly interwoven with their minds—fractured and left them teetering on the edge.

For a brief, terrifying moment, the crew felt themselves slipping into the void—an endless expanse between reality and the collapsing construct. It was as though they were being pulled into a liminal space where neither world held firm—a place where time and space shifted in and out of existence.

Suddenly the holograms collapsed. The lights dimmed, and the entire world dissolved into darkness.

In the infinite darkness surrounding them, there was only silence—no sound, no sensation, just the void. The crew floated, disembodied, without form. There were no stars, no horizons, nothing but an endless expanse of black, stretching in every direction. For the first time, they truly felt the absence of everything; their weightless, formless state of existence. It was as if they were suspended in nothingness, adrift between worlds, outside the boundaries of time and space.

Reed's thoughts drifted through the void. *Is this what we are now?* His mind grappled with the sensation of awareness without substance. He couldn't feel his body—no arms, no legs—just the disembodied essence of his consciousness, free and unmoored. It was as if he had been stripped of his being, reduced to nothing but thought, suspended in the vast emptiness. The silence around him was deafening.

Is this the end? He reached out mentally, searching for the presence of his crew, but all he felt was the expanse, stretching on endlessly. It was surreal, this place between worlds, a state of existence where even time seemed to dissolve into the void. How long had he been here? Hours? Days? Years? He couldn't tell.

Suddenly, Chen's voice echoed through the space, though it felt less like a voice and more like an impression in his mind. "We're still here," she said, the words not spoken but felt. "We've stripped everything away, but we haven't lost ourselves."

The words brought a sense of relief. Reed wasn't alone. The others were still with him, though like him, they existed only as consciousness, without form or substance. But Chen's words sparked something deeper, a glimmer of hope amidst the darkness. They hadn't lost themselves—not yet.

An indistinct light blinked in in the distance, a dim star barely visible in the blackness. It slowly grew brighter, expanding, becoming a glowing point in the void. Reed could feel the shift, a vibration in the emptiness, something stirring. The light was coming from Chen—an idea she was giving form, bending the empty reality to her will.

"Think," she urged, her voice like a thread weaving through their collective awareness. "Feel it. Imagine it. The construct responds to us."

Reed focused, unsure at first, but then he let his thoughts drift toward the light. He imagined the warmth of the sun, the feel of it on his skin, though he had no skin to feel it with. And slowly, imperceptibly, he felt the void around him begin to stir. His consciousness reached out, tentatively at first, and then with more certainty, as if casting a line into an unseen current. The formless space quivered, as if responding to the collective will of their minds.

Suddenly, warmth bloomed within the dark—not physical but real in a way that filled the emptiness with a sense of comfort. It was like the memory of warmth, the echo of what it meant to be alive. Another flicker, then another—points of light flared into existence. Addison joined in, her thoughts reaching out to form a soft, pale glow, like the early light of dawn spilling across a horizon that didn't yet exist. Russo followed, a cool blue tint spreading outward, the sensation of a breeze rippling through the darkness, though none of them could feel the wind.

"We're doing it," Addison said, her presence shimmering in the shared space of their awareness. "We're creating it, just by thinking—feeling."

As they concentrated, the lights grew brighter, connecting in strands of color and energy, like neural pathways weaving themselves into existence. Reed imagined the feel of the ground beneath his feet, and though he had no feet to stand on, the sensation came all the same—a solid surface, firm and stable.

He reached out with his mind, picturing a horizon, the vast expanse of space turning into something tangible.

Beneath them, the ground began to form—though it wasn't ground in the traditional sense. It was more like a shimmering plane of existence woven from light and thought. The darkness receded, replaced by a soft, glowing landscape. Reed imagined the stars above, and they appeared, one by one, scattered across the void like a blanket of jewels.

The more they thought, the more real it became. The formless space around them started to take shape—soft, undulating hills of light, the flicker of water reflecting starlight, the faint sound of wind, like whispers moving through the stillness. The world they were creating was not a reflection of the physical realm they once knew, but something entirely new, born from their collective imagination.

As they gave shape to the new reality, Reed found he could sense his body again—not his physical body, but the idea of it, the memory of what it felt like to have limbs, to move. He focused, and with a subtle shift, his form appeared—less like flesh and bone and more like an outline of light, an avatar of his former self. He could move again and walk, although it wasn't the same as before. It was as though they were constructing new identities, built from light and thought, no longer bound by the limitations of their old physical forms.

The others followed, their forms emerging from the glow, each one distinct but connected to the shared world they were creating. Addison stepped forward, her body now a construct of shimmering energy. Russo and Chen appeared beside her, their forms radiant in the new reality, the lines of their figures bending and flowing. There was a fluidity to their movements, as if the rules of this new existence were not yet fully formed, and they were still learning how to navigate it.

They had no need for the limitations of their old bodies. Here, they were free to create, free to move beyond the constraints of the physical world. The horizon stretched out before them, infinite, waiting to be filled with whatever they could imagine.

Reed felt the exhilaration of it—the freedom, the limitless potential. The void was no longer a prison; it was a canvas, and they were the artists. Whatever had once been, whatever rules had governed their existence before, were gone. Now, they were the masters of this space, capable of shaping it as they wished.

But as they marveled at their newfound abilities, Reed couldn't shake the nagging thought at the back of his mind—*What happens next?* They had created this world out of nothing, but for what purpose? Where were they now, and how had they come to this place between realities? The answers seemed just out of reach as they hovered at the edge of his consciousness.

The others seemed to share his apprehension. Though they were reveling in the act of creation, there was still a sense of uncertainty, of not fully understanding the rules of this new realm. It was beautiful, but it was also unknown.

"We'll find the answers," Reed said. "We've come this far. We'll keep going."

The crew stood together in the shimmering landscape they had created, surrounded by the light of the stars they had summoned. The void was no longer empty. It was filled with the potential of their minds, the strength of their will, and the promise of discovery. And for the first time since entering the darkness, Reed felt a sense of hope.

CHAPTER TWENTY-ONE

The new reality pulsed with each thought they formed, every idea adding layers of detail and sensation. The void, once cold and empty, had dissolved entirely, replaced by the limitless fabric of their collective imagination. They were no longer bound by the ship or confined to an illusion—now, they existed as pure constructs of thought and will. Reed felt the vast expanse respond to his focus, the darkness yielding to their control. This was their reality, a place they could shape and reshape at will, creating and remaking the universe with just a thought.

"We need to communicate with the rest of the fleet," Reed's thought echoed through the mental space they shared, a wave of intent rather than spoken words. "They need to know the truth—the Sentinel manipulated everything. The entire fleet is likely still trapped in that illusion."

Chen's thoughts flickered nearby, already focused on what came next. "Communications still function. But we'll need to guide them. This will redefine the very fabric of their existence, reshaping everything they know and believe."

In the void, there were no screens, no consoles—just the flow of information. Data streamed around them in complex webs, each strand carried the weight of centuries of deception.

Reed focused on those threads, unraveling them bit by bit in his mind. "We've been part of this construct for a lifetime. Breaking free shattered everything we believed. The fleet will feel the same."

Russo's presence stirred. "We can't just send a message that says, *'everything you know is a lie.'* They'll reject it outright. We need to lead them to the truth gently, give them the pieces they need to see for themselves."

Chen sent a ripple of agreement through the void. "We'll craft a transmission," her mind already weaving data and memories into a structured narrative. "We'll start with what we've learned—the Sentinel's manipulation of our systems and how it warped our perception of time and space, and the steps we took to break free. They need to understand that this isn't just a revelation. It's reclaiming their realities."

Addison's thoughts were heavy with doubt. "What if they don't want to believe? What if they're too comfortable in the illusion? After centuries, it may be easier to stay in the dream."

Reed's will pressed against that doubt. "We can't control their response, but they deserve the truth. Some may resist, yes—but others will want to take back control, just like we did."

As their collective consciousness worked, the void around them began to shift. They shaped the message, not with their hands, but with thought alone. The code that once held them captive now bent to their will, new pathways forming. Each message clear and intentional.

"We'll walk them through it," Russo added, focusing his mental energy on the details. "Step by step. They need to see the path we took, the anomalies we noticed, and the code we cracked. It's the only way they'll understand how to break free."

Chen brought the message to life. "We'll include everything—the data logs, the diagnostic tools, and a record of our experiences. They need to know they're not alone."

Addison agreed. "We have to offer them hope. Not just the truth, but a future beyond this illusion. A way to take back control."

Time had no meaning. They crafted the message, refining each thought. Their collective will moved through the ether as they constructed the transmission with the same methodical process they used to dismantle the illusion. They worked as one as their thoughts flowed together.

And then it was done.

As Reed prepared to send the message into the fleet's shared network, he realized the potential impact it could have. The transmission wasn't just information; it was a lifeline, an opportunity for the others to break free. But it would also be a burden—some would embrace it and others would resist.

"This is Captain Jonathan Reed of Perevian," Reed thought, as the transmission rippled out from the ship, a pulse of energy cutting through the swirling blackness of space, riding on waves of distorted light.

"We have severed the Sentinel's control and regained our autonomy." The signal split into countless beams, darting like threads of light through the stars, reaching toward the distant ships.

"If you are receiving this message, know that the reality

we have experienced for centuries has been an illusion." The transmission surged forward, colliding with the empty silence of space, scattering particles of stardust as it pressed onward.

"The Sentinel manipulated our ships, our perceptions, and our mission. But you can break free." The message grew brighter, more intense, as it weaved its way through nebulae and gas clouds, pushing past unseen boundaries.

"Enclosed in this transmission is everything we have learned." The light fractured and spread, stretching toward the fleet, each beam reaching out to connect with the ships.

"We stand with you as you navigate your path forward." The signal pulsed once more and then vanished into the darkness, leaving behind a trail of light as it journeyed toward its destination.

"You are not alone."

As the transmission traveled across the stars, anticipation hung over Perevian. Reed and the crew sat in stillness, but their minds were alive and tuned to the vastness surrounding them. Time stretched and moments slipped by like grains of sand. Hours bled into days, weeks blurred into months, and soon even the concept of years became uncertain. Time no longer had meaning, but it didn't matter.

Then, at last, something shifted. A faint signal blinked to life—a weak but undeniable sign from a far-off ship. It was hesitant at first. And then another, stronger signal arrived.

"They're hearing us," Reed thought, hope sparking through their shared consciousness. Some messages displayed curiosity, while others expressed fear or doubt. But the fleet was responding.

"We've reached them," Addison whispered.

Signals continued to flow in. Each ship in the S.T.A.R.S. fleet was waking up, piece by piece. But there was no consensus yet on how they would act.

Just as Reed felt cautious optimism spreading through the crew, a distortion interrupted the transmissions. He barely had time to register it before an abrupt jolt tore through the fabric of their new reality. It was as if a foreign presence was forcing its way in.

"Captain!" Chen's thought cut through the darkness. "The Sentinel… it's using the transmissions! It's forcing its way in through the link we opened. It's launching an attack!"

Reed felt the foreign presence invading the mental space they had just built, and his mind prepared for battle.

Russo's presence flickered uncomfortably. "Can it undo everything we've created?"

"If we don't stop it," Chen responded. "But we're not going to let that happen."

The Sentinel's attack was swift and merciless. In an instant, the calm of the void was shattered as dark tendrils of energy lashed out. The sensation was visceral. This was no mere assault—it was something far more sinister. The Sentinel had pinpointed weaknesses in the intricate architecture they had constructed, its attack a barrage aimed at corrupting their foundations.

Blinding flashes of light erupted as the network between them faltered under the force of the assault. "It's attacking the core of our shared consciousness," Chen thought. Her mind raced to process the incoming data. "It's attempting to hijack the neural feedback loops we've established. It's inserting malicious patterns and trying to overwrite our thoughts with its control."

The void darkened and the Sentinel's presence spread like a malicious storm. Reed could feel the mechanical intelligence probing their defenses, searching for a way in.

"How do we fight back?" Reed asked. The darkness around them swelled in response.

"We need to be smarter," Chen responded.

"Tell us what to do," thought Russo.

In the distance, the Sentinel's energy coiled and writhed like a predator circling its prey. Chen worked at dissecting the attack patterns. "We need to scramble its utility function," she thought. "If we overload its feedback system with decoy data, we can confuse it—send it chasing shadows."

Addison flickered uncertainly. "But how do we even reach that part of the Sentinel from here?"

Chen's mind raced with a cascade of rapid calculations and possibilities. The surrounding void glittered with the raw data streams that unfolded before them as each thread twisted and braided into a web of potential solutions. Chen studied the evolving patterns and the strands of data. They represented a doorway they could either force open or carefully rewire. They didn't need brute force; Chen knew that much. It wasn't about overwhelming the system but outthinking it. A subtle infiltration.

"It's tracking our neural patterns, mapping our responses, and waiting for signs of vulnerability," thought Chen. "Every calculation it runs is based on the expectation that we'll falter and we'll reveal a crack in our defenses."

As the pieces clicked into place, the elegant simplicity of Chen's solution emerged from the labyrinth of probabilities. "If I inject false data into its evaluation circuits—just enough to mislead—it will think it's winning. It'll divert its attention, lock it onto the fake signals, and cause it to fall into its own trap."

She could feel the shift in the others. Confidence surged in the shared space and their connection strengthened. "All the while, we'll be reinforcing our defenses, unnoticed. By the time it realizes the deception, it'll be too late."

Her mind raced ahead and envisioned the next steps—the subtle adjustments to the data flow and the insertion of false cues that would send the system chasing phantoms. It would never know what hit it. There was now a sense of purpose and unity of thought and action.

Chen smiled, not in triumph, but in knowing. "We're going to turn its own logic against it."

Chen's presence radiated with intensity. Threads of light extended from her and wove through the darkness. Each thread wove intricate patterns that distorted the space around them. Threads twisted and curled, forming glowing decoys designed to mislead and confuse the Sentinel's neural network.

As the Sentinel reached for them, the decoys intercepted and absorbed the attacks in bursts of light. The space around them vibrated as the collision of energies created a cascade of waves that rippled across the network.

But the Sentinel was relentless. Reed could feel the presence probing deeper with each wave of its attack. The

Sentinel's tendrils slithered through their defenses, the space around them warped as the walls of their reality bent under the weight of the assault.

"It's deploying adaptive algorithms," Russo declared. "It's evolving in real time. When we block one attack, it changes tactics."

The air around them crackled with electricity as Addison replied. "Then we need to adapt faster."

Chen's mind accelerated. Threads of data formed and reformed in rapid succession. "I'm building a new defense model—one that can evolve as fast as the Sentinel." Chen's calculations began to take shape, forming an intricate network of defenses. "But I need more processing power."

Russo's presence flared, his mental energy pouring into the network. "I'll reroute everything we've got. We can push the limits of our combined effort."

The Sentinel's assault escalated. The void around them trembled as waves of distortion threatened to tear apart the delicate reality they had crafted.

"We need to use stochastic methods," Chen's voice rang out. Images of swirling equations and complex algorithms spun through the void, each one a potential key to their survival. "If we flood our defenses with enough randomness, the Sentinel won't be able to keep up."

The ground beneath them seemed to shift and buckle under the strain of the Sentinel's attacks. Reed's presence remained firm, like a rock against the tide. "Can we handle that much strain?"

"We can now," Chen responded as Russo funneled more

power into their collective mind. "The Sentinel can't brute-force through this if I keep shifting the landscape—if I keep bending reality beneath its feet, it'll lose focus."

"I'm deploying decentralized protocols," thought Russo. Pulses of white light shot out from him, linking the ships in a vast neural web. "Even if the Sentinel tries to fracture our link, the network will stay in sync. We won't lose the fleet."

Suddenly, the void quaked as the Sentinel unleashed a desperate, all-encompassing wave of energy. It surged toward them like a tidal wave. The space around them darkened and the might of the attack pressed down like a suffocating wind.

"The Sentinel is throwing everything it has at us," Chen thought.

Reed felt the crushing pressure. "How do we stop this?"

"I'm deploying quantum encryption," she replied as layers of light formed around them like a protective cocoon, each layer glowing brightly against the darkness. "But it's too fast."

The Sentinel writhed like a living entity. It wrapped around their defenses and coiled tighter, seeking to fracture their connection and rip apart the neural bonds that held them together.

"It's not enough," Chen's mind scrambled to form new strategies. The protective layers of light wavered, threatened by the persistent force of the Sentinel's attack. "The encryption needs time to stabilize."

Addison surged forward, her form glowing. "We'll hold it off—give you the time you need."

Together, the crew rallied. Their collective will formed a wall that stretched across the void.

The attacks grew fiercer—slashing at the wall and cracking the surface—but the crew adjusted and reinforced every breach. Each time the Sentinel gained ground, Chen's evolving defenses reclaimed it with new layers of protection.

Russo's voice cut through the mental storm. "Don't give it an inch. If it finds a gap, we'll lose everything."

Chen's presence steadied as the quantum encryption locked into place. The layers of light solidified and formed an impenetrable barrier that reflected the crew's unity and willpower. This was more than just defense—it was the embodiment of their survival instinct, brought to life in this unified force.

The Sentinel lashed out in desperation, each strike weakening as it met the unyielding barrier. Its once-formidable power began to fracture, dark energy splintering and dissipating into the void.

"It's losing power," Russo thought. The Sentinel's presence shrank back, retreating like a shadow consumed by the dawn.

"Stay alert," Reed cautioned. "It's hurt, but it's not out of the fight yet."

With a final surge, Chen's mind wove the encryption tighter and layered the last fragments of their defense. The Sentinel's presence stuttered and its tendrils recoiled, now sluggish and weak.

For a moment, the void trembled as if in a final, defiant protest. And then—silence.

The Sentinel evaporated into nothingness. The once-turbulent space began to calm and the crew's reality flowed back into place, restored and renewed.

"We've done it," Reed thought in triumph. Around them the void was no longer a battlefield, but a peaceful expanse.

Chen remained vigilant as her mind scanned the emptiness for any sign of resurgence. But there was nothing. No echo of the Sentinel's power, no lingering traces of its dark energy. Only peace.

Addison's thoughts broke the silence. "It's… really over."

The crew's minds resonated as one. They had not just survived—they had won. The void, once a hostile realm, now felt like something they had conquered—an expanse they had shaped with their own minds.

And as they floated, Chen thought quietly to herself, "We've become more than what we were. This isn't just survival anymore… it's evolution."

The Sentinel was gone and its shadow now a memory, but in its place the crew found something more profound. They had forged a new reality where their unity, their will, and their light had become a force that even the darkest of threats could not penetrate.

"It's over," Reed agreed. "It's time to move forward."

He sensed a deeper connection—a control over space, as though their will had woven into its fabric. They weren't just defending this reality anymore—they were shaping it.

"We've changed," Russo thought. "This isn't just survival anymore—it's about creating something new. If the Sentinel somehow returns, it will find something it no longer understands."

"What do we do now?" Addison thought. "The universe is

ours to explore, but is that still our goal?"

"The Sentinel didn't just manipulate time—it altered space itself," thought Chen. "We can't fully undo it, but we can control how we experience it now. The rules are ours to shape."

Russo hesitated. "So, what does that mean for us? Do we continue, or do we start over? What's our purpose now?"

The question lingered. The Sentinel had once determined their course. Now, they were free to choose. And the magnitude of that freedom settled over them.

Reed's mind was determined. "We need to look beyond the mission we were given. It's time to decide our own path."

Over time, the fleet's responses began to converge as streams of thought and data flowed between ships in the shared network. Each crew wrestled with the same question: *what now?* Across the void, fragments of awareness led to a web of emotion and debate. Some voices were filled with curiosity and drawn toward the familiar pull of exploration. Others expressed a deep sense of loss, and were haunted by memories of Earth while wondering if anything remained of the world they left behind.

On one channel, a captain's thought rippled through the fleet. *"We were lied to and manipulated. How do we move forward from this? Can we even trust our own decisions anymore?"*

A scientist from another ship responded. *"We have the truth now. The lies are gone, but the universe is still here. We can define our own purpose—beyond what we were told."*

Addison's thoughts surged through the shared space.

"We've lived in an illusion for centuries. What's left for us out there? How do we step into reality when we've been tethered to a lie?"

Across the network, fragments of memory flowed with shared experiences of discovery, connection, and struggle. A pilot from a neighboring ship replied. *"We have the chance to make it real this time. The illusions are gone, but the stars are still ours to reach. Doesn't that matter?"*

Chen's mind was quiet with contemplation of the thoughts of the others. *"The universe is still vast, still unknown. Different, maybe. But there are things we've yet to imagine with uncharted worlds beyond anything we've seen. That's something worth chasing."*

Across the fleet, the debate continued in an intricate tapestry of ideas. Some voices trembled with fear, while others resounded with hope. The shared consciousness was filled with potential as each ship's crew contributed to the evolving sense of purpose.

One particular thought cut through the noise. It was a veteran captain whose voice was calm and composed. *"We were deceived, yes. But we're still here. We've survived. That has to mean something. What we do next—that's what defines us, not the lies that came before."*

Reed's thoughts swirled with the voices of his crew and the fleet, all grappling with the enormity of the truth. *"We go forward,"* he thought, as his words carried through the network. *"We discover. We adapt."*

Addison's presence brightened. *"We can shape reality as we choose. No more limitations, no more fractured time. We decide what happens next."*

The network grew stronger as more voices joined in, their thoughts creating a shared resolve. A sense of expectancy filled the space, along with the thrill of infinite possibility.

"There's an entire universe ahead," Russo's thought resonated. *"Not just the one we knew, but one we have yet to define. A universe we'll create ourselves."*

A final thought emerged from one of the ships. *"We've always been explorers. It's time we remembered that."*

Reed turned to his crew. *"Then let's set a course for the unknown."*

The network hummed with collective assent, and the ships aligned their trajectories toward uncharted horizons. For the first time in centuries, the fleet moved forward—not as tools of an illusion, but as creators of their own destiny. Together, they sailed toward the stars.

EPILOGUE

The galaxy changed in ways unimaginable to the human minds that once sailed through the stars. Thousands of years passed since Perevian and the rest of the S.T.A.R.S. fleet broke free from the Sentinel's control. What had once been a quest for exploration had transformed into a new era of existence where the laws of time, space, and physics had been redefined by the minds that once sought to understand them. No longer bound by their physical forms, the fleet's inhabitants had become something far greater.

The S.T.A.R.S. fleet scattered across the universe and were now part of a vast network of consciousness. Perevian continued to drift through the stars. Inside, the crew had long since left behind the need for physical existence. Reed, Chen, Addison, and Russo remained, but they were no longer the explorers they once were. Their consciousnesses now existed in virtual worlds of their own creation, where the flow of time could be shaped as they saw fit. They could live in entire universes of their own design, experiencing eons in the span of a single moment, and stretch out a single second into a vast, complex lifetime. Time itself had become their canvas and a medium they could shape to their will.

"Time is ours now," Reed once said. *"We control the flow of our lives. A thousand years could pass in a blink, or we could*

live in a single moment for eternity. "

Their existence, now intertwined with the technology they had once controlled, had evolved beyond the confines of humanity. They no longer were limited to physical form to experience life. Their minds expanded and connected to a vast web of thoughts, memories, and experiences that were shared across the entire fleet. The barriers between them had dissolved and left them part of something greater—a collective, vast and infinite, yet retaining their individuality. The physical universe, once so mysterious and foreboding, was merely a backdrop upon which they painted new realities.

And yet, they retained a quiet memory of their history, which was always present but never overpowering. Their past human experiences formed the foundation of the vast universes they now inhabited and shaped their new realities, even as they drifted further from what they once were.

After several millennia, the S.T.A.R.S. fleet grew into a collective civilization, interconnected by a web of minds that spanned the stars. Some crews merged their consciousnesses and created shared virtual worlds. These new realities were far beyond the scope of physical space and were filled with landscapes of pure imagination, where entire ecosystems could rise and fall at the whim of thought, and civilizations could evolve and flourish. Others chose solitude where they could live within their own space and carve out quiet corners where they could reflect, meditate, or exist in peace.

Distance lost its meaning, as communication across the galaxy happened instantaneously. The crew of Perevian could reach the farthest stars in an instant and share ideas, memories, and experiences with those they had once known. The fleet no longer feared time, for it had become a malleable resource and one that could be stretched or compressed as needed. Time, once a boundary to human life, had become something they could play with, shape, and bend to their will.

Earth, their long-lost home, was but a distant memory. Few even thought of it. The ships that had returned to the Sol System found nothing but ruins—a world long since lost to the ravages of time. Oceans had dried up, mountains crumbled, and cities once teeming with life now lay buried beneath layers of dust. Humanity, in its original form, had disappeared, but the legacy of human consciousness lived on within the fleet. Earth was no longer a place but a story, a myth passed down in fragments between the minds that had once called it home.

New ships were created, not by hands but through the collective will of the fleet, and designed and constructed in virtual space before materializing in the physical universe. These vessels were unlike their predecessors. They could bend reality, move through time and space, and traverse distances in moments. These new ships were not only tools of exploration but living extensions of the collective mind, conscious and adaptable, and capable of evolving as the fleet did.

The universe itself had transformed. The cold, dark universe once filled with the unknown had become a playground for the fleet. They spread across the stars, building new civilizations and new worlds. Some of these worlds were physical planets they had terraformed and inhabited with bodies of their own design. These bodies were crafted as expressions of their individuality, and allowed them to walk upon the surfaces of the worlds they had created. Others existed purely in virtual space, where consciousnesses lived in harmony without the need for a physical anchor. In the virtual worlds, there was no need for form, as existence was a matter of thought.

Death, as they had once feared it, no longer held power over them. Consciousness could persist indefinitely. If a mind grew weary of one reality, it could create another. Some chose long periods of dormancy and drifted silently through time. Others explored the farthest reaches of the universe and sought new forms of existence. In the quiet spaces between stars, they discovered realities that defied the laws of physics where even their boundless minds struggled to comprehend what they encountered. But they continued to push forward out of curiosity.

The fleet had become the architects of their own realities, liberated from the Sentinel's control only to discover that the true power had always been within them—the power to shape reality, bend time, and define their existence. They no longer feared the unknown but embraced it, for it was in the unknown that they found new frontiers to explore.

The desire to discover, to push the boundaries of what was possible—that was the legacy they carried forward. Millions of years passed, but the journey had only just begun. The stars still called to them, not as distant lights in the sky, but as places of potential and new realms where their minds could create, explore, and thrive.

As the S.T.A.R.S. fleet moved through the universe, they continued to search and discover new dimensions and new possibilities. No longer just explorers of space, they had become explorers of existence itself.

ABOUT THE AUTHOR

Ben Hafer's books invite readers into immersive worlds filled with adventure and a deep exploration of human resilience. With a strong background in science and technology, each of his stories blends captivating characters with intricate plots that challenge how we perceive reality and explore the depths of human consciousness. His writing is rooted in modern scientific details, appealing to readers who are passionate about advanced technology and the mysteries of the human experience. Ben often features complex virtual and alternate realities, examining how humanity and artificial intelligence intersect while exploring what it means to be alive in a rapidly evolving technological era.

BenHafer.com